GANGSTA

Bloomsbury Publishing, London, Oxford, New York, New Delhi and Sydney

First published in Great Britain in September 2004 by Bloomsbury Publishing Plc
50 Bedford Square, London WC1B 3DP

This paperback edition published in September 2017

www.bloomsbury.com

BLOOMSBURY is a registered trademark of Bloomsbury Publishing Plc

A CIP catalogue record for this book is available from the British Library

ISBN 978 1 4088 9500 9

Typeset by Newgen Knowledge Works Pvt. Ltd., Chennai, India
Printed and bound in Great Britain by CPI Group (UK) Ltd, Croydon CR0 4YY

13 5 7 9 10 8 6 4 2

For those who care
for those not here

Benjamin Zephaniah
on writing *Gangsta Rap*

Why did I write Gangsta Rap?

I was fascinated by the amount of young people excluded from school who had loads of talent and who then went on to succeed in their chosen careers, usually creative careers. I was in a similar situation myself when I was excluded at 13 and the teacher called me a "born failure", so I wanted to go into the life of a young boy in a similar situation. Ray is, on the one hand, a bad boy, a boy you wouldn't want your daughter to bring home, but actually underneath there is goodness and real talent. So I wanted to explore what could happen to him if he was given creative freedom and how he could be inspired by a head teacher who had the vision to recognise his talent.

I love Rap music. Many people say that teenage boys are not interested in poetry but Rap is simply street poetry. Why do kids get embarrassed when you call it poetry? I used to. I love poetry, but poetry reminds lots of kids of dead slow words written by dead white men. Rap tells it as it is. It might grate or upset you, but people who are studying youth trends should just listen to Rap music as that's where it's at. Rap is street poetry owned by young people. Nowadays every kid on a street corner is a rapper and that's all good.

I also wanted to explore the gun culture. In some areas where black people live there are more guns than food. In many inner city areas kids no longer get into scraps and come home with a bloody nose or a black eye, now it's a shooting or at the very least a stabbing.

Some studies have shown that black kids are highly intelligent when they start their education but by the time they've left they are at the bottom of the pile – why is that? I can partly answer that question from my own experience of school where I found the system far too rigid. When I objected to the teacher's version of black history starting with slavery, I was told that that's how she was told to teach the subject. When I objected to being told that infrastructure of civilisation started in Europe, I pointed out that Ancient Egypt had a social security system and a sewage system. I feel that everyone is taught a biased inflexible version of history and I know it's not the teachers' fault – they're boxed in by the thing called the curriculum. My instinct says it's based on a need to pass exams. Are kids failing school, or are schools failing kids?

Simply what do you do with talent that's living on the wrong side of town?

CHAPTER 1

School, What School?

Ray was woken up by the sound of his parents shouting at each other downstairs. He pulled the duvet over his head so that he could not hear them, but after five minutes his alarm clock rang anyway and he was forced to face the day. He dragged himself out of bed, went to the top of the stairs and shouted, 'Give it a rest, will you.' His parents heard him, but carried on.

Back in his room Ray searched through his massive collection of CDs until he found his favourite Tupac Shakur album, 'Me Against the World'. Dressed only in his boxer shorts, he strutted around the room rapping along with Tupac, imagining that he was on stage and the CD player was his audience. Tupac was Ray's hero. Ray knew every word of the track and rapping along with him made Ray feel as if Tupac were in the same room as him. When his music was on he could no longer hear his parents arguing, but before the first track was over he could hear the sound of his sister Kori singing along to the R'n'B singer

Beyoncé in the other room. Ray turned his volume up. Kori turned her volume up. Ray turned his volume up even more. Kori turned *her* volume up even more. Ray turned his volume up until the room began to shake. Kori turned her volume up until the house began to shake.

'What the hell do you two think you are doing?' shouted their father from the landing. He was a short stocky man who had shaved his head the moment his hair had started to go grey, and had obviously spent a lot of time pumping iron in his youth. He stood in a position from where he could shout into both bedrooms.

'This is no rave, this is not a discothèque business you know. What are you trying to do, shake the house down?'

Both CD players went silent.

'She started it,' Ray said, opening his bedroom door wide to see his angry father standing there.

Kori stormed out of her room. 'He started it with that hip-hop rubbish,' she said as she locked herself in the bathroom.

'What hip-hop rubbish?' Ray shouted in the direction of the bathroom. 'It's better than that stuff you play, that stuff doesn't say a thing, that stuff sounds like babies crying. And hurry up and get out of the bathroom, other people want to use it too.'

'If the music I play sounds like babies crying, yours

sounds like dogs barking,' Kori shouted at the door.

'Oh yeah,' replied Ray. 'You wait until I get my rap band together, we'll teach you about good music. All that stuff that you listen to does is brainwash you.'

'You and your so-called band. It will never happen Ray, and if it does you'll be crap.'

Their father stamped his foot down hard. The house shook. 'Both of you shut up, and you, Ray, you should know better. I told you to start being an example to your sister, didn't I? And put some clothes on.'

'You should know better,' Ray said, turning his back on his father. 'Every morning this week you and Mum wake me up with your arguing.'

Ray could see that his father wanted to lash out. He had hit Ray before but this time he managed to control himself.

'Who do you think you are talking to, boy? Don't you talk to me like that. You are only a boy, do you understand? A boy, so don't come giving me your backchat.'

'It's true though,' Ray said fearlessly.

'I said shut up.' His father stamped his foot again.

'At least Kori and me make noise with music,' Ray said self-righteously.

His father stood in the doorway and shouted at the top of his voice, 'I will make a noise on your head if you don't shut up. Now get dressed and piss off to school, boy, and I hope you learn some manners when you're there.'

'Yes, Dad, I'll piss off to school, just like you said, and I'll be an example just like you.'

His father didn't reply. He looked hard at Ray and then turned and went downstairs.

Ray got dressed and after shouting Kori out of the bathroom he went downstairs and sat at the breakfast table with the rest of the family. The atmosphere was tense. His father spoke to Ray without looking at him.

'You have to learn some manners you know? You won't live long in this world if you don't have some respect for people.'

Ray's mother looked at his father. 'Respect, what you know about respect?'

'I know a damn lot more than anyone in this house,' Ray's father shouted, standing up. 'This is my house and I don't get no respect here.'

'You don't know what respect is,' Ray's mother shouted back.

'And you don't know what manners is.'

'And you don't know what it takes to be a father and a husband.'

'And you don't even know what it takes to be a real woman.'

Ray stood up, rocking the table, and shouted over them. 'You know what, you two make me sick. Every day you arguing, every day you go on and on at each other, from morning till night that's all you do, and you want respect? I'm going to school.'

Ray left the room, picked up his coat in the hallway and left the house, slamming the door behind him. Kori left a minute later, and she stayed a minute behind him all the way to school.

Kori was fourteen, a year younger than Ray. Their parents believed that Ray could have been a role model for her, and they had encouraged her to learn from him, but it soon became clear that they were two completely different people. So she continued to watch him, but from a distance.

It was a long, lonely school day for Ray. He missed his two best friends, Tyrone and Prem, and by the last lesson it was beginning to show. It was history and Ray was just not interested. He looked out of the window watching aeroplanes in the sky and waited for the lesson to end. Mr Harrison, the history teacher, spotted him.

'So, Ray, I take it you know all there is to know about the Roman Empire?'

'No,' Ray replied quietly.

'Well, pay attention and you may learn.'

Ray continued to look out of the window.

'Are you listening?' Mr Harrison said, walking towards him.

'No, I'm not,' Ray replied.

'Well, I have an idea,' Mr Harrison said, still walking. 'Why don't you stop looking out of that window, turn your face round to the front of the class, turn your brain on, and then try listening – you could learn something.'

Mr Harrison was now standing over Ray. Ray looked up. 'Well, I have an idea too. Why don't you shut up?'

The class became suddenly quiet and then noisy. The pupils had heard similar exchanges before, but some were still shocked by Ray's words. Others giggled and laughed. Mr Harrison turned to face the class.

'OK, you lot, be quiet.' His normally pale face was reddening with anger. The class waited for him to explode. 'There is absolutely no reason why you should talk to me like that, Ray. All I'm asking you to do is to pay attention.'

Ray continued to look out of the window. 'And all I'm asking you to do is leave me alone.'

Mr Harrison raised his voice. 'Right, Ray, turn and face the front. I don't know what your problem is, but I cannot allow you to disrupt the rest of the class like this.'

'Well, if you leave me alone you can carry on with your stupid class, can't you?' Ray said, still looking out of the window.

'How dare you talk to me like that? Get out now.'

Mr Harrison was beginning to shout.

Ray stood up. 'Yeah, that's cool, 'cause I'll talk to you how I like and you can't do anything, and if you think you can, come, see if I don't box you down.'

'Are you threatening me?'

'You can call it what you like, I'm just telling it as it is. All I'm saying is you can't do nothing to me.'

Mr Harrison pointed to the door. 'We'll see about that.'

Ray pushed his desk and chair away with his feet and headed out of the room, pushing past Mr Harrison who followed him into the corridor, leaving the rest of the class to talk amongst themselves.

'I don't know what has come over you, Ray, but you cannot speak to me like that.'

Ray looked everywhere except at Mr Harrison. 'You got the problem, you're always picking on me, so if you pick on me I'll talk to you how I want.'

Mr Harrison dropped his voice and tried to sound as reasonable as he could. 'Look, Ray, I'm not picking on you, and let's not make this a personality thing. You are in a lesson, a history lesson, and all I'm asking is that you take part in that lesson.'

Ray turned to face him. 'No, stick your history, who cares about history?'

Mr Harrison strode off. 'Right, that's it. Follow me.'

Ray followed him to the head teacher's office where

Mr Harrison explained the reason for Ray's behaviour to the head teacher, who was sitting in his large leather swivel chair. Ray stood in front of the desk, and Mr Harrison stood next to him with folded arms.

The head teacher, Mr Lang, got straight to the point. 'Now, Ray, you have already had three temporary exclusions and a spell in the Learning Support Unit. Let's face it, I told you what would happen if you came before me again. Do you have anything to say for yourself?'

'No.'

'Well, you leave me no alternative. This is not the first time that you have threatened a member of staff and as always you show no remorse, so from today you will be permanently excluded from this school. I simply will not tolerate this type of behaviour. Your parents will be contacted by the local education authority who will advise them as to what will happen next, but the simple fact is that you are no longer a pupil here. You must understand, Ray, this is for your own good, and the good of other pupils.'

'Shut up,' Ray growled as he walked towards the door. 'You know what you need, you need a beating, you big pussy, look at you. You leave me no alternative but to buss your lip but you're lucky I'm in a good mood.' Ray slammed the door behind him so hard that pictures fell off the walls and the head teacher jumped.

For a moment Mr Lang stared at the closed door. He cared about the pupils and had spent a lot of time on Ray. Now it seemed like it was all going down the drain. Ray had slammed doors on him before, but this felt like it could be the last time.

Outside the school Ray took off his tie and put it in his bag. He hung the bag on his shoulder for a moment but then took it off again. He looked at it, thought about its contents, and then stuffed it into a large rubbish bin that was already full of sweet packets and soft drinks bottles. He walked with a bounce, taking off his jacket and undoing his top shirt buttons as he went. It was all about making himself look like someone who had just finished school rather than someone who had been excluded. He was free. As he walked through Stratford shopping centre he looked at every girl between the ages of thirteen and nineteen as if he were in love with them, and in his mind he thought that they too would love him if only they knew how bad he was.

On West Ham Lane he went into Flip Discs, his regular hang-out stop, a small music shop specialising in hip-hop. The shop was run by Oswald Jolly, known to all as Marga Man, a Jamaican-born reformed bad boy who weighed nineteen stone before breakfast. No one knew where he had got the name Marga Man, not even Marga Man himself, but it seemed that back in Jamaica someone was being ironic. In Jamaica 'marga' means skinny, very skinny. Marga Man was big, very big.

Leaning over the other side of the counter, listening to music, were Tyrone and Prem, Ray's best friends. Tyrone looked like a younger version of Marga Man, a bit large and a bit menacing, until the moment he smiled, when, like Marga Man, he became charming and cuddly. But Tyrone didn't talk much. He was a thinker; he always looked as if his mind was working overtime. Prem really was marga. Thin, fit, energetic and good-looking, he was less funny than he thought he was but he always tried to look on the bright side of life, even when things looked very dark. He also believed he could look after himself. One of his cousins once represented India in a world-class karate tournament and Prem claimed that this cousin had taught him many karate skills – but he never mentioned that this was when he was eight years old, and that all that karate had long been forgotten.

Tyrone and Prem turned round like two cowboys in an old Western movie to see Ray standing inside the shop.

'What's up, Ray?' said Tyrone, surprised. 'You suppose to be at school, guy.'

Ray smiled, walked over to them, and with his right fist clenched he touched fist. 'I don't do school no more.'

All three broke into laughter. Marga Man stood nodding his head to the beat, pretending not to listen to them.

'What you saying, guy?' said Prem.

'I told you man, I don't do school any more. I'm like you now, excluded.' Ray stretched the word out.

'What happened?' asked Tyrone.

'Well, you know that Mr Harrison, I had to deal with him, you know what I'm saying. I had to show him the truth. Then that headmaster bloke, he wanna try come on some authority trip, so I just deal with him too.'

They laughed more and touched fist again.

'So what is it, how long for?'

Ray stepped back and threw his arms open. 'I told you, I'm like you now, permanent exclusion.' Once again he dragged the words out. 'Permanent exclusion, this is no long weekend, this is no go home and calm down. I told them where to stuff their school and that's it.'

Marga Man turned the volume of the music down low and folded his arms. 'What you mean, all three of yu now not going school?' His voice was deep, his accent heavy Jamaican, the type of voice that had never made any attempt to sound more English. 'Listen, all I know is dat if you three roam de streets is trouble, yeah man, big trouble, and de tax payer will not foot de bill.'

'No, Marga Man,' Ray said, rocking to the beat. 'We ain't going to roam the streets, we're going to hang out with you in here.'

Marga Man quickly turned the music right off. 'You mad? No way, yu not hanging here. Hey, let me tell yu something. I survive Trench Town Jamaica, I survive women wid beards in New York, I survive de British immigration system, but I can't survive yu three, no sirs. Yo, look, I run a respectable business here.'

The three boys laughed as Marga Man tried to hold a serious face.

'Respectable?' said Prem. 'I bet most of these CDs are pirates.'

'Yeah,' Tyrone continued. 'One of your Jamaican pirate friends got his computer and just made up copies to order.'

Marga Man pointed to various CD racks. 'Every musical biscuit in dis joint is legal, me is an upright citizen, you see? Me is what dem call boni fido.'

The laughter got louder and now the boys began to strut around the shop, teasing Marga Man.

'Marga Man,' said Prem, 'it's bona fide, not boni fido. Boni fido is a dog or something like that.'

Marga Man now cut a smile as he saw the funny side. 'I don't care what you say, me is a pillar of de community. Tax payer is me. One day I shall be Lord Mayor wid gold round me neck and Rolls-Royce outside.'

'Yeah, one day you'll own a pet shop,' said Prem. 'With a nice little dog in it called boni fido.'

'Get out of me shop,' Marga Man shouted, but still smiling. 'Now I permanently exclude you. Move, I expel you for ever.'

'Yeah, yeah, OK, let's go,' said Ray. 'But we coming back later, Marga Man.'

Marga Man turned the music back on, then shouted over it, 'I told you, you permanently excluded.'

'But Marga Man,' Prem pleaded. 'We coming back with some nice bitches for you.'

'I don't care 'bout bitches, is money I deal wid, I out to mek a living. If yu want to bring me any bitches bring me some bitches wid money, bring me woman who want to buy records, bring me some consumer types.'

'Later,' they all shouted back as they left the shop.

'Look after yourselves, you guys,' Marga Man said as he watched them leave.

This was typical of the kind of banter Marga Man and the boys always had. Marga Man was a father figure for them. Even though they all had fathers, Marga Man was in tune with their way of life. They could talk to him about things their real fathers would never talk about. His knowledge of the world meant that they would listen to him and respect him much more than other adults. And Marga Man had the best music

13

shop in town. He didn't just rely on regular distributors, he had contacts in the hip-hop business all over the world, and that meant that he would receive discs long before most high street stores would and get music from smaller, more radical labels that would never be released in Britain. So this piece of east London was the boys' connection to the rest of the hip-hop world.

The boys made their way down West Ham Lane towards their homes. Prem was still asking about Ray's exclusion. 'So you're really out?'

Ray was getting fed up. 'How many times do I have to tell you, yes.'

'And you really did deal with Mr Harrison?'

'Yes.'

'So what your parents gonna say? Did they threaten to send you back to the Caribbean like mine were going to send me to India?' Prem asked.

Ray thought for a moment, then shrugged his shoulders. 'I don't know, they'll probably say what they said when I got excluded before.'

Tyrone thought for a moment, trying to remember what Ray's parents had said before, but he couldn't remember. 'What *did* they say before?'

'I don't know,' Ray replied, after a moment. 'They don't talk to me about these things.'

* * *

It was true. After all Ray's previous exclusions his parents had barely spoken to him. His father's attitude was, *He made his bed, let him lie in it*. His mother's instinct was to side with Ray but she tried to convince herself that his father knew best. Prem and Tyrone had been excluded for pretty much the same reason as Ray. They too had just lost interest in school and after a couple of exclusions Prem had decided to verbally terrorise every teacher in sight. Tyrone had quietly backed him up with clenched fists and a macho stare.

Tyrone was an only child. His parents did try to talk to him but they simply couldn't control him. They tried threats, they tried beatings, they tried the church, and they even considered sending him to relatives in Trinidad, but they changed their minds when he calmly threatened to kill the family cat. Now they had reached the point where they would try to do their best for him in the hope that he would see the dead-end street that he was on and change his ways of his own accord.

Prem came from a working-class, trying hard to be middle-class, Indian family. He had an older sister at Newham College, a younger sister in primary school, his father worked in a travel agency, and his mother was proud to be a mother, although not so proud of him. His parents felt very let down by their only son leaning towards black culture and by his indifference to education.

Tyrone and Prem lived on the same road, and when the boys had come to the road where Ray lived, Ray led them into a spontaneous rap session, freestyle.

Ray:

I know I'm getting older as I look over my shoulder
And my lyrics just get bigger and my lyrics just get bolder
Like musical rebel full of bass and full of treble
Take it brother Tyrone, take it to another level

Tyrone:

You gotta hear me when I say just be cool X-Ray
I'm the guy the girls admire so I gotta take it higher
And any boy come challenge me that boy got to retire
But if you want come rap with me I promise to inspire

Prem:

Well I could rap in Hindi but for now I'll say nameste
And I'm worried 'bout the future 'cause the girls are out to
    get me
Some of them want kidnap me and some want tek me on
    safari
Some of them dress up in mini, some of them dress up in
    sari

Ray:

The moral of the Hip-Hop is the Hip-Hop never does stop
'Cause it travels from the bottom and it goes right to the
    top
So do it to the fullness, never let your rap be shallow
Now I'm going to see my parents and I'll see you guys
    tomorrow

They burst into laughter and touched fist.

'We got it going on,' said Prem. 'But I think we should still think of a name for ourselves. Whoever's heard of a rap band with no name? When you have a name people know that you're serious.'

'The name will come with time,' said Tyrone.

'Yeah, first we gotta get the style right, you know what I'm saying? Then the rest will fall into place,' Ray said. 'See you tomorrow, round the music shop.'

Tyrone and Prem nodded in agreement and went on their way. Ray turned to go home. He couldn't show it to the others but he was apprehensive about the future, and he walked down the street rapping to himself in a whisper until he reached his house. He let himself in and went to his bedroom.

CHAPTER 2

Home, What Home?

Ray was alone in the house. He lay on his bed looking up towards the ceiling listening to every word of Tupac's rap and carefully analysing his style. As he listened he day-dreamed about the day when he would have his own rap band and rap about the things that he cared about. Most of Tupac's raps were about the hardship of the young black male trapped in the ghetto by the oppressive system. There were words used and references made that Ray didn't understand, but he tried hard to keep up with Tupac until he was disturbed by the doorbell.

He ran downstairs and opened the front door to his sister. He didn't even look at Kori, and she didn't acknowledge him. He just turned away and ran back upstairs.

'Where's your key?' Ray shouted down to Kori.

'I forgot it,' she replied to the empty space in front of her.

Within seconds Ray was back with Tupac. But it wasn't long before the sound of Kori singing along to

Beyoncé came seeping through the walls. Ray turned his volume up. Kori turned her volume up. Ray turned his volume up even more. Kori turned her volume up again. Ray turned his volume up until the windows began to rattle. Kori turned her volume up until the walls began to move. Ray's instinct was always to turn the volume up any time Kori invaded his hear space, but there was a problem: Kori had a much better sound system than Ray. Ray's system was given to him as a birthday present by his mother. He had had to pressure her for it, and it was the cheapest one in the shop, but Kori had bought hers with her own money. She had made sure that she got the system she wanted by working in a shoe shop on Saturdays and during the holidays. She still had the job; it now paid for her clothes, hair-dos and tickets to concerts.

Ray was completely outclassed. The power of Kori's superior sound system made Tupac's angry raps sound like desperate whispering. Ray made a tactical retreat by turning his volume down, and in recognition of his gesture Kori turned her volume down. Ray had to live with it: Tupac could be heard, but Beyoncé would make her presence known in Tupac's quieter moments.

It wasn't long before Ray could hear his mother moving around downstairs, so he left the CD playing and went down to see her. She had just come back from the supermarket where she worked as a cashier. Ray stood in the kitchen doorway watching her fill the cupboards with the discounted food that she always brought home on Friday afternoons.

'Hello Mum,' Ray said quietly.

His mother had a feeling that something was wrong. Ray never said 'Hello Mum' unless something was wrong or he was in need of something.

'What's up with you?' she said, waiting for his reply.

'I'm OK,' he replied.

'What's wrong?'

'Nothing.'

'Don't tell me nothing, what's wrong?'

'Nothing, I just got excluded from school.'

'Oh no,' she said, turning towards him. 'Not again. How long for this time?'

'No, Mum, it's different this time, this is permanent exclusion. It means I can't go back to that school again.'

His mum was more confused than angry. 'What? I don't care what they call it, they can't just kick you out of school. What do they expect me to do, stop work to look after you? On Monday morning you will be going back to school and that's that.'

'I'm not going nowhere, Mum.'

'You will go to school. I will not have you walking

up and down the streets like before.'

Then Ray flipped. He shouted so loud Kori heard him over the music in her room.

'It doesn't matter what you say, I'm not going to school, they don't want me and I don't want them. They can stick their bloody school. Their school is boring, their school stinks and I'm not going there.'

His mother shouted back. 'You and your big mouth, I can see why them kick you out. Maybe I should kick you out too. You think you're a man, you think you're big, you wait till your father comes here, you wait. Listen to the way you speak to me.'

Ray headed towards his bedroom, slamming the door again and kicking everything in sight as he went.

Kori was at the top of the stairs. 'What's going on, Ray?'

'I got excluded, didn't I.'

'Oh, Ray,' she sighed. 'What happened?'

'That Mr Harrison, I had to put him in his place. He come telling me about where I should look, and what I should do and all that foolishness.'

'Ray, he's the teacher,' Kori pleaded. 'Can't you control yourself? He's only trying to run the lesson, you can't just do what you want, you know.'

'Don't you start. Just 'cause you let people walk all over you doesn't mean I do.'

'It's not about letting people walk over you, it's about education.'

'It's about your education, not mine. I don't need education.'

Kori turned to walk into her room. 'Yeah, you know everything don't you?' she shouted back over her shoulder.

'Yeah,' Ray replied. 'And if I need to know anything new, Tupac will teach me.'

'You're stupid, Ray,' Kori shouted as he went into his room. 'You're so stupid.'

It wasn't long before Ray's father came home. The house was noisy. Upstairs Ray had gone from playing Tupac Shakur to playing Snoop Doggy Dogg. Downstairs his dad was shouting at his mum because his boss had shouted at him, and Mum was shouting at Dad because Dad was shouting at her. This was quite normal for a workday; they always came home and expressed their frustrations in these ways. It could be worse. When Kori brought her friends home, and when Ray brought his, everything would go to another level.

'Come on you two, get your food,' Ray's mother shouted from the bottom of the stairs.

At the table there was very little conversation until Ray's mother began to try to get Ray to speak. 'Ray, talk to your father.'

'Yeah,' replied Ray, but he just continued to eat.

A couple of minutes later she tried again. 'Ray,

haven't you got something to say?'

'No,' Ray said.

'All right,' she said in resignation. 'I'm not saying anything.'

Ray's father, who had been giving the impression that he wasn't listening, now stopped eating and leaned back into his seat. 'Right, what is it?' He looked towards his wife.

'Don't look at me,' she said, before shovelling some rice and peas into her mouth.

'Nor me,' said Kori, making sure she was not involved.

'Well?' said Ray's father, looking at him.

'It's nothing. I got excluded from school, that's all.'

'That's all?' his father asked unconcernedly, leaning forward to meet his food. 'They've kicked you out before, and they'll kick you out again, and you will go in and out like an old criminal.'

'No, Dad, he's been kicked out for good,' Kori said.

'What you mean, kicked out for good?' said their father, going way back in his seat again. 'They can't just kick him outta school for good. This is England and every boy must go to school, even if he is a no-good layabout like this one.'

'I'm no layabout,' said Ray.

'You are,' said Kori.

'Yeah, you can talk, you had two boyfriends at the same time. That means you're a slag.'

23

'I didn't, and I ain't a slag.'

'Shut up, you two,' shouted Ray's mother. She looked towards his father. 'They said he can't go back to school, so he can't go back to school. We can't force them to take him back.'

'They took him back before.'

'But this is different from before, before it was . . .' Ray's mother hesitated.

Kori obliged. 'Temporary exclusion.'

'Yes, temporary,' his mother continued. 'And this is . . .' she hesitated again.

'Permanent.' Kori obliged again.

'Yes,' she continued. 'That means that the school don't want nothing to do with him.'

'And I don't want nothing to do with them,' Ray added.

'Leave him,' said his father. 'That's what I say, leave him and let him fend for himself.'

'He's a child, Marvin, he cannot fend for himself.'

'Well, he keeps telling everyone he's a man, so let's see how man he is, let's send him to work, make him pay his way.'

'He's not a man, he's a boy,' Ray's mother shouted.

'I'm not a boy,' said Ray.

'Shut up,' said his father.

'He's not a boy, or a man, he's a teenager,' said Kori.

'Shut up,' said their mother. 'As far as the law is

concerned he is a schoolboy, and he's too young to work anyway.'

'Just because he's excluded from one school that doesn't mean he's excluded from all schools. What they do is they find another school in the area to take him,' said Kori.

Ray stood up and headed for the door, knocking his chair over as he did so. 'You lot are talking rubbish. It don't matter what you, or anyone says, I'm not going to school.'

'You see,' said his father, pointing in Ray's direction. 'That's why them don't want him in school, he has no manners, he has no respect.'

'Yeah, and he has no parents,' said Kori.

Ray's mother went pale. 'Kori, what are you saying? What do you mean by that?'

Kori held her head down. 'I'm sorry, Mum. But you can't just keep shouting at him. Try talking to him. That's the problem, he thinks that everyone is shouting at him, his teacher, his head teacher, his mother, his father. Shouting doesn't work with him.'

'Nothing works with him,' said her father.

'Kori has a point,' said her mother, in an effort to try and get her husband to take a different approach. But Kori's father wasn't having it.

'She has a point, does she? Never mind the point. He's a failure, it's as simple as that.'

25

Kori tried again. 'Dad, I know he's a bit messed up but –'

'Yes, you're right he is a bit messed up,' her father said, interrupting, 'and that's being kind to him. I could tell you a lot more things that he is.'

Kori stood up and left the room. Her father shouted after her. 'You just make sure you don't turn out like him.'

For the rest of the evening life carried on as normal: music blared, and the usual arguments raged over who took what from the fridge, who was disrespecting who, and the volume of the music. Ray and his father drank a few cans of beer and fell asleep in front of the television where Ray slept for a couple of hours until his mother reminded him where his bedroom was.

Ray had planned to sleep for as long as he could the next day, but the sun shone brightly through the curtains and Kori was up early playing music and preparing to go to her Saturday job. By the time Ray made it downstairs his father had gone to the bookmakers to bet on some horses. His mother had just read a letter from the school notifying her of Ray's dismissal and was now sitting reading her favourite magazine.

'Can I have some money Mum?' Ray asked.

His mother continued to read as she spoke. 'You don't even say good morning and you're asking me for money. What do you want money for?'

'I just wanna go out.'

'Out where?'

'Just out.'

'You don't need money to go just out.'

'Please, Mum, you know what I mean.'

'I got a letter from your school today. Ray, why can't you just get on with your work at school and stop making life difficult for everyone?'

'That school crap, Mum. It's that stupid school that makes life difficult for me. Mum, can I have some money please?' As Ray finished speaking, the doorbell rang. He looked out of the window. It was Tyrone and Prem.

'Please, Mum,' he pleaded as he went to open the door. 'Wait, I'll be out soon,' he said to Tyrone and Prem.

He went back to his mother. 'Please.'

She pointed to her purse on the table in front of her. 'Take five pounds.'

'Five pounds?' Ray said loudly. 'Mum, that can't even buy me a CD.'

'I thought you said the money was for just going out?' she said.

'Come on, Mum, please.'

'OK, take ten and get out.'

Ray grabbed the purse and took a ten-pound note out. 'That will do I suppose.'

He ran upstairs and quickly got himself ready. On the way out he stopped off in the kitchen and grabbed some biscuits before shouting to his mother, 'I'm gone.'

The boys headed for the park where they sat around chatting up girls as they passed. Then they started rapping freestyle to each other, each trying to show the others their superior wit, observation and rhyming skills. But as always there was no obvious winner. All three of them made claims and all of them knew that any one of them could have won, depending on what the judges would stress as most important, and there were no judges anyway.

From the park they went to Flip Discs. There they listened to the latest recording that Marga Man had obtained from America. DJs from near and far visited the shop during the day, but Marga Man had his favourite customers, and these were the DJs who would be the first to hear the freshest cuts.

The only things the boys had eaten all day were biscuits and crisps washed down with a variety of fizzy drinks. At 8pm Marga Man shut the shop and took the boys to the burger bar a couple of doors down.

'You got some wicked beats,' Tyrone said, with his mouth full of burger.

'You got some nice raps,' Marga Man replied, biting into a burger twice the size of everyone else's.

'The difference is,' Ray said, looking at his burger and wishing it was as sweet as the biscuits he had eaten earlier, 'you can make money selling your beats, but we can't make money selling our raps.'

'Talking about money, how much money you guys got?' asked Prem.

'What you wanna know for? You can't have any of my money,' said Ray.

'Don't joke,' said Prem seriously. 'DJ Rapcity is playing at the Rex tonight, let's go. Seven pounds in before midnight.'

'I got seven,' Ray said.

'I got seven,' Tyrone said.

'And I'm not going,' Marga Man said. 'You just be careful, don't go getting yourselves permanently excluded from there. When dem guys exclude you it hurt, yeah man, it hurts bad me a tell you. Have you ever been excluded at de end of a boot?'

After killing some time in the burger bar Marga Man left for home and the boys headed towards the club. It was early but Prem insisted that an early arrival would be to their advantage. He had a plan. Before the club opened they circled it and identified a suitable exit door. They waited for the club to open, and Prem paid his money to get in. Ray and Tyrone waited outside, and as the club began to fill up Prem made his way to the exit door. Ray and Tyrone had waited for almost an hour and they were beginning to get impatient, but when Prem could see no security staff he lifted the bar that opened the door. Ray and Tyrone were relieved to see the door open, but as it opened, a loud, piercing alarm went off.

'Hurry up,' said Prem. 'Stay low.'

They entered quickly, staying as low as they could. Fortunately the club goers around them were willing to turn a blind eye, and although it took less than a minute for security guards to arrive, when they did so the boys had disappeared into the crowd. All Ray and Tyrone had to do now was avoid any contact with security staff because, unlike people who had paid their entrance fee, they had no ink stamp on the back of their hands.

Once they had found a corner to rest, Ray had a go at Prem. 'You didn't say there was an alarm on the door.'

'I didn't know,' Prem replied. 'There wasn't one the last time I did it.'

'You did it before?' Tyrone asked.

Prem laughed. 'Loads of times. Why pay for three people when you can pay for one?'

'The bouncers here are massive, did you see them?' Ray held his hands apart to emphasise width. 'If they get you they kill you.'

'No, they don't,' said Tyrone, scanning the dance floor. 'They only kill you if you try to kill them, normally they just slap you up a bit and throw you out. Anyway, let's circulate.'

'Yeah,' said Ray, 'let's circulate. I see some bitches that look like they want some training.'

In fact the girls didn't need them; the girls were getting on fine without them. They were not amused when the boys pushed their way in front of them to try and impress them with their dancing. Ray had a habit of dancing very close to girls he didn't know and quite often he was forced to back off when bigger boyfriends arrived on the scene. The boys were among the younger people in the club so without more back-up they were vulnerable to attack, and they knew it. They spent most of their money on non-alcoholic drinks, and left the club without any of them obtaining the phone number of a female. But they'd had a great time and they rapped happily as they made their way home.

They decided not to meet on Sunday, but as none of them was going to school on Monday the plan was to meet then and move between the park, the shopping centre and the music shop.

It was half past one. Ray said goodbye to Tyrone and Prem and walked down the street to his house. He unlocked the front door and quietly went up to his bedroom. He put on a CD on low volume and sat on his bed to take his shoes off. But then his father walked in. He was angry, his eyes looked crazed.

'Who do you think you are, coming home this time of the morning like you own the place?' he shouted.

'OK, keep your head on, you don't have to shout,' Ray said, trying to hide how startled he was.

His father made no effort to keep his voice down and Ray could see how angry he was. 'Who you talking to like that? Don't get me mad you know.'

'You're mad already.' Ray was pushing his luck – he could smell alcohol.

His father went over to the CD player and pushed the whole unit off the table, causing an almighty crash. Ray's mother came to the door.

'What's going on, Marvin? The noise woke me up.'

Kori joined her mother in the doorway. She was frightened, she held her mother's arm tightly.

As Ray's father answered he kicked the CDs that had also fallen on the floor. 'This boy thinks he can speak to me however he likes, and he can't. That's what's going on.'

Ray jumped up and stood over the electronic mess that was on the floor. 'Look what he done Mum, and I didn't do anything.'

'Didn't do anything? He come in here after one o'clock, put on music, answer me back, and him thinks he hasn't done anything.'

'Shut up! I haven't done anything, and you're drunk,' Ray said, looking down at the mess of his hi-fi as if his world was broken before him.

But his father was taking no more. He stepped over to Ray and slapped him across the back of his head. 'Don't tell me to shut up.'

'I will,' Ray shouted defiantly. 'Shut up, you drunk.'

His father lost his temper completely. He picked up one of the shoes that Ray had just taken off and tried to pull Ray down to the bed to beat him with it, but Ray wasn't having it. He began to struggle to try and get away but his father struck him with the shoe on his back.

'You can't beat me any more, I'll fight you back,' Ray shouted as he swung a punch towards his father's stomach.

His mother stepped in and grabbed his father to try to separate them but they rolled over the bed all hanging on to each other. They were quickly joined by Kori, who grabbed hold of Ray. Kori screamed for them to stop, but they continued grappling. All four rolled off the bed and ended up on the floor. Ray's father managed to get Ray face down on the floor with his arms behind his back.

Ray was getting desperate. He twisted and wriggled until he got in position, then he opened his mouth as wide as he could and bit down on his father's arm. The bite was so hard he felt his teeth tear through his father's shirt, but it wasn't enough, and he bit harder. His father screamed and loosened his grip. Ray was now in tears, and his father was vowing to kill him.

Ray jumped up with Kori still trying to hold him, but he threw her to the ground. As quickly as he could he grabbed his shoes, one from off the bed and one from the floor, and ran down the stairs and outside. He didn't stop running until he got to the top of the road. Suddenly it was quiet, it was peaceful, but, as he walked, shoes in hand, clothing torn, reality hit him. He had nowhere to go.

CHAPTER 3

Out on the Town

The night wasn't cold, but Ray needed light and a roof over his head. For a while he tried to convince himself that the streets made him free, as free as he had felt when he walked out of school, but then it began to get colder and he had no jacket.

He seriously began to consider what he should do. He thought about going to Tyrone or Prem's house, but it was so late, and he would also have their parents to deal with. He considered going to Marga Man's place, but Marga Man lived miles away in Walthamstow, and he wasn't even sure if he could remember the address. And then he thought about going back home. Home was where he wanted to be, with his CDs, warm in his bed, but his pride wouldn't let him, so he walked.

At West Ham Park he climbed over the fence and sat on a bench in the middle of the park. The unfamiliar sound of the night animals made him nervous. Although he knew the park well, he only knew it by day. The park at night was a new world, and he had never experienced such darkness alone. He wasn't used to being surrounded by sounds he didn't know. Cars, trains and police sirens didn't scare him, but the sounds of city foxes moving in hedges kept him on edge, and hedgehogs rustling through leaves on the ground was the sound of the unknown.

When Ray couldn't take any more, he left the park and went to Stratford bus station. It was light, there were people there, and a machine to buy a bar of chocolate. After checking how much money he still had, he came up with an idea, one that would mean him being warm and getting a roof over his head. After a short wait, the N25 night bus arrived. For one pound Ray had a ride right into the heart of London.

The closer Ray got to central London the busier it got. On Whitechapel Road, market traders were already beginning to prepare for the next day, and ambulances were busy ferrying the wounded to hospital. The bus had to stop for five minutes at Aldgate East while two car drivers took their road rage out on each other, and then for another five as the police arrested them both, along with a passer-by who tried to convince the police that their employer was the devil and that they should go to hell.

By the time Ray arrived at Oxford Circus the bus was packed. He had been to the West End many times before, and he had been there at night, but never at this time of the morning, and never alone. He walked down Regent Street to Piccadilly Circus; it was an uneventful walk, nobody looked at him twice. At Piccadilly Circus he spent a few minutes being dazzled by the lights before he sat down under the statue of Eros to watch buskers playing West African music. As he sat watching and listening, a man who reminded him of his father came and sat next to him.

'Hey, you wanna earn some money, youth man?' he said, looking Ray up and down like a piece of merchandise.

'Doing what?' Ray replied.

'That all depends how far you wanna go, youth man. If you wanna earn a bit sticking cards in phone boxes, I can set that up, you wanna do deliveries, I can work that for you, and if you want some serious shit, and I'm talking about serious money, money for the bank, I can get you some modelling work, you know what I'm saying?'

Ray looked away from him. 'No.'

'Hey man, don't be like that. Ask me about the possibilities or career prospects.'

'I said no, guy, now leave me.'

The stranger spoke with excitement as he tried to keep his voice low. 'Listen, youth man, I know all the right people, I know people who could set you up nicely if you need help. Do you have somewhere to stay?'

Ray stood up and shouted, 'What's wrong with

you? I told you to leave me alone. Don't get me vex, just move from me, right.'

The stranger stood up and two men who had heard Ray began to laugh. They moved towards them. One of them put his arm around the shoulder of the stranger.

'Are you still at it, Midnight?' he giggled. 'Still trying to lead the young and beautiful to the promised land?'

'Hey, Midnight,' the other man added. 'If you wasn't so ugly you could sell yourself.' They all began to walk off in the direction of Leicester Square and the man with his arm around Midnight looked back and shouted, 'Don't worry mate, he's just working overtime.'

Ray had had enough, but to his relief daylight was beginning to show. As the road cleaners and refuse collectors began to prepare the streets for the day shift he took a slow walk back down Regent Street, and there he boarded the very same bus that had brought him in. He was in desperate need of some sleep and kept nodding off, but the jerks of the ride and the stopping and starting of the bus just about kept him awake enough for him to be aware of where he was on the journey. Back at Stratford station he searched his head for more ideas but by now even his mind was tired. He sat on a bench and eventually fell asleep, his head bowed.

* * *

It was a strange sleep. One part of his brain seemed to be sleeping whilst the other was aware of the build-up of passengers around him. He could hear the buses arriving more frequently, and he began to feel the sun as it warmed the air.

The waking-up process was a slow one. First, without moving his body, he switched on his mind. When he felt that his mind was strong enough to control his body, he shook his head, then he raised his shoulders and moved them in a circular motion. He clenched and opened his fists, which were placed between his legs, and took his feet from under him and stretched them forward. Then he lifted his head as far back as he could until he was looking up at the bus shelter. Breathing in deeply, he moved his head from side to side and stood up.

He had only slept for just over an hour but the station was now a different place. Even at eight o'clock on a Sunday morning it was lively. Ray went to the newsstand, bought a packet of biscuits and began walking once again. This time he headed for Tyrone's house, which was just a couple of streets away from his own. To kill as much time as possible he walked slowly, stopping to look in the windows of as many shops as he could and watching people much more than he usually would.

* * *

Tyrone's father didn't like Ray – he thought that Ray was the bad influence who was leading Tyrone astray. So when he opened his front door to find Ray standing there, he wasn't happy.

'What you want?'

'Could I speak to Tyrone please?' Ray didn't like Tyrone's father either, so this was as polite as he could get.

'Wait there,' Tyrone's father said, closing the door.

Ray was left standing on the step, but this was what always happened when he called for Tyrone. Ray had been inside the house in the past, but only when Tyrone's parents weren't there. When Tyrone opened the door, Ray could see that he had just woken up. All he was wearing was shorts and a vest and he was still rubbing his eyes.

'Ray, how come you get up so early? We said we'd meet up on Monday?' As Tyrone spoke he realised that something wasn't right. 'What's up? You look rough.'

'Got kicked out.'

'What, your parents kicked you out again?'

'No, he didn't kick me out again, I got into a fight with him and I left. The man come mash up me CD player, and throw all me CDs on the floor.'

'What if he calls the police?' Tyrone asked.

'Look how many times he's kicked me out, he's not gonna call the cops. He's probably really glad that I've gone.'

Tyrone could feel his own father lurking in the background. He pulled the door behind him until it was almost closed. 'So what you gonna do?'

'I don't know,' Ray replied despondently.

'We got to have a plan, look at the state of you.'

Ray looked down at his slept-in clothing.

'I know.'

'Do you want to borrow some of my clothes?' Tyrone asked.

Ray sounded surprised. 'No, guy, look how big you is.'

'Well, I got a plan,' he said. 'Wait here, I'll get dressed.'

Ten minutes later, Tyrone came out. He handed Ray a few biscuits and they began to walk, with Tyrone leading the way. But Ray had to stop him when he turned down the road where Ray lived.

'You mad or what, where you going?'

'Don't worry, I got a plan. Trust me, you're safe,' Tyrone said reassuringly. 'This is the plan,' he continued. 'We get some girl off the street to knock for your sister and get her out here, and then when she comes we can get some stuff for you.'

As they waited at the top of the road Ray saw Lizette and Thara going to their singing lessons. They were friends of Kori's so it was easy for them to go to the house and get Kori out on the pretence that they needed to speak to her.

When Kori saw Ray, she pleaded with him to return home, but Ray and Tyrone pleaded with her in turn to go back to the house and bring some of Ray's belongings out. They won. Kori went back to the house and filled two carrier bags full of various items of his clothing. She put his lightweight coat under her arm and made her way back. It was easy to bypass their parents, as their mother was watching a cookery programme, and their father was still in bed. Even as Kori handed Ray the bags she continued to plead with him to come home, but Ray had made his mind up.

'Where to now?' Ray asked Tyrone as Kori left them.

'Marga Man to the rescue,' Tyrone said, as if announcing the arrival of a super hero.

When they arrived at the music shop Marga Man was busy serving customers. The boys hovered around until they had gone, then they started to make their presence felt.

'Marga Man, it's us. Long time no see,' Tyrone said.

Marga Man folded his arms, leaned his head back, and looked down his nose. 'I never expect to see you guys until tomorrow. So, what's up?'

'Nothing,' Ray said.

Marga Man laughed. 'So how come you look like a

wild dog's been playing wid yu? Yu can't fool me yu know.'

Ray realised that there was no way he would be able to hide anything from him. 'Had a fight with me dad didn't I, and I left home, that's it.'

'Fight with yu dad? Left home?' Marga Man made it all sound so ridiculous. 'So you're still fighting? And all right, you left home, but tell me now, do you have anywhere to live?'

'Never mind that,' Ray said.

Tyrone started thinking practically. 'Marga Man, let him use the washroom.'

'What washroom?' Marga Man said. 'There's no washroom here, here there is a toilet wid a sink in it, no washroom here.'

Tyrone saw the funny side of it but didn't think it was that funny. 'You know what I mean, he needs to change and wash up.'

Marga Man nodded in the direction of the toilet.

It must have been the smallest toilet in Europe, almost impossible to turn in, and changing in it was very much like changing in bed. When it was cold in winter Ray changed in bed, so he was practised, and he managed. When he came out there were customers searching through the racks. Tyrone and Marga Man had smirks on their faces.

'Ray, how come you take so long?' Tyrone asked, trying to hold back the laughter.

'You try prettying up in there, it's no changing room you know. There's no mirrors and no dressing table in there you know,' Ray said.

Marga Man fanned the air in front of his nose and grimaced. 'Hey man, you stink up me toilet.'

'It's the biscuits,' Ray replied, rubbing his stomach. 'It's like biscuits, chocolate and hamburgers all mixed up, does stuff to your belly man.'

'Ease up,' Marga Man said quickly. 'Never mind de details, just open de windows and let in some pollution.'

'And don't let any customers go in there for the rest of the day,' Tyrone added. 'Can I call Prem?'

Prem was the only one of the three that owned a mobile phone, and when he received the call from Tyrone he was in the shop within half an hour. Tyrone and Prem then took Ray into the shopping centre to get something to eat. They stayed around the shopping centre for a while and then they made their way to the park to tease more girls. By mid-afternoon they were back in the music shop. The question of where Ray was going to stay if he insisted on not going home kept coming up, but it kept being pushed aside, unresolved. Prem and Tyrone both considered sneaking him into their homes, but it was too risky. Prem's sisters could not be relied on to keep secrets, and if Ray were to be caught in Tyrone's house they had no reason to believe that Tyrone's father would suddenly feel compassion towards him.

Marga Man usually closed the music shop around eight o'clock, depending on the level of business, but Sunday always meant early closing, at about six. Ray picked up his bags from behind the counter and the boys helped Marga Man roll down the shop shutters. As they hovered around him Marga Man could feel that they were not eager to leave.

'You guys want to eat?' Marga Man asked.

The boys looked at each other and, seeing that none of them reacted in any way, Prem chose to speak for all of them.

'No, we're cool.'

'So where you going now?'

'Just hanging out,' Ray said.

Marga Man looked towards the bags Ray was carrying, and said, 'Yu don't have any choice but to hang out, yu don't even have a plan of action, do yu? Listen, I'm going down to Rock It Science Studio to check a brother, yu want come?'

There was no hesitation; they all said, 'Yes.'

'OK come, but yu must work out a plan. Yu look like three leaders who don't know where to go.'

The studio was a short walk away in a converted factory in Burford Road. After pressing a few buttons and whispering a couple of passwords they were in. The studio was owned and run by an aging ex-musician who had never lost his afro and still dressed and sounded as if he were in a seventies soul band.

'What's happening Bunny,' Marga Man said as they touched fists, shook hands, and hugged.

'Everything's cool man,' Bunny said. 'Everything's just cool, and you?'

'All right man. Business is OK, sun is shining, and love is lovely. Hey, meet de crew.'

Marga Man introduced Bunny to the boys, and after some small talk Bunny began to play various pieces of music that he had been working on. It was the first time any of them had been in a recording studio. For over an hour they sat listening to R'n'B and soul music. The boys nodded reluctantly, but Bunny was loving his creations.

It went quiet for a moment and Bunny stood up. Reaching for a digital tape high on a shelf he announced, 'This you have to hear. This is the right tune, all it needs is the right vocals.'

He put the tape on and started to dance around the control room like an upright snake. 'Good, isn't it?'

'Nice tune,' said Marga Man. It wasn't his favourite type of music, but he could get into the groove.

The boys just looked at each other. Not laughing was becoming hard work, so every time Bunny's back was turned they giggled quietly. It was a slow instrumental, a sweet track, a perfect example of the kind of music Ray and the boys didn't like. When it stopped playing, Bunny looked at Ray, excitement etched on his face.

'So what do you think, nice groove or what?'

Ray came straight out with it. 'Not my kind of thing, but it's all right.'

'What you mean, all right? That's good music, young blood, you're too young to know real music.'

'Careful,' said Marga Man. 'These guys listen to music every day, I can't get them out of my shop.'

'So what you into?' Bunny asked, looking towards the boys. 'Reggae, drum an' bass, garage music, house music, living room music?'

'Hip-hop,' Tyrone said. The others nodded in agreement.

'Hip-hop,' said Bunny. 'Got plenty of that. What, do you kids sing?'

'No,' said Prem. 'We kids don't sing.'

'I can do hip-hop.' Bunny started searching his shelves. 'Got plenty of hip-hop.' He took a tape and began to play it. Now all heads were nodding. The tune had very little melody, but it had an irresistible beat and a bass line that could destroy the weak-hearted.

As the music began to play, Ray had a flash of inspiration. 'Play it again,' he said, with his eyes closed.

Bunny rewound the tape and let it run again. Ray began to improvise a rap over the track. It was about kids that are misunderstood by their fathers, and fathers who pay no attention to their sons. He opened his eyes halfway through and for much of the rap he was staring at his carrier bags. Marga Man, Tyrone and Prem were struck by what Ray was saying and by the intensity of the lyrics. Bunny jumped around the studio, unaware of the significance of what Ray was rapping. When the rapping was done there was silence until Bunny voiced his opinion.

'That was so cool, yeah man, that was something else. Hey, do you wanna record that jive? We can run it right now.'

'No,' said Ray.

Bunny pointed to the vocal booth. 'Come on, man, let's lay it down one time.'

'No way,' Ray replied quite sharply.

But Bunny wanted to capture the moment. 'Hey blood, we can do that vocal tonight, man, and you'll leave here feeling as good as I do.'

'Leave it out,' said Prem. 'He said no, let it rest.'

'Yeah, Bunny man, let it rest,' said Marga Man.

Bunny became aware that something was up. He backed off and searched through some more tapes. 'No problem. Hey, I got another one, check dis.'

They listened to more music and then went back to West Ham Lane. They arrived at Marga Man's car near the music shop.

'So what do you think of my man Bunny?' Marga

Man asked, as they stood around the car.

'He's got some good ideas,' Ray replied. 'Some of his tunes are a bit antique but some of those other beats kick it nicely.'

'He looks like he knows his stuff,' said Prem.

It was time to leave, but Ray wasn't prepared to spend another night in the park and on the buses. They still hadn't discussed a plan, so the others had no idea of what Ray was about to say.

'Marga Man, I need a favour.'

'How much do you need?' Marga Man went for his wallet.

'No,' said Ray, 'I need somewhere to sleep.'

'I know dat.' Marga Man laughed aloud. 'Hey man, yu want to come home wid me? Me wife will kill yu and den she will kill me, she dangerous. Listen Ray, go home, make peace wid your old man. Dat's best, yu know it.'

'No way.'

'So Ray, what do you want me to do?'

'Just for a couple of nights, let me stay in the shop.'

'In de shop?' Marga Man shouted back. 'You're joking?'

'Hey, not a bad idea,' said Prem.

'Yeah,' Tyrone added.

'No way, yu spend all day in there and now yu want to spend all night in there? Soon you'll be kicking me out and moving in wid some of dem wild girls I see

49

you chasing. Ray, think about what you're doing, reason wid yourself.'

'Marga Man,' Ray said in a raised voice, 'you don't understand, man. It doesn't matter how much I reason with meself, right now I can't reason with me dad, so it's like this – if I can't stay in the shop I'll just have to hang out on the streets, 'cause I'm not going back home.'

Marga Man thought for a while. 'Is a place of business, there's nowhere to sleep there.'

'I'll sleep between the racks in the shop, or in the storeroom. I won't disturb a thing Marga Man, just for a couple of nights, till I sort meself out.'

Marga Man trusted Ray, he knew that he would do no harm to the premises, but he had other concerns. 'Listen, I will let yu stay, but I don't want no trouble from your father. You is under sixteen so there must be an illegal thing here and I'm too old to go prison now. But I will trust yu. But please don't get me in trouble, me have enough troubles already.'

'Thanks Marga Man, respect,' said Ray.

Marga Man decided not to drive home for a while. They all went to a convenience store to stock up on drinks, crisps and biscuits. In the music shop Marga Man recited a list of do's and don'ts to Ray and left him to bed down. The floor was hard but Ray was happy to have a real roof over his head.

CHAPTER 4

Girl Trouble

For the next couple of days Ray slept in the music shop. Tyrone and Prem spent as much time as they could with him, and Marga Man kept them all fed. On the third day Kori turned up at the shop. Marga Man was out and about, and Prem, Tyrone and Ray were behind the counter stacking CDs.

She walked straight up to the counter. 'Ray, I've been looking everywhere for you. You have to come home.'

'Do you wanna buy some real music?' Ray said, waving a CD around.

'This is no time for joking, you know. Come on, you must come home with me.'

Tyrone and Prem continued their work. Ray put the CDs down and leaned on the counter. 'What for, so that Dad can have another go at me?'

'Never mind Dad, Mum wants to see you.'

'It don't matter what you say, I am not going home.'

Kori turned towards the door. 'OK, I'll tell her that

51

you don't want to see her.'

'Listen,' Ray shouted over the music. 'No, Kori, just don't tell her that you've seen me, don't say nothing. You ain't seen me, right.'

As Kori walked towards the door she said, 'I haven't seen you but you should know that you can't run and you can't hide,' giving a customer who was entering the impression that she was speaking to her.

As the customer passed Kori, she looked back at Kori, then she looked towards Ray. Ray pointed his finger to the side of his head. 'Don't worry,' he said. 'She's on medication.'

When Marga Man returned to the shop the boys took off for the park. They arranged to meet up with him later at the Calabash Caribbean takeaway on Vicarage Lane. It was mid-afternoon and a perfect time for the boys to hit the park. The local girls' school had begun to empty out and the boys wanted every girl that walked through the park to know they were around. They teased, questioned or simply made noises without let-up, never stopping to consider why none of the girls had come rushing over to throw themselves at their feet.

'This is it,' Ray shouted, jumping up to stand on the seat of the park bench. 'This is it, they is some sweet bitches, and I know which one is mine.'

Tyrone and Prem looked in the direction of where

Ray was looking to see three girls who had just entered the park.

'Now don't tell me these bitches weren't made for us,' Ray said, dancing around. 'Look, they're coming right to us, drawn to us like a magnet. The one on the left is mine all mine, Tyrone you should go for the one on the right, she looks like she come from Trinidad, and Prem you go straight for the centre. It's a community service thing.' Ray was referring to the fact that two of the girls were black and the one in the centre was Asian.

'All right,' Ray said as they got closer. 'Let's service the community.'

As the girls reached them the boys jumped off the bench and blocked their way. Each one stood in front of their designated girl.

'What's your name?' Ray said to the girl in front of him.

'None of your business,' she replied, looking straight back at him.

Tyrone tried to be more courteous. 'Can I carry your bag?'

'Excuse me, let me pass.' The first girl was not allowing herself to be entertained by Ray in any way whatsoever.

Prem asked what he thought was a more intelligent question. 'So how was school today?'

'At least we go to school,' said the girl in front of

him, who stepped past him and began to walk on.

'Hey, come here, I just wanna talk to you,' Prem said, reaching out and tugging her arm.

'Take your hand off me,' she said sternly.

'Hey girl, I only wanna talk to you.'

'Don't girl me, and take your hand off me right now.'

Prem let her go.

'That bitch got plenty of bark,' Ray said to the girl in front of him. 'So you got a boyfriend or what?'

'Move out of my way,' she said, noticing that the other two girls had now passed their obstructions. 'If you don't move out of my way there will be trouble.'

Ray smiled. 'Listen, there's no need to get heated, we're just saying hello. Let's walk for a while.' He put his arm round her.

She threw his arm off and pushed him away. 'Don't you touch me.'

Ray staggered back a few steps before he regained his balance, but as soon as he was steady on his feet he lunged forward and pushed the girl, who fell to the ground. She stood up straightaway, angry and determined, and tried to push him back, but he was too strong, he pushed her over again. As she lay on the ground the other two girls shouted at Ray to leave her alone but he just shouted back.

'No bitch pushes me and gets away with it.'

The two girls that were standing helped the girl

from off the ground. When she was on her feet she shouted back at Ray.

'Yeah, and no dog pushes me and gets away with it. Look at me good and remember what I told you, you won't get away with that.'

The Asian girl linked arms with the other two and led them away. 'You're in trouble,' she said in a low voice as she passed Prem.

The boys began to circulate around the park, harassing girls as they went, and it wasn't long before they cornered another three. The boys tried to persuade them to meet up with them the next day. The girls told them that they had already got boyfriends who wouldn't approve of them hanging out with other boys, but they struggled to name their boyfriends. This encouraged the boys to try harder, but they were getting nowhere.

Tyrone and Prem began to get restless, they wanted to move on, but Ray insisted on giving one of the girls the phone number of the music shop. He talked about Flip Discs as if it were his shop, inviting the girls to call him any time. Ray was putting on a pretty good show until the moment he was handing his chosen one the phone number.

A powerful kick struck the middle of his back and he fell to the ground. He felt like he had been struck by a car, and he was stunned and hurt. The girls screamed and ran away. Tyrone and Prem's attention focused on Ray, but as they moved towards him Tyrone was attacked by two boys and another two went for Prem. The boy that had kicked Ray was joined by another and now they both stood over him and kicked him anywhere they could. With two boys going at each of them they stood very little chance. Their attackers were older than them, a mixture of Asian and black guys. They had come for revenge, and they had the element of surprise. Ray was overwhelmed with kicks, Prem had been badly winded and Tyrone was bleeding from the mouth. But they tried to fight back. Tyrone and Prem managed to stay on their feet, though all they could do was lash out wildly in the hope that some punches and kicks would connect, but very few did. Ray tried to roll away, but the more he rolled the more the guys followed him. He tried to kick at them from the ground to little effect.

'That's enough,' said the boy who had first kicked Ray. He looked down at Ray and pointed at him. 'Now you should know that you don't mess with my sister. This is just a warning. If any of you touch any of those girls again we'll turn you into statistics.'

Ray managed to get on his feet. All three began to back off. One of the Asian boys pointed to Prem. 'We know you,' he said, almost laughingly. 'We know where you live, we know your sister, and we know where she studies.'

Prem shouted back. 'What can you do? If you touch my sister it will be more than us three.'

'Bring who you want, we'll take you out any time, any time.'

'Yeah,' Tyrone said, wiping blood from his mouth. 'Six of you come, attack from the back, 'cause that's the only way you could do it. But you can't come face to face, you can't come one to one.'

'Come on then, me and you, one to one,' said another of the attackers, pushing his way forward.

Tyrone clenched his fists ready for another round, when one of the attackers shouted, 'Run, police!'

All nine of them made a run for it but all exits were blocked. West Ham police station was just over the road and it looked as if every police officer from the station was chasing them. They scattered but they were all captured. Two police vans screeched up to the park gates and they were all put in the vehicles. As Ray was entering one of the vans he looked across the road and saw the three girls they had stopped earlier looking on. The girl that he had pushed to the ground looked right at him just as she had done in the park.

In the station they were all held and questioned separately. All of them admitted to the parts they had played. Tyrone, Prem and Ray claimed it was harmless fun that had just gone a bit too far, and their attackers claimed that the girls had been humiliated and that it was therefore their duty to defend the honour of their sisters and cousins. For the police it was all pretty straightforward. Everyone had to promise not to do it again, accept a caution, and then they were free to go.

But there was a problem. Ray, Tyrone and Prem, along with two of the other boys, were classed as juveniles and their parents had to be notified. It was also necessary for their parents to go to the police station to witness their discharge. At this point Ray, Tyrone and Prem were put in a room together to wait. The two boys from the other gang were in the room next door, so part of the time was taken up with the two groups shouting abuse at each other. But soon an adult came and the opposition was set free.

An hour had passed without anyone showing up and the boys had started freestyling when the door was opened and a police officer entered with Prem's mother and Tyrone's mother. Prem could see that his mother had been crying. Her eyes were still watery and the bright scarf that matched her turquoise sari was wet with her tears. Speaking just made her weep more.

'You should feel ashamed of yourself. You get thrown out of school, then you end up in a police station. What next?'

'They attacked us,' Prem said.

'But you attacked girls,' his mum shouted back. 'Young girls on their way home from school.'

'We didn't attack them,' Prem reasoned. 'We were just talking and messing about with them.'

'Girls are not for messing about with. How would you like someone to start messing around with your sisters?'

'Girls are not all perfect you know. You think they're all angels don't you?'

'That's enough,' his mum said. 'Let's go.'

Tyrone's mother just nodded her head and calmly said, 'I'm not saying anything to you.'

'OK,' Tyrone said. 'Don't say anything.'

All three of the boys began to walk towards the door when the officer put his hand up in front of Ray as if he were stopping traffic. 'I'm afraid you can't go.'

'What are you talking about can't go, there's the adults, there's the door, let me out.'

The policeman signalled the two mothers and the other two boys out of the room. 'I'm afraid not. You need a guardian or one of your parents to sign you out. They have been notified but they haven't shown up yet.'

'They know me,' Ray said, looking at the door that had just been closed by Prem's mother. 'They can sign me out.'

'I'm afraid not. The adult must be related to you,' the officer said as he left the room.

When the officer locked the door behind him, Ray was on his own. No friends, no police, just an empty room with its own little toilet. If there had been windows with bars and whitewashed walls it would have been a cell. But there were no windows, only artificial light, and the walls were painted a shiny sky-blue. A padded bench ran across the back wall.

For a while Ray rapped to himself, entertaining an invisible audience, but he couldn't keep it up for long. He was tiring and it was a tough audience. It wasn't long before he was lying on his back on the bench listening to the background noise: a mixture of phones ringing, keys jingling, doors slamming and cries for freedom from other arrested people.

Ray fell asleep and was woken by a police officer standing over him and calling his name. He sat up to see his mother and father standing by the door. Ray addressed his father.

'What do you want?'

'I want to leave you to rot in here, that's what I want,' his father said convincingly.

'Just go, then,' Ray snapped back.

'Look at you.' His father was beginning to lose his temper.

Ray returned fire. 'Look at you.'

'Look at the both of you,' his mother said. 'You're like two babies. Come on, I want to get out of this place.'

The police officer listened, uncomfortable in the midst of a family feud. Ray stood up and walked out. His mother signed for him and they left the police station. Outside the station, Ray's parents turned to face home and Ray turned towards the music shop.

'Where are you going?' asked his mother.

'I'm going about me business,' Ray replied, looking down the road.

'What business?' his mother said. 'What kind of business you have?'

'Leave him,' said his father. 'Just leave him, let him live on the streets. That's all he's good for.'

'Shut up,' his mother shouted at his father. 'No wonder he doesn't want to come home.'

'He doesn't want to come home because he's a tramp, he's a negative. Him and his friends, they are all negatives.'

'Shut up,' she said. 'And you Ray, come home, you heard what the police said, we're responsible for you.'

Ray's father walked away and left his mother standing pleading with Ray to go home.

'Your father's upset, Ray, he doesn't mean what he's saying. He doesn't know how to deal with these things. Come home, Ray, we can talk things over.'

'He doesn't know how to talk,' Ray said, looking in the direction of his father.

'Well, talk to me,' said his mother.

After a few more words of reassurance Ray decided

to go home with his mother. They were silent for most of the time, but every couple of minutes Ray would ask her a question which she would answer using no more than a few syllables.

'Has anyone been in my room?'

'No.'

'Are my CDs all right?'

'Yes.'

'Is my CD player working?'

'Don't know.'

'Has anyone messed with my stuff?'

'No.'

'Has anyone called for me?'

'Yes.'

'Who?'

'School.'

'Why?'

'Checking that we got the letter.'

'What have we got to eat?'

'Food.'

CHAPTER 5

The Sunday Educational Supplement

A report published today reveals some alarming figures about exclusions in schools in England and Wales. The report, published by The Nation Foundation, an organisation that works with excluded children, identifies the reasons for the high levels of exclusions as verbal abuse, violence towards teachers and non-teaching staff, damaging of school property, bullying and possession of cannabis.

The authors of the report highlight the fact that an exclusion from school is often only a symptom of deeper problems within the child's life, and that in most cases simply taking the pupil out of full-time education can cause more severe problems for the pupil in the future. The report states that an excluded child is most likely to be a teenage boy, although the number of girls is increasing rapidly. Eighty-three per cent of excluded children are male and over two-thirds of them are aged between 13 and 16. It also found that a significant number of excluded young people are involved in crime, which means that the real cost of exclusions is very difficult to calculate.

The government has recently stated in its Green Paper on welfare reform that reducing the number of exclusions from schools is a specific target in its battle to tackle social exclusion, but today's report questions its approach by saying that 'the government is looking for a panacea when there isn't one'. It claims that a lack of inter-agency coordination has exacerbated many of the problems faced by socially excluded young people, and concludes by advocating a multi-faceted approach that would shift the balance towards prevention rather than using what it calls 'the drastic surgery of exclusion'.

The Education Secretary said his department was looking into the report and would respond to its recommendations in the near future.

CHAPTER 6

Positivity

When Ray and his mother arrived home Ray went straight to his room. Someone had made an attempt to tidy it up, but that was unimportant – the first thing Ray attended to was his CD player. It had been put back on the table, but the wires at the back were tangled and had not been reconnected. Ray connected the wires and put a CD in. He felt a great sense of relief when it started to play.

'Good job,' he said as he began to check his CDs. When he noticed that one was missing he went and banged on Kori's door. 'Where's my CD?'

'You only just back and you started already?' came the shout back from Kori.

'Just give me my Busta Rhymes before I bust ya nose.'

Before Ray had time to say anything else the door opened, Kori's hand reached out holding the CD, and Ray took it from her without either of them saying anything further.

* * *

Although he was very hungry, Ray avoided sitting at the table with the rest of the family that evening. Instead he waited until his father was in front of the television, then he persuaded his mother to re-heat the rice and chicken. Ray ate it like it was the first meal he had had for weeks. At times he loaded his mouth with so much food that it was hard to chew, as it was like trying to swallow cardboard. It took him a while before he began to realise that he simply didn't have enough saliva to cope with the contents of his mouth, and then he added orange squash to the mixture to lubricate its passage.

His mother watched him quietly for a while, then left the room. When she returned she had a letter in her hand which she put on the table as Ray ate. Ray wiped his mouth with the back of his hand and picked up the letter. It was from the school, calling his parents to a meeting.

Ray's mother stood over him as he read the letter. When he had finished reading she took it from him.

'Obviously your father's not going to go, but I made an appointment with them for tomorrow, after work.'

'Good luck,' Ray said, as he continued to eat.

'What do you mean, good luck? This is no joke,' his mother said as she poked her finger into his shoulder.

'I'm not joking either,' Ray said, still chewing

chicken. 'I hope the meeting goes well.'

She began to wave the letter in front of his face. 'This is not about me, you know, this is about you.'

'Well, if it's about me then forget it, because I know I'm not going back to that school.'

'Listen to him,' his father shouted from the living room. 'I told you to forget him. Next time he ends up in the police station we should just leave him and let him rot there.'

His mother sat on the chair next to Ray and pulled it up until she couldn't get any closer to him. It was uncomfortably close for Ray; he froze as she spoke softly to him.

'Please Ray, I beg you, come with me. Never mind your father, never mind your friends, just do it for yourself, and for me. I can't take it any more. They said it will be a relaxed meeting where you will be listened to, nobody will be shouting at you, and anything that you have to say will be taken seriously. Please.'

She reached out and held Ray's arm as it rested on the table. Ray had not felt the touch of his mother for years. It had a calming effect on him, it relaxed him with its warmth, but she was shivering, and when Ray looked into his mother's eyes he could see that she was a mother who was worried about her son.

'There's nowhere else to go,' she whispered.

'OK then, I'll go,' Ray replied, staring at her hand.

After a day of avoiding his father, Ray had a great sleep. For a short while he was woken when his parents prepared for work and Kori prepared for school, but then he went straight back to sleep and he slept right through until two o'clock. It was great being in his own bed. Ray had told himself to sleep until he couldn't sleep any more, and that's just what he did.

When he did get out of bed he got into a hot bath and soaked for twenty minutes. Then he had a shower and washed his hair. He oiled his skin with baby oil, he oiled his hair with Mr Cool hair gel, and he wiped some of his father's Afroslick aftershave around his neck. He was smelling, he was oily, and he was greasy, but after only being able to wash in a sink for the previous couple of days he was happy.

Ray began to wonder what had happened to Tyrone and Prem. He rang Marga Man at Flip Discs. Marga Man had heard about the incident at the park and their detention at the station from other kids who had come into the shop, but he had not heard from any of the boys themselves. Then Ray rang Tyrone's home and Prem's mobile but there was no reply from either of them, so he spent most of the afternoon putting his CDs in order and lazing around the house until his mother came in from work to take him to the meeting at school.

* * *

When they arrived at the school most of the students had left. Ray liked the idea of walking into school dressed in his big clothes, but his pride in looking so big was matched by his embarrassment at being with his mother.

When they arrived at the headmaster's office, Prem and his mother were sitting outside. The two mothers greeted each other.

'What are you doing here?' Ray asked, moving quickly to sit next to Prem.

'Had a meeting with Mr Lang, didn't I. Tyrone's in there now.'

'So what are you waiting for?'

Prem looked a little unsure. 'Well, I don't know, he said that he wants to see me again.'

Tyrone and his mother came out and Ray and his mother went in. The meeting was short. Ray's mother was told exactly why Ray had been excluded, Ray was told why the school could not put up with his behaviour any more, and they were both given a lecture on the job market and why a good education was so important.

Then Mr Lang's plan became apparent. He formally ended the meeting but went on to say that he would like Tyrone, Prem, Ray and their mothers to have a discussion together. Ray and his mother agreed and so the others were invited back into the office.

The boys and their mothers sat in a semi-circle

around the head teacher's desk. As Mr Lang looked at them from his seat even the mothers looked as though they were in trouble. Noticing how uncomfortable everyone looked, he stood up and went to the front of the desk.

'I want to drop the formality and just have a chat with all three of you whilst your mothers are here,' he said, as he pushed papers aside and half sat on his desk with one foot still firmly on the ground. 'All three of you have broken almost every rule in the book and now, within the same week, all three of you have been permanently excluded from this school. The truth is that I don't believe that there'll be any drastic change if you are simply passed on to another school. Let's face it, none of you have apologised, none of you think that you have done any wrong, and it almost seems as if you are happy to be excluded.'

Ray, Prem and Tyrone looked at each other, all with a hint of a smile on their face. Their mothers looked at them without the slightest hint of one on theirs.

Mr Lang saw this. 'What I am about to say may seem rather strongly worded, but it's the truth. On paper you have failed, and you are going nowhere. If we follow the statistical logic your visit to the police station will be just the first of many. You may not want to read it, but the writing is on the wall. But I wanted to bring you together today because I know that deep down you are three highly intelligent boys. Deep down I believe that your actions, these actions that so many of us find intolerable, are in fact reactions to something else, or the lack of something else.

'Now, I didn't ask you here for a counselling session. I'm not a psychotherapist, and I don't want to rummage through your "emotional baggage" or anything like that, but before I consider what to do next I thought that it would be fair if I gave you a chance to speak. The last thing I want is for you to leave here saying you were not listened to. I want to give you this opportunity to tell me where you want to go from here, and if there is anything at all that I can do, I promise you that I'll do anything to help you, within reason.'

The boys and their mothers just looked at each other in silence. There was a knock on the door. 'Not now,' Mr Lang shouted, keeping his eyes on the boys. When they had finished looking at each other they all turned back to face Mr Lang.

'So, nothing,' Mr Lang continued, looking at the boys, going from one to the other and back again. 'We'll just move you on to another school, who may move you on to another school, and they will probably move you on to another school. Because you don't like school, you have no idea about what you want to do in life. It may even be fair to say that you have no talent and no ambition.'

'Rubbish,' said Ray, frowning back at Mr Lang. 'We got ambition, you just can't cope with it. We got skills, we know exactly what we're gonna do. Right now we're just killing time.'

'So what are you going to do?' asked Mr Lang.

Ray leaned forward and rested his elbows on his knees. 'We're gonna be the baddest motherfucking hip-hop band in the physical world gezza, and your daughter's gonna love us.'

His mother slapped him across the back of the head. 'What are you saying, how dare you speak like that? I am going to wash your mouth out with soap myself and then I'm going to hand you over to your father.'

Even Tyrone and Prem were shocked by what Ray had said, and they moved on their seats uncomfortably as their mothers waited, ready to pounce at any false move or word. But Mr Lang was relaxed.

'It's OK. I want him to feel free to express himself, but I should tell you that my daughter's into grunge music and a bit of the old punk rock. So you want to form a hip-hop band?'

'That's right,' said Ray. 'And you can't deal with that.'

'OK, I have to confess I have never been into a recording studio,' Mr Lang said, shifting on the table. 'But I do know that music-making at its best is an art that requires independent thinking, teamwork, mathematics, an enquiring mind, and knowledge of the relevant technology, so I want to make a suggestion.'

'Oh no,' Ray said, punching the other two playfully. 'He wants to be our manager.'

The boys smiled. Mr Lang smiled. The mothers didn't.

'I'm a bit busy at the moment,' Mr Lang continued, 'but you could think of me as your consultant. Look, I think that you could really benefit from joining a Social Inclusion Project. You have to attend every day, you'll have to do maths and English and other things that are on the curriculum, but you can also do music technology as your central subject. You will be able to study music and have access to people and materials which would normally be very expensive.'

'No,' said Prem's mother firmly. 'My son is going to be a doctor, not a music techno person.'

'That's right,' said Tyrone's mother. 'My son is going to be an airline pilot, so another school will be just fine.'

Ray's mother stayed silent.

'What's your son going to be?' Mr Lang asked her.

'My son is going to be a rapper,' she said, knowing that her idea of the perfect son was not going to be.

'You sound pretty sure. Why do you say that?' Mr Lang asked, focusing his gaze on Ray's mother.

'I know because it's the only thing that he cares about, he does nothing else. He can't cook, he'd live on biscuits if he could, he never does his homework, he just listens to music instead, and he spends all his money on rap music. If he doesn't become a rapper, he won't become anything.'

'And you don't mind if he becomes a rapper?' asked Mr Lang.

'Well he's not going to be an airline pilot or a doctor, so he can be a rapper. Look, I want him to be something, because something is better than nothing.'

Prem's mother began to get vocal. 'I am not going to allow my son to go to some place to turn some knobs on a big stereo and shout over some boff boff bang bang noise that they call music.'

'It's not shouting, Mum, it's called rapping,' Prem said.

His mother slapped him on his head. 'It's shouting.' She turned towards Mr Lang. 'I tried to get him to sing a nice Hindi song and he wouldn't. I mean if he could sing a nice Hindi song maybe I could get him in a film in India – you know, a Bollywood film. I have a cousin who is a big Bollywood star, he said Prem is good-looking and he stands a good chance of becoming a film star too, but no, Prem doesn't like Hindi films, Prem doesn't like his own culture, he wants to do that shouting rapping thing to that Jamaican music.'

The moment she said 'Jamaican music' there was silence. Tyrone and Ray looked at each other, their parents looked at each other, and Prem looked highly embarrassed.

Mr Lang leaned forward and in a quiet voice said, 'It's American music, Mrs Sharma. Reggae comes from Jamaica. Reggae started with mento music, then that became ska music, then there was bluebeat and then reggae. Dancehall evolved from reggae, but you will find that in Britain dancehall is called ragga. Now some people claim that the roots of rap can be traced back to Jamaica and from there back to Africa, but there is no doubt that hip-hop music comes from America, and the biggest market outside America is France. But having said that, one has to give credit to our lads here, for in the last few years Britain has begun to develop a very distinctive style of hip-hop, and in my opinion it won't be long before we begin to see some great, innovative artists on the scene. So, to sum up, Jamaica is the home of mento, ska, bluebeat and reggae, and the roots of hip-hop are in America and not Jamaica, but its branches are spreading inter-nationally – or should I say outernationally?'

The boys looked at Mr Lang, amazed by his knowledge. Ray nodded in agreement.

Everyone was impressed, except Mrs Sharma.

'Sorry, but I don't care where it comes from. Children need education.'

'But Mrs Sharma,' Mr Lang said reassuringly, 'they will still be receiving an education, the only difference is that it will be more practical and less theoretical, and it will also be more tailored to their needs. I can assure you that they will be doing most of the things you find in any other school, but just at a different pace.'

'So where's this Social Inclusion place?' Ray asked.

Mr Lang got up from the desk and sat in his high-backed leather swivel chair. He used his feet on the ground to turn the seat from left to right and from right to left, still trying to be as informal as he could.

'You will remain pupils of this school but you will become recipients of what we call our Off-Site Provisions. The actual centre you will attend is called Positivity and is based at Hamilton Road, just off Manor Road. The people at Positivity have a whole range of experiences. Some of them experienced exclusion themselves when they were in school, and they will listen to your needs and develop a programme to suit you.'

Ray and Tyrone nodded positively. Prem was expressionless.

'I'll give it a go,' Ray said.

'Me too,' said Tyrone.

Mr Lang looked to the parents. Ray's mother nodded.

'OK,' said Tyrone's mother.

Mr Lang could see that Mrs Sharma was uneasy. 'Listen, Mrs Sharma, all being well, Ray and Tyrone can start at the beginning of next week. You can take some time to think about it, talk about it at home. I'll make arrangements so that if you decide to go ahead Prem will also be able to start on Monday, but only if you say so.'

Back home, Ray's father showed no interest in the subject when his wife explained the situation. Tyrone's father thought that the boys should have been separated, but he was willing to go ahead with the idea. Mr and Mrs Sharma stayed awake until two o'clock the next morning talking about what they should do. In the end they decided to allow Prem to attend the project, believing that it was the best option open to them.

Ray kept avoiding his father as much as he could – when they did cross paths they hardly spoke. Ray spent the next few days in the music shop helping Marga Man out and freestyling in the park with Tyrone and Prem. When they told Marga Man about the head teacher's plan he was impressed.

'Yeah man, sound good to me. So have all your parents agreed to it?'

'Yes,' they said in unison.

'My parents took a bit of time coming round,'

added Prem. 'But what can they do? I'm not gonna be a doctor, and I'm not gonna be a Hindi movie star.'

'Everyone's all right,' said Ray. 'Because we'll be getting some kind of education, and we'll be off the streets.'

'And one more thing,' said Tyrone, 'we will be doing what we like, music, and everything will be based on that.'

'Yeah man, dat's why it sound good to me,' said Marga Man. 'But you must take this ting serious yu know.'

'We're so serious,' said Ray. 'When it comes to music you can't get more serious than we.'

The boys had now become known to the police. On Thursday night as they walked home from Flip Discs they were stopped and searched and on Saturday in the shopping centre they were stopped and questioned, and on both occasions the police called them by their names. But the boys had agreed between themselves that they had to try their best to stay out of trouble. It was tough, but they succeeded.

By the end of the week they had all received information about the Positivity Centre and on Monday morning all three arrived at the centre with their mothers. The receptionist took them into a large open-plan office where they were introduced to Sam, an energetic Asian woman dressed in a black tracksuit who bounced around the office introducing them to her colleagues. The boys and their parents politely nodded and shook hands with the staff, but as they sat down in a corner to be briefed by Sam the staff members' names had formed a nameless blur in all of their memories.

The parents were once again reassured that what the centre had to offer was worthwhile before they left, leaving Sam and the boys to talk about the programme that the centre had in mind for them. Some of the more formal lessons were to be taken in rooms owned by the local college and in community centres nearby. Their maths lessons would be based around music theory and their English lessons would also include reading books on the subject.

Soon the main topic was raised.

'Right,' said Sam, handing each of them an A4-size piece of paper. 'We have a great relationship with this studio, which is based in East Ham. It doesn't mean much to me, but this is a list of the equipment that they have there. I'm told that it's all good, and we've had no complaints in the past.'

The boys read down the list but most of it meant nothing to them either. Ray stopped reading and put his paper on the floor. 'Never mind all that, who owns the place?'

'Well,' Sam said, smiling, 'it's run by a wonderful

guy called David Oak. Have you ever heard of a band called The Strolling Rollers?'

'No,' they replied in unison.

'Nor had I, but David Oak used to be their bass player. Apparently they had a hit with a song called "Honey Sugar Baby", or something like that, and they were on *Top of the Pops* once – well, that's what he keeps telling me.'

The boys looked at each other suspiciously.

'He's expecting us to pop in and see him,' Sam continued, 'not to work, just to introduce yourselves.'

After a brief tour around the centre, which was also home to other groups involved in theatre and youth activities, Sam drove them in the project's minibus to the studio. It was called Firehouse. When they went inside, Sam pointed out David Oak, who was working with a female singer who couldn't sing. They stood for a while and watched as she tried again to get at least half of the song on key.

'You're doing great, baby!' David said every time he re-wound the tape. 'One more time now, baby. Let's go for it.' When he ran out of words of encouragement he told her to, 'Take five. And get some coffee.' He was a large guy whose eyes, nose and lips were barely visible through the hair that covered his face.

'I've been expecting you guys,' he said, reaching out to shake hands. 'I captain a nice little ship here.

We got good analogue and digital recording facilities. We got Pro-Tools Logic Audio Platinum four point seven running off the PC in a 48-channel Mackie desk, with some great off-board gear, and we got a great live room. Do you know Tommy Hurst?'

Everyone shook their heads.

'Well, he used to be in a band called Silver Fish. They were big in the seventies. He records here all the time. And David Essex. Well, he hasn't recorded here yet, but he said he will. Do you know much about recording?'

Everyone shook their heads again, including Sam.

'Well, don't worry. There's nothing about recording that I don't know. I've done it all, me. Hard rock, soft rock, boy bands, girl bands, I've done some of that old reggae stuff as well, yeah, I like a bit of the old reggae jeggae. This is how I like to work with all the kids that come through here: first I get you to know how the board works, then we go on to the off-board stuff, effects units, compressors, samplers and patch bays. Once you've done all that I'll get you to lay some tracks down. Do you write your own stuff?'

'We create our own stuff,' said Ray. 'We'll write it down if we have to, but freestyling is how we create, we got music on the mind all the time, you know what I'm saying? The words just come from the lung to the tongue, you know?'

'I hear you, and that's what I like to hear. When

you lay your tracks down if you need some help I'll play a bit of bass for you, and if you need singers I knows loads of birds who sing, nice birds too.'

Sam had heard this all before and she knew that once David started talking it was difficult to stop him. She told David that this was just a visit to say hello and that she would be in touch, and they left the studio. As soon as they were outside the building Ray spoke his mind.

'I ain't working with that guy. No way. What you guys say?'

'He's weird,' Prem said. 'I don't think he's all there.'

'He's a bit eccentric, but he's all right,' Sam said. 'We use him a lot for our service users.'

'What's a service user?' Tyrone asked.

'You,' she replied.

'Service user. Well we don't want to use his services,' said Ray.

'It's not just about equipment, he doesn't know where we're coming from,' said Tyrone. 'It's obvious.'

'Yeah, and if he was so great, why hasn't David Essex recorded with him already? Who's David Essex anyway?'

Sam did know who David Essex was. As she was explaining, Ray was thinking up an idea. When he was clear about what he had to say he interrupted.

'Listen,' he said, looking at Sam. 'You have an

arrangement with this guy, right. He owns this studio and you do some kind of a deal with him over the amount of studio time you allow your –' he stressed the words '– service users to use. Is that right?'

'Yes, that's right,' said Sam.

'OK, so why can't we use another studio?'

'Because we have an arrangement with this studio,' said Sam.

'Well, this is what I say. All this stuff about doing maths and English is fine, but we want to do this music technology thing in Stratford in a studio we know already.'

Prem and Tyrone nodded enthusiastically.

'Yeah,' said Prem.

'Yeah, with Bunny,' said Tyrone.

Ray continued, 'All you have to do is arrange your arrangement business with our man in Stratford and that's it. There's nothing so special about that studio. There's nothing special about that David guy.'

'There is,' said Sam.

'What?' said Ray.

'Well, we have inspected him. He had to pass a test, and he knows how to work with the service . . . people we send to him.'

'Well,' said Ray, 'you can go and inspect Bunny. He won't mind being inspected. Actually I think he would like to be inspected.' The boys laughed.

Sam didn't think it was that funny, but she could

see the sense in Ray's idea. 'OK. I'll have a word with the guys back at base, and we'll see what we can do.'

Sam went back to Positivity and put the proposal to her colleagues, and the boys went straight to the recording studio and explained things to Bunny. Bunny was happy with the idea. He was pleased to have an opportunity to work with the boys, and even more pleased because he would be getting paid for his services.

When the boys told Marga Man, he praised Ray for his logical thinking. He knew that the boys wanted to do nothing as much as they wanted to do music, and that leaving them to roam the streets, or even serve in the shop, was a waste of their talent.

The next day Sam and a colleague went to Bunny's studio to make sure that Bunny was willing and able to work with the boys. They were happy with what they saw, and after the boys received the good news at the centre they went on to give the news to Marga Man.

'Everything's cool,' Prem said as they walked up to the counter.

'It's all done, guy. No problem,' said Ray. 'From next week we take up residence with Bunny.' There was a little celebration with much touching of fists but then Ray went behind the counter and turned the music down. 'Listen. Let me talk. I think we should have a plan.'

'Yu full of ideas,' said Marga Man, all smiling and jolly.

'This is serious. We gonna be in the studio three times a week. Bunny's the engineer, he's gonna be in control of the equipment and teaching us how to use it at the same time, right?'

Everyone nodded yes.

'I say we should take this for real and record some serious stuff. We got studio, we got engineer, we got the beats and the lyrics and we got Marga Man. Marga Man, you know about music, you know what music should sound like in a car or on a CD player, you know what's happening on the scene, so you should be our producer.'

'For real,' said Tyrone. 'For real.'

'It makes sense to me,' said Marga Man, now becoming quite serious. 'I feel we can do some nice nastiness if we really put our minds to it, but it depends on how serious you are. If I have anyting to do wid dis I don't want to mess about. I'm too old to waste my time.'

'And we're too educated to waste any time,' said Ray. 'If you don't produce us we'll have to ask our head teacher to.'

There were laughs all round.

'I'm your producer,' said Marga Man. 'What does your head teacher know about hip-hop?'

'Actually, he knows a lot,' said Tyrone. 'More than

our parents.'

'But not as much as you,' Prem added quickly.

That night the boys sat on the wall outside Ray's house freestyling and talking about future possibilities. And there they decided that the time had come officially to adopt the names that they had wanted to adopt for so long. Prem was now Prem de la Prem, Tyrone was Pro Justice and Ray was X-Ray-X. Together they were to be called Positive Negatives.

CHAPTER 7

Studio Time

The first full week on the project went well. The boys not only attended the studio in the time slots that had been arranged by the project, they also sometimes stayed late into the night to watch and help Bunny as he worked with other bands. The English lessons were adapted to their interests and as well as reading technical books they practised writing letters to record companies and answering letters from fans and agents. In maths they worked out the tempo of music by studying the BPM – beats per minute – and they studied percentages by examining the kind of royalties they could expect to receive if their records were selling in the shops.

In the second week the boys began to really get serious. Ray summoned Marga Man to the studio to hear an idea they were working on. With the help of Tyrone and Prem, he improvised the rap idea. It was about them taking their place in the hip-hop world – at times angry, at times humorous, with a memorable chorus. As soon as Bunny got a metronome click up on the computer Ray played a bass line in on the keyboard. Bunny began to run around the studio saying that he had a sample of drums somewhere that would fit the bass line perfectly, but Ray stopped him, insisting that they play in their own drum beat from the drum machine.

Marga Man left the studio and the boys crowded around the drum machine punching in their ideas. Over the next couple of days they tried various melodies and added some percussion, and by the end of the week they had completed the backing track. They put it on CD and over the weekend they practised their lyrics to perfection.

After attending lessons the next Monday the boys went to see Marga Man in the music shop. As soon as the shop was empty they put the CD in the player so that he could hear the backing track. As it played they looked towards Marga Man, waiting for his response, but he just nodded his head expressionlessly to the beat. When it was finished he raised an eyebrow and said, 'It nice, man.'

'Nice?' said Ray.

'Yeah, it's nice,' Marga Man said calmly.

'That's a killer beat,' Ray said, pointing to the player.

'It's a nice killer beat,' Marga Man said, just holding back a smile. 'OK, tonight you put de vocals down.'

* * *

That night they had a long hard session in the studio. The rap they were recording was called 'War Cry'. They had adopted a style whereby they would take it in turns to rap verses, and when the main person was rapping his verse the others would join in on single words to give emphasis. They had three verses each and they did the choruses together, but it wasn't easy. After all the practising they had done they believed that they could get it done in one or two takes, but Marga Man pushed them hard. There were several times when Ray was convinced that they had got it right, but when he looked through the soundproof glass into the control room he would see Marga Man nodding his head, switching on the talkback system and saying, 'It good, but you can do better than that. One more time.'

About two hours into the session they did a take that Marga Man seemed happy with. He called them into the control room to listen to it. Bunny pumped up the volume and they listened to the track. They all loved it.

'It nice,' said Marga Man. 'But it's not angry enough. Let's do it one more time.'

'What?' Ray huffed in disbelief. 'What you mean, it's not angry enough? The joint's OK guy, what do you reckon?' he said, looking at Tyrone and Prem, who were quick to agree with him.

'I like it,' said Tyrone.

'Yeah, it's OK,' Prem added.

'Ssh,' Marga Man said, putting his finger in front of his lips. 'Let me tell yu something.'

The boys leaned forward on their seats. Marga Man leaned forward on his seat to meet them and he spoke to them very quietly as if he were passing on some top-secret information. Bunny began dusting off equipment in order to look as if he wasn't listening.

'Of course you like it. I like it too and of course it's OK, but there are plenty tunes out there dat are OK. I'm not working wid yu to do just another OK tune. I'm here to do something extraordinary, you know what I'm saying, extra ordinary, I want to produce something dat is super sonic. Now I'm de producer and I'm telling yu dat yu have some great lyrics over a great beat, but right now yu not doing de lyrics justice if you don't put more emotion into de performance. If you are happy wid what yu have dat's OK, dat's cool, you've done your thing, I can go home to my wife and you have your track. But don't put my name on it. I don't do OK. If yu want to do something extra ordinary, super sonic, get back in there and put some aggression into de tape.' He looked at Prem. Prem looked away. He looked at Tyrone. Tyrone looked away. He looked at Ray. Ray looked straight back at him.

'Let's go,' said Ray to Marga Man, keeping his eyes on him even as they left the room.

This time it was different. The group were fired up. This take was the one. Ray clenched his fist as the words shot from his mouth. The others, fed on the intensity of Ray's performance, began to perform in a way they had never done before.

Marga Man called them back into the control room and this time he was all smiles.

'Yeah, man. Dat is super, super sonic. You feel it?' he asked, holding his right fist up.

'I feel it,' Ray replied, touching his right fist with Marga Man's.

This time when they listened to the track they were all in agreement. It was a great recording.

They got home at eleven o'clock that night. The next day was spent in classrooms, but the day after that they were back in the recording studio doing the final mix. This would determine the heaviness of the bass, the amount of special effects that were to be used, the prominence of the vocals, and the overall sound of the track. Marga Man directed Bunny as he turned the knobs and pressed the buttons. The boys threw in comments and said their piece, but Marga Man had a fixed idea of what he wanted. When he was done everyone was happy.

Bunny cut a copy for each of the boys on to CD, but Marga Man warned them not to make too much noise about the recording. They should play it, study it, but they should not play it to everyone that they knew. Marga Man had plans, but to execute his plans it was important that the boys kept up their work. He wanted to make sure that every track that the boys recorded was as good as the first one.

Over the next couple of weeks the boys attended every class as required and they spent as much time in the studio as they could. Most of the time they concentrated on learning recording techniques and understanding how all the equipment worked. From time to time Marga Man would make appearances at the studio to see how they were progressing and, although the boys' parents had concerns about the late nights, the amount of time they were spending in the studio, and their lack of interest in anything else, there were no complaints. For the first time they could see that their sons were waking up in the mornings feeling like they had purpose, and returning home at nights feeling like they had accomplished things. Ray's father still only spoke to him when he had to, but there were no big arguments, and he was never at home long enough to bother his sister.

One afternoon as the boys were being given lessons

on how to sample sounds by Bunny, the phone rang. Bunny asked Ray to answer it. It was Marga Man.

'What's up?' asked Marga Man. He sounded very serious.

'Nothing,' Ray replied, 'everything's cool.'

'When are you leaving de studio?'

'Soon,' said Ray. 'Then we were going to go back to the centre to talk to Sam about how things were going.'

'Don't move until I get there,' Marga Man said, worrying Ray with the low tone of his voice.

Tyrone and Prem could see that something was on Ray's mind. 'What's the matter?' asked Prem when Ray had hung up.

'I don't know,' said Ray. 'Marga Man was on the phone and he sounded real serious. He said we gotta stay here until he comes.'

Twenty minutes later, Marga Man walked in and the boys sat around him to hear what he had to say. Bunny went to leave the room so that they could talk alone, but Marga Man stopped him.

'Bunny. You too, sit down man. I want you to hear dis, dis involves you.'

Bunny sat down like a naughty schoolboy.

'I'm gonna get straight to de point,' Marga Man said, panning around the room looking at all four of them. 'I have good news and bad news. What do you want first?'

There was no reply, only a puzzled look on all their faces.

'What do you want first?' he said again, raising his voice and sounding a little like a schoolteacher demanding an answer.

'OK,' Bunny said, 'stay calm brother. Hey, let's get the bad news out of the way first.'

'All right,' said Marga Man. 'Today I have not made a single penny because my shop was closed. Yeah, I had to spend the whole day in a meeting talking to a well-educated hippy boy and a man in a suit. Meanwhile my shop was closed and my customers went elsewhere.'

The boys looked at each other, even more puzzled, not understanding what this had to do with them. Bunny was just as confused, but felt that he should try and move the conversation on.

'Sorry to hear that, Marga Man, but don't worry, things will pick up. Flip Discs is number one, we know that, they know that. Don't worry brother, the customers will come back. How about the good news?'

Marga Man panned around the room again, looking at all of them so seriously that they all felt the proverbial shiver run down their spines. 'De good news?' he said.

The silence was loud. Bunny nodded his head

encouragingly. Marga Man stood up and produced the biggest smile they had ever seen him accomplish.

'We have a record deal.' He raised both fists and shook them. 'Yeah man, we got a record deal. I played "War Cry" to some guys at Deaf Defying Records and they loved it. They can put it out more or less straightaway, but den they want a full album from us, with first option on another CD within two years.'

The boys were stunned by what they were hearing. It took them a few seconds to take everything in, but they could see that Marga Man was not joking.

'What, they want a whole CD?' asked Tyrone.

'Listen man,' said Marga Man, 'they want it as soon as we can get it done, so let me tell yu how it's going to work.'

Marga Man went on to tell them how they were going to work together and what would be the chain of command.

'I am de manager and producer. I oversee de recording and I negotiate wid de record company and de other suits. Bunny is de engineer. He will make sure de place is ready for yu to record in and he will do his best to make sure dat yu have all de equipment yu need. You are who you are,' he said looking at the boys. 'Yu write de raps, yu rap the raps and your faces go on de CD cover.'

He took a large book out of a bag that he had with him and handed it to Ray. It was heavy and bigger than any book that Ray had ever read. Ray looked at the front of the book. It was called *Music Business Arrangements*.

'Read it,' Marga Man said, smiling. 'You're de spokesman for de band so yu have to know about de business, and when yu have all read it I want yu to tell me what kind of arrangement we should have between us. It's up to you.' Marga Man stood up and began to leave the room. 'Now I'm going,' he said. 'You guys start working. Your public awaits you.'

CHAPTER 8

The Business Trip

The boys were becoming obsessive. Every chance they had, they were in the studio, and they continued helping Bunny out when he was working with other bands. When that wasn't happening they would go into one of the spare rooms to write lyrics.

Ray carried *Music Business Arrangements* with him everywhere he went, and he would read it whenever he could. He read it before he went to sleep at night and as soon as he woke up in the morning. Their teachers also used it as a tool for their English and maths lessons, and the band would discuss issues raised in the book with each other. Their general knowledge of the music industry was increasing greatly and they were recording beats at a rapid pace.

When the band felt confident that they understood the major points from the book that would affect them, they went to the music shop to see Marga Man. It was after a period of intense work and they hadn't seen him for a few days, but as always Marga Man was pleased to see them and he expressed how much he had missed them in his own way.

'So what do yu want? Whatever it is, take it and go, I want pretty people in my shop,' he said, waving them back into the street.

'That's why we're here,' said Ray. 'We come to add beauty to your life.' He put the book down on the counter and Marga Man knew exactly why they were there.

'OK,' Marga Man said, turning the music off. 'Dis is a business trip.'

'Yes, we come to buy you out,' said Prem.

Marga Man took a set of keys from his pockets. 'Take it, take everything lock, stock, and two thousand CDs. It won't cost yu a ting, all yu have to do is give me a job, one wid guaranteed wages. Dat way I may earn more dan I'm earning now.'

Ray rested his hand on the book as if it were a book of sacred holy scriptures. 'We read the book. Then we talked amongst ourselves, and we talked with our parents, and we've decided we wanna run this thing as a collective, an equal split for all members of the band. We see you as a member, it's as simple as that. Bunny said he can't fully commit himself to the band because of other stuff, but he's happy to get a bit of work from us when we need him. So that's it, a four-way split.'

Marga Man got serious again. 'Are yu sure 'bout dis? Dat's not necessary yu know. Are yu sure you've read de relevant sections in de book?'

'Yeah, we know,' said Tyrone. 'We took the music agreements book to the centre and studied it hard, and then we took it home and done some homework. We know what we're saying.'

Ray kept his hand on the book and spoke with genuine sincerity. 'We know that managers normally get a percentage and producers work on a points system, and we know that those are two separate jobs. But we also know that you're more than a producer and manager to us, you've always been there for us, so we want to do this in a cooperative style.'

'Yeah guy,' Prem added. 'We all got our jobs, we all got our responsibilities, but we're all equal. That's the way we want to run it.'

'Well, you guys sound like you know what you're 'bout,' said Marga Man. 'I got a meeting with Deaf Defying Records next week and I want yu to come. But first if we're gonna do dis ting properly I want to draw up a contract for ourselves saying dat we want to work on a cooperative basis, and I want dat contract signed before we sign wid de record company. Yes we are friends, but if we want a sound business relationship wid dem we must have a sound business relationship wid each other. So paperwork must be done.'

After spending so much time studying the book the band knew exactly what he meant.

The next week Sam from Positivity gave the band a day off so that they could go to the record company with Marga Man. To the band's amusement the company office was above 'Lickit', an adult shop in the heart of Soho. One could never have guessed that the building housed a record company. The name on the silver intercom box on the door simply said DDR.

'What kind of a record company is this?' Ray said as Marga Man announced his arrival to the receptionist via the intercom.

'It's an independent one,' Marga Man replied.

Inside was another world. The brightly painted walls were covered with silver, gold and platinum discs, and with giant posters, the type normally seen on billboards. The receptionist led them into a side office. A man moved quickly towards Marga Man as they entered the room.

'Hey, Marga me mate, how you doing? How's the wife?' he said, shaking Marga Man's hand vigorously. Marga Man had the kind of look on his face that said, *I know you, but not that well*.

'Meet de boys,' Marga Man said, disconnecting his hand. 'Pro Justice, Prem de la Prem and X-Ray-X.'

The man shook their hands vigorously. 'Great to see you, how ya going, glad you could make it. I'm Wayne, but they call me Skelly. I'm the A and R man, which usually means spending a lot of time in damp clubs drinking cheap beer and listening to naff bands, but as you see this is a small company so I do a bit of everything – contracts, promotions, making coffee, washing-up, that sort of thing.'

Skelly was short and loud, mixed race with short dreadlocks. He dressed like a children's entertainer. His red tracksuit bottoms and multi-coloured shirt dazzled their eyes and as he strutted around the office Ray couldn't help thinking that he was saying, *I may look like I'm an idiot, but I'm important, I've got my own office.*

'Please be seated, lads,' he said, pointing to the four seats that had been pre-prepared. 'It really is great to see you here; as soon as I heard the tape I thought that this was for us. We know that hip-hop is about to go big in Britain and we want to be at the forefront of this. Positive Negatives is the best I've heard yet and we want to back you all the way. Your sound is refreshing, it's musically inventive, it has attitude, and it's as good as anything coming from the States.'

'And we want to keep it that way,' said Ray.

'Hey, we've only got the money, you've got the talent,' Skelly said, smiling insincerely.

'Yeah,' said Ray, very sincerely. 'But we don't want you coming to tell us that we gotta water down our sound to get radio airplay our anything like that. We know what we want to do and if you want to give us money to help us that's cool, but your money can't buy our soul.' Ray sat back, feeling pleased with himself. He felt in control, he knew that he represented the talent, he felt a confidence that he had not felt before, he felt right, he felt powerful.

Skelly was trying hard to sound as friendly as he could. 'No way mate, that's not what we're about. You do what you do, it's your thing, you have complete artist control. There is no debate about that. All we do is give you the money and you make the recording. Once we have the product all we have to do is let the public know how great it is. You concentrate on the art.'

'For real,' said Ray.

Skelly went on, 'And I think we'll have no problem promoting you. There's a big gap in the market and there's not much competition right now. I would like to be able to get to work on the single straightaway, and I already have some ideas. The really good news is that the powers that be have given me a substantial budget to work with.'

Marga Man folded his arms and rested back on his seat. 'Can we have simultaneous releases in other territories? We tink dat we should hit de States at de same time, and even Canada. Dis is not just a British ting yu know, Positive Negatives have a universal message for people all over.'

'No problem, my man,' Skelly answered eagerly. 'Both "War Cry" and the album will be licensed for release in the States, Canada, Australia and France, and if all goes well we have other European territories in sight. And more good news: all those territories will have separate promotional budgets.'

'And what about tour support?' asked Marga Man.

'Of course,' replied Skelly. 'We are keen to support any touring the band wants to undertake, we think touring would be a great idea. And by the way guys, you got a great name, kids are going to love it,' he said, doing a double thumbs-up.

'This is not just a kids thing,' Ray said.

'Yeah, no gimmick thing,' Prem added, with Tyrone nodding in agreement.

'No way,' said Skelly quickly. 'Of course not, this is for everyone. Hey, before you go, let me introduce you to someone. We don't see him that often, so let's catch him while he's here.' Skelly led them out of his office into another room where a man in his late thirties was sitting behind a large oak desk. 'This is Duncan,' he said. 'The powers that be, the boss.'

'I'm not the boss,' said Duncan, 'I just own the company. Pleased to meet you.' He stood up and reached over his desk to shake everyone's hands. He looked surprisingly timid, with thinning black hair and stubble on his face. His sharp black suit would have looked fine in one of the major companies, but made him look slightly out of place in an independent record company's office.

'This is not a large company, but we're like a family here,' said Duncan, sitting back in his chair under a picture of a gold Lamborghini. 'And we like to take care of our artists. Has Skelly been looking after you?'

'So far so good,' replied Marga Man.

'Good, that's the way we do it. And Skelly, what's your plan of action?'

'I think the best way of marketing the band is to go straight for the hard core hip-hop fans, regardless of age of course. We know that the band will attract many kids but we would also expect that a high percentage of the consumers will be people between the ages of sixteen and thirty. It's also very important that we try to get all those people that buy American hip-hop to start investing in local product,' said Skelly.

'Product?' said Tyrone.

'Yeah, and consumers?' added Ray.

'Don't worry,' said Skelly, 'it's all just jargon that we use in the business.'

'Don't let the jargon worry you, just be rappers and don't let anything stand in your way,' said Duncan. 'If you don't mind me asking,' he added, fiddling with his fountain pen, 'what age are you?'

'Why do you want to know, is that something else that can be marketed?' Ray asked.

'Don't worry,' said Duncan, sensing friction, 'you certainly won't be hyped up because of your age. It's all going to be about the arrival of British hip-hop.

The Western Alliance may be on their way, but you have arrived.'

'Who's the Western Alliance?' Ray asked, looking around his crew.

'They're not very good,' said Duncan.

'They're a rap group from west London who have just signed to Damage Limitation Records. They're led by a guy called Dragon, half-black, half-Chinese, looks tough, sounds tough, but he can't rap. Don't worry about them, they can't touch you guys anyway,' said Skelly.

After five minutes of talking about the state of British hip-hop, Duncan promised the boys that they would make lots of money together, then he excused himself and left for another meeting. Skelly assured Marga Man that they were in for a long and prosperous relationship and promised that the contract would be in the post within the week.

As the band made their way slowly back to the East End in the rush hour traffic there was plenty of talk about Duncan and Skelly.

Ray started by asking, 'Hey Marga Man, that Skelly guy, was it him who you played the CD to when you got the deal?'

Marga Man nodded.

'But you called him a suit, he didn't look like a suit to me. I couldn't even imagine seeing him in a suit.'

'Don't be fooled by his disguise. Under dem pyjamas dat yu see him wearing there's a businessman, just like de other boy. Dem have one ting on their mind, believe me. Look, let me tell yu someting. I only meet him once before and now him asking me how's me wife, him know nothing 'bout my wife, never see her in him life. And yu see the way him shake me hand? Dat's not because him love me yu know, dat's not because him care about me family and their well-being yu know, dat's because him smell money. So any time you hear dem people talk about how much dem want to do for you, or how great yu sound, or any time dem start talk about a long and prosperous relationship, remember de bottom line is money. Dem is spending money on yu to mek money for demselves. Trust me.'

That night, back in the studio, the band did a remix of 'War Cry', guided by Marga Man. They changed the snare drum sound and gave the percussions a more prominent position. The attitude and tone of the rap sounded the same, but after taking out some of the more melodic elements the new mix was minimalist but more danceable.

Marga Man had arranged for a photographer to come in and photograph the boys as they worked. The idea was that photos of them at work would give the impression of a hard-working band, but the boys couldn't resist doing a bit of posing. After all, they were a rap band.

A week later, after Marga Man had completed the process of registering Positive Negatives as a cooperative company, he took the first steps towards opening a company bank account. All he needed to complete the process was the signature of the boys' parents. And then the contract arrived from Deaf Defying Records. The band discussed it with the aid of the music agreements book, checking the advance payments and the percentages they were to receive, and making sure that all of their territorial concerns had been incorporated into the deal. They were happy with it, they signed it, and Marga Man delivered it by hand to the record company with the master tapes of the recordings.

For the first time in their lives the boys felt a real sense of responsibility. It was the first time any of them had signed a legal document, it was the first time any of them had entered into a business agreement, and it was the first time they had seen any value placed on what they were doing. They were all feeling quietly nervous but they were all feeling good. All they had to do now was record the album.

CHAPTER 9

In the Public Domain

The time had come for the school to see how things were going. Bunny was sent an assessment form that he had to fill in and the boys and their parents were asked to attend a meeting with Mr Lang.

On the day of the meeting the boys and their mothers lined up outside Mr Lang's office. As before, none of their fathers made an effort to attend, but there was a father figure – Ray had insisted that Marga Man come along. The mothers and Marga Man were uneasy together. The mothers were all aware of him and his music shop, and they would have all preferred for the boys not to spend so much time there, but they were also aware that if they were not spending their time in the music shop they could be hanging out in places which were a lot more unsavoury.

And then there was Marga Man, of the same generation as the mothers, but feeling like one of the boys.

Marga Man waited outside whilst inside Mr Lang

congratulated the boys on the feedback he was receiving.

'I told you it would be fine, but this is outstanding,' Mr Lang said, pointing to three folders on his desk. 'Not a bad word about any of you, just praise, praise, and more praise. I am thoroughly delighted, and I hope that you are too.'

'Things are cool,' said Prem.

'Yeah, just cool,' Ray added.

'Good, very good,' said Mr Lang.

'If things are so cool and so very good, when will my son be sitting his exams?' asked Mrs Sharma as if she were continuing her speech from the last meeting.

'It is possible,' said Mr Lang, 'that we could get to the stage where, if we all agreed, the boys could be given a kind of probationary period back in school. But they would have an awful lot of catching up to do, and I think we have some way to go before we get to that stage. But I have no doubt in my mind that the approach we are taking at the moment is the best.'

It didn't matter what Mr Lang said, Mrs Sharma remained unsure. 'So what stage are we at now?' she asked. 'I am worried; worried that he won't be a doctor or a proper singer. I ask him to play something on the sitar and he can't, then I ask him to sing for me and all he can do is play me a CD with that hipordy hopordy music.'

'One minute, Mrs Sharma. Yes, I have been

informed about the CD that they've recorded, and also the record deal. This is very exciting. Tell me more,' Mr Lang said, turning his attention to the boys.

'Yeah,' Ray said, as if he were bringing someone on stage. 'At this point in the proceedings I would like to introduce to you our producer and manager. You see we formed a cooperative and our fourth member is right outside. Can he come in?'

'Of course,' said Mr Lang.

Ray went and opened the door. 'Yo, Marga Man, step forward.'

Marga Man was seated, the back of his head resting on the wall and his eyes closed, giving Ray the impression that he was sleeping. There was urgency in Ray's voice.

'Marga Man, get it together, man.'

Marga Man opened his eyes. 'I'm here, man and it's all together.' He stood up and followed Ray into the office.

'This is my man, Marga Man,' Ray said, full of pride. 'Producer, manager, overseer and businessman extraordinaire.'

'Easy on de extraordinaire business, me is just a hustler man, just a survivor,' Marga Man said as he adjusted his clothing.

Mr Lang stretched his arm out over his desk to shake Marga Man's hand. 'Pleased to meet you, I have heard about you. I heard that you helped the boys to record a CD and that you're being a great inspiration to them.'

'Not really,' Marga Man replied modestly. 'They get on and do their thing and I just hold it all together. They create de beats, they write de raps, and it was they who decided to form de cooperative, so they are de creative force, I is just like a spectator throwing in comments from de side line.'

'I'm sure you're much more than just a spectator,' said Mr Lang. 'Tell me about this track that you have recorded.'

Marga Man looked around the room for a CD player. 'You want hear dis bad beat?'

Mr Lang was keen. 'Yes, of course, that would be wonderful.'

'It's unhealthy, you wait until you hear it,' said Mrs Sharma. 'It's very loud.'

Marga Man couldn't see a player. 'Where can we go to play it?'

'Right here,' said Mr Lang, pointing to his computer. 'This thing has two forty-watt sub woofer speakers. It's, erm, well it's heavy.'

Marga Man went and stood by the computer. He put his hand in the inside pocket of his jacket as if to get the CD, but he kept his hand there and began to make a speech.

'Yes, well, right now I have something to say, is a

little announcement ting yu know. Now, for de first time, right here, right now, I can show yu de finished CD single, in its own case wid photographs, artwork done, and everything.' He took the CD out of his pocket and held the front cover so that all could see.

'Yes,' said Ray, on seeing himself posing on the front cover in front of the other two.

'Now that's cool,' said Tyrone.

'Nice one,' said Prem.

'Nice what?' said his mother.

'It's just nice,' said Prem. 'That record's going to be in the shops soon.'

'That's right,' said Marga Man. 'And dat's another ting, we have a release date two weeks from today, and next week we need two days to do a video shoot. The idea dat I put to dem is dat we do de shoot local, partly in de studio and some in Epping Forest, and they went for it. And one more ting, there is a very large cheque in de post.'

'Yes.'

'Nice.'

'Great,' the boys all shouted as they touched fists.

'Yes, very good,' said Mr Lang. 'So now, let's hear this bad beat.'

Marga Man put the CD in the drive drawer and let it play. The boys' heads started nodding, the mothers listened impassively, and Mr Lang wasn't happy with the sound. He went over to the computer, guided the cursor to the Stop button, and began to play the CD again. This time he raised the volume, and then he pumped up the low frequencies on the bass.

The boys beamed happiness, the mothers didn't, and Marga Man looked like a jolly Jamaican Father Christmas as he began to produce copies of the CD from various pockets of his multi-pocketed coat and hand them to all present. Various degrees of interest were shown as the mothers examined the artwork. Mrs Sharma even managed a very slight smile, but as Mr Lang listened to the recording he knew how much work had gone in it. When the two mixes had been played he stood next to Marga Man to say his piece.

'This is really superb,' he said. 'I'm very impressed. I knew that you had been getting on well on the technological side of things, and I knew you had plans to record, but I must say I had no idea that you had gone this far. Well done, all of you, well done.' He clapped his hands four times before he realised that no one was joining in with him, then he stopped. 'Well, that will be all, unless any of you have any questions or concerns that you would like to raise.'

'Yes, I have a concern,' said Tyrone's mother, directing her words at Marga Man. 'You are supposed to be managing these boys, and now you make a record and you have a bank account and business and all them things, but who are you? I am not being funny, I don't want to cause offence or anything like that, but we only hear about you, we don't know you. All we hear is that you're cool, and you're safe, and you're sound, but that is not enough, especially now that you've gone into business with our children and that money is involved. And another thing that I wonder, are these boys ready to actually go into a business arrangement now? They are just children.'

'That's right,' said Prem's mother. 'Me and my husband have talked about this already at home, but now that we are all together we should talk about it. This is important.'

Marga Man responded confidently. 'Yes, I can understand what you're saying, and if I was in your position I would ask de same questions. All I can say is dis. I care 'bout these boys too, like you I don't want to see dem on de streets doing nothing, and I don't want to know dat dem ending up in de police station. But I know dat what dem love is music, and dem have musical skills of de highest order. Yes dem can do dis music ting without me, but I know 'bout de business side of tings, I can guide dem. We have set up our business in a cooperative way, but yo, dis wasn't my idea, dis was de way de boys wanted it. And yu know what, although it is a co-op, it is set up so dat if de main body of de band is not happy wid de manager they can sack him any time. So as soon as they are not happy with me dem can get rid of me. I can't get rid of dem, but dem can get rid of me as quick as Jack Flash.'

'Well, that sounds pretty reasonable to me,' Ray's mother said. 'But what about the money that you just get, and money that you will get in the future? Who is in control of all that?'

'OK,' Marga Man continued. 'As was de wish of de boys, we have equal control, is like we are all directors. The arrangement I set up wid de bank says dat all cheques must be signed by two people. Now when it comes to buying equipment or other tings like dat, we must all agree upon it, and de money will come from de account. When we decide to pay ourselves again we must all agree on de amount and we will all get an equal share, unless we agree otherwise. For example, right now I am proposing dat de boys take out some money from de payment we are about to receive in order to get some clothes. They need to look cool yu know, video shoots and tings like dat demand sharp-looking brothers. I will not be including myself in dis withdrawal 'cause I look cool already.'

The boys laughed.

'And I also tink dat after dem work so hard de boys need some spending money, not too much, just enough to give dem a chance to taste de good life, yu know what I mean. So de way we doing tings is simple and straightforward, I know dat we can make dis ting work so everyting must be above board, transparent yu know, boni fido.'

'It's bona fide,' said Prem, trying to whisper across

the room, 'not boni fido.'

Mr Lang began to straighten the files on his desk. 'Well, that sounds like a wonderful idea to me, but to be perfectly honest I think those are things you can talk about between yourselves. I'm a little pushed for time at the moment, so if you don't mind I think we should wrap up now.'

Outside Mr Lang's office Marga Man began to pull brown envelopes from his multi-pocketed coat. He handed one to each of the mothers.

'Dat is bank business. De bank needs de signatures of de parents because of de ages of de boys yu see, so just sign de form and everyting will be cool. If yu have any questions just ask me, or seek advice from an independent financial adviser, as they say in de commercials. Don't worry, all is good. '

Tyrone and Ray's mothers took the envelopes with some hesitation, but Prem's mother kept her hand firmly at her side.

'Is nothing to worry about. Tink of it like dis, yu son is a businessman now, a director, we doing tings properly, boni fido. And him don't really have nothing to lose 'cause there is no up-front financial investment, him only investing him talent.'

Prem's mother slowly held out her hand.

'Yes, missus,' Marga Man said, nodding his head and handing her the envelope. 'Strictly business.'

*　　*　　*

That weekend the boys went on a shopping spree. On Saturday they explored Stratford and Ilford shopping centres before heading for the West End where, despite having to travel by bus, they really began to act like a rap band. In the past they would have been looked upon as suspicious in most of the shops but now they were desirables, and the cheesy chat-up lines they delivered to the most beautiful shop assistants were greeted with smiles as they were accompanied to changing rooms. The clothes they were trying on had to work well in movement, and so the boys entertained many other customers as they danced in front of mirrors. On Sunday they went for haircuts. Each haircut was different – each one of them wore a different map of tramlines on their head.

Come Monday they were back in the classroom but on Tuesday it was time to start the video shoot. There was no concept to it and no story, just a performance to camera with a few extra-big men to make it look a bit tough, and a few skinny models to make it look sexy, all provided at the expense of the record company. It was harder work than the band had thought it would be – they thought that they could get through it all quite quickly, but the director made them do several takes of every section. And they didn't like miming. When they had to mime for the indoor shots away from the public it wasn't too bad, but they felt silly when they began to shoot in the park and crowds gathered to see what was happening.

Word was beginning to get around. The three boys who had become known for their confrontational behaviour and for continually chasing girls were now generating positive rumours. But these became more than just rumours three weeks later when, one week after its release, the single 'War Cry' was at number nine in the charts. Radio stations all over Britain were constantly playing it and it was receiving considerable airplay around the world too. To the boys' delight it was even being well received by both commentators and fans in North America. However, the video turned out to be disappointing for the boys, as the female models' butts and crotches seemed to take up more scene time than the boys themselves. It was played on a couple of Saturday morning kids' shows, but when the band received an offer to appear on *Top of the Pops*, the video was forgotten and they had to have their first major debate.

Top of the Pops was the most important music programme on television. Many pop bands' greatest wish was to appear on the show because of the exposure it would bring and the sales it would generate, but it was also seen by some as the place that represented the worst elements of pop music culture.

Bands with the best-looking kids would have pride of place, alongside bands that brought with them the most formulaic dance routines or, even worse, a whole troupe of wriggling navels. The hand-picked audiences always consisted of the most clean-cut white kids, with a few token funky representatives from the ethic minorities thrown in, and the bands were made to mime to the songs.

Miming brought about some of the most embarrassing moments of the programmes. Some people even mimed to songs that they had never sung, either because the original singer was a session singer, or because the original singer just refused to go on the show. Some bands made a point of refusing to do the show, especially the bands who wanted to project a rebellious, independent or alternative image and thought that going on the show would damage their credibility.

The Positive Negatives called a meeting in the music shop on the subject. It was time for the meeting to start but Tyrone had not yet turned up so they decided to start without him.

Ray was the prime objector. 'Marga Man,' he pleaded. 'I don't think we should be doing this, this is not us, this is rubbish. Can't you get us on MTV or something like that? We want some television that's more street.'

Marga Man knew that convincing Ray was going to

119

be difficult. 'MTV are going to start playing de video, and dat's cool for reaching foreign parts, but there's nothing like appearing on *Top of the Pops* for getting to de British kids. Tell me, do yu know how many concerts yu would have to do to reach a million people? Dis programme reaches millions of kids, doing dis programme once is like doing a thousand concerts. Yu gone to number nine wid very little mainstream publicity, dis will tek yu to another level.'

'The programme stinks,' said Prem. 'It's for babies.'

'The programme pays,' said Marga Man.

'It may pay,' said Ray, 'but you can't deny it Marga Man, the programme doesn't matter when it comes to rap music.'

'Are you joking?' Marga Man laughed. 'People die to get on it.'

'And people die on it,' said Prem.

Tyrone entered the shop. He wasn't in a hurry, and Ray noticed. 'Tyrone guy, you're late man, where you been?'

'Sorry man, had to pop into the Positivity Centre,' Tyrone replied calmly.

'What you doing there?' Asked Prem.

'I just had to do something.'

'What?' asked Ray.

'Nothing much. What's happening here?'

'Do you want to do *Top of the Pops*?' asked Ray.

Tyrone answered without hesitation. 'I don't mind.'

After much debating Ray came up with a compromise. 'OK. This is what I suggest. No dance routines, no dancing girls, and no miming, we do the programme using an instrumental backing tape but we must do the vocals live.'

Marga Man checked with the producer of the programme at the BBC and was told that it was fine. Rap groups and some of the heavier rock bands had played live in the past, as had some of the more soulful artists who really could sing. It was a matter of insisting.

After appearing on the programme the next week the band found it very difficult to move around their own area. Kids would bring other kids to look at the houses where the local rap heroes lived. They were being asked for autographs on the streets, but more importantly, their parents began to give them some respect. Ray's father tried not to show it but he was quietly pleased to see that his son was making a name for himself, although he was still no closer to Ray.

When he could, Marga Man would drive the band around, in order to save them from being seen too much on the street. They began to use taxis to take them to the Positivity Centre and the recording studio, and they were now all equipped with state-of-the-art mobile phones. Radio airplay was one thing

– it was great for the band to hear their tune being played in public places – but their appearance on *Top of the Pops* meant that the public could now match the voices with their faces. Positive Negatives had arrived. Kids wanted to dress like them, kids wanted to sound like them, and graffiti in praise of the band began to appear on trains and inner-city walls nationwide.

CHAPTER 10

Live at the Rex

The week after the band appeared on *Top of the Pops* they really did hit the top of the pops. 'War Cry' stayed at number one for four weeks. The record company was happy, the boys were happy and Marga Man was happy, but not happy enough. He knew that the band could not wait too long before releasing an album, so to the record company's delight Marga Man got the band recording in the studio even as they were still riding the high of the single.

They recorded thirteen more tracks. Marga Man had pushed them to the limits of their performance, and Ray made sure that they drew on all their experiences from their short lives to write the raps. The result was 'Collective Security', a hard-hitting, lyrically-crammed, angry album, that had nothing positive to say about anything, yet still had listeners admiring the band's lyrical skills. The album had tracks on it that dealt with being in school, being out of school, leaving home, street fights, boredom and being locked up in a police station. Marga Man employed a local artist to do the artwork for the CD sleeve, which was approved by all.

The record company gave a release date, but the release of the album was going to be different from the release of the single. Now the band were known, now people were waiting for the beats, and doubters needed to know if they were a one-hit wonder, or if they could sustain the quality of the first single over another thirteen tracks.

The day after the record company announced the album's release date, Marga Man turned up at the studio to see the band.

'Right,' he said, as the band sat around him in the control room in the circular configuration which was now automatic. 'I have an idea for de release of de album.' He paused. 'Your first live gig.'

The boys checked each other optically and nodded positively, as did Bunny.

'Now I've been checking out de scene,' Marga Man continued. 'On de date of de release we could get de Brixton Academy, we could get de Dominion Tottenham Court Road, we could get de Marquee, de Scala, or de Hammersmith Palais, but we not doing none of dem. Your first gig is going to be right here, in Stratford, at de Rex. Yes, man, mek dem come to de East End, record company, press, everyone man, mek dem come to us. We call de shots now.'

And that's the way it was. People were not only waiting to hear the album, they now also wanted to know if the band could pull it off live. Due to the album and the gig being promoted concurrently, the band were now taking up large amounts of room on billboards on the streets. They were still spending lots of time in the studio but now they were practising for the live show.

There was no room for second takes, they could no longer refer to the words on paper. It all had to be memorised. They soon learnt that they could not simply perform standing still like they had been in the studio; they now had to fill a large stage and learn how to control their breathing so that they didn't resort to shouting or just burn out. This was getting physical. Ray came up with the idea of going through an exercise session before they began rehearsals, consisting of press-ups, sit-ups, running on the spot, jumping jacks, stretches and martial arts-style kicks and punches. He had also come up with a motto for the band which was quickly adopted and even managed to make it on to the sleeve of the CD. *Let wordy great minds think alike, sweet Hip-Hop be our guiding light.* When they said the motto they would stand in a circle and touch their fists, and if Marga Man and Bunny were around they too would join in.

* * *

On the day of the gig, none of the band members could hide their nervousness. It was noticed by all their families, many of whom were going to attend the concert. Prem's older sister had planned to go with three of her friends, Tyrone had given a backstage pass to Sam and a couple of his close relatives, although it seemed like his whole extended family were going – at least those that were under thirty. But it wasn't until Ray was leaving his house that afternoon for the sound check that Kori asked him if she could go.

'Of course you can go,' Ray said. 'I think you can still get tickets at the door.'

'No,' said Kori. 'I'm your sister. I wanna go with my two friends Lizette and Thara, they're your biggest fans.'

'Are you one of our biggest fans too?' asked Ray with a big grin.

'Yeah,' she replied, placing her hands on her hips and kissing her teeth. 'I think you're wicked. Now can we get on the guest list or what?'

'Yeah, OK.'

'And can we have backstage passes?'

'Yeah, OK. Mum,' Ray shouted back into the house. 'Do you wanna come to our concert?'

His mother made her way to him. 'No thanks, I don't think I could take all that loud noise. But good luck anyway.'

'Thanks Mum,' Ray said, turning to leave.

'Why don't you ask your father?' said his mother.

'Because I don't want to,' replied Ray. 'Any time I try to tell him what we're doing he doesn't care, so I don't think he's gonna start caring now.'

'You could be wrong,' said his mother.

'I wish I was,' said Ray, walking away.

The band met at the music shop and then went on to the Rex with Marga Man. At the venue they began to sense how great the task ahead for them was. Although they had been to the Rex before they had only seen it from the dance floor when it was full. When they stood on the stage and saw the size of the large empty hall, it was hard for them to imagine that later that night the place would be full of people who were there for one reason – to see them.

They watched as the massive PA system was wired in and lighting people went about their business. Then Bunny arrived. He went behind the mixing console and they did their first sound check. After each of them had their levels checked by shouting 'check one, two' into the microphone, they performed 'War Cry'. It was strange performing to a large empty hall, but they really used up the space they had on the stage, and it was beginning to feel good.

After the sound check Marga Man and the band went to an Indian restaurant on Romford Road. All the food that they ate was given compliments of the manager.

When they arrived back at the Rex, Marga Man drove slowly past so that the boys could see the people waiting to go inside. The queue seemed endless, and ticket touts were looking for trade. A couple of policemen watched quietly, not letting anyone know that there were two vans full of geared-up police two blocks away.

Marga Man drove the boys round the corner to the stage door, but even there people were waiting. A security man moved a plastic bollard that was strategically placed to reserve a parking place for them and within seconds they were out of the car and through the stage door. In the dressing room they changed into the clothes they were going to wear on stage – they were all dressed differently, but the colour they had agreed on was brown.

The hall was pumping to the hip-hop that was being played over the PA system, in contrast to the dressing room, where, semi-insulated from the sounds in the hall, the boys laughed and joked to cover up the tension of waiting for their call. Marga Man would come to the dressing room every fifteen minutes to make sure they had their drinks and were happy, but it wasn't long before he came to tell them to prepare for action.

The boys began to walk around the room like athletes getting ready to compete. Ray began to shadow box as if limbering up for a fight, Tyrone began to get serious, and Prem went through a series of deep breathing exercises.

The next time Marga Man entered it was with Skelly from Deaf Defying Records.

'This is it,' said Skelly. 'Go for it, lads.'

'Go rock de people,' Marga Man said, stretching his clenched fist into the centre of the room.

The boys gathered around, and reaching out and touching fist they all shouted, '*Let wordy great minds think alike, sweet Hip-Hop be our guiding light.*'

'Your public awaits you,' said Marga Man.

'Let's do this,' Ray said, as Marga Man and Skelly led them out of the room and towards the stage.

As they neared the stage the music got louder and the heat became more intense. People they had never seen before touched them as they passed by, wishing them good luck and telling them to go for it. Without seeing the crowd the boys could feel the excitement. Marga Man stopped them behind the stage curtain.

'Wait here. Your mics are in place. As soon as I announce yu, hit de stage. I'll be right here if yu need me. Make a joyful noise, your public awaits you.'

Marga Man walked on to the stage and immediately the music stopped. Before he even spoke the crowd clapped, and when the clapping stopped there was silence.

'Dis is de night yu have been waiting for. Dis is a night yu will not forget. Tonight yu are witnessing de future, because tonight yu are seeing de first live performance of de best hip-hop band in de land. Yes, people, put your hands and hearts together, and focus your minds, because yu are about to be charged wid de wonderful sound of Positive Negatives.'

The crowd went absolutely wild; the clapping was overtaken by whistling, chanting and other guttural sounds. The boys hesitated as if savouring the moment, but then when they walked on stage everything went up another level. Willing the crowd on even more, Ray took his microphone and said, 'We're Positive Negatives and we wanna hear ya make some fucking noise.'

Having been given permission by X-Ray-X the noise of the crowd increased once more, and this time, just as it seemed the energy level had reached its peak, the beat kicked in. The first thing to hit was a heavy bass note that vibrated through all the bodies present. Then the band began to rap, starting altogether on the chorus.

Chorus:

We are the Positive Negatives

We live the Hip-Hop philosophy
So if you wanna live
You gotta know not to fuck with we,
We come out of the East
Where we are not ethnic minorities
So just leave us in peace
We are the immoral majority

Ray:

My name is X-Ray-X
So be careful how you flex
My name may be really short
But the meaning is complex,
I used to freestyle in me bedroom
But me daddy got me vex
The teacher kicked me out of the classroom
Now I'm rapping in the Rex

Tyrone:

My name is Pro Justice
Yeah Pro Justice that is me
And I'm the only person that
I ever want to be,
Like the sugar in your coffee
And the sugar in your tea
As long as you don't stress me

I'm your lovable sweetie

Prem:

They call me Prem de la Prem
And I like to rap with them
We started off in Stratford
But we'll reach Jerusalem,
Because we're full of raw ambition
So remember when I say
We are rappers on admission
So we'll see you in Bombay

Chorus:

We are the Positive Negatives
We live the Hip-Hop philosophy
So if you wanna live
You gotta know not to fuck with we,
We come out of the East
Where we are not ethnic minorities
So just leave us in peace
We are the immoral majority

It wasn't a rap that appeared on the album, but one written specially for the night as a way to introduce themselves. When that rap was over, the crowd hardly had a chance to applaud before the second track kicked in. Ray spoke over the first few bars of the beat.

'Wanna introduce you to my man Bunny doing the mix over there.' He pointed to Bunny at the back of the hall. 'And I wanna thank you all for buying this next jam, this one dedicated to the enemy of the youth, this one called "War Cry".'

And so the beats continued, relentless, and the themes got stronger and stronger. The boys loved the big stage, they strutted up and down it as if they lived there. Not an inch of it was left uncovered. Soon they found themselves performing at ease without having to think too much about the words, they knew they were made for it. Non-verbal communication took over, each one knew where the other was going, each one knowing exactly when to take the lead.

The set lasted for an hour and a half, and they finished by performing a rap called 'Eastside Story', which Ray dedicated to his hero Tupac Shakur, calling it a rap about thug life on the streets of east London, and the crowd loved them even more.

The boys left the stage, leaving behind a crowd that just didn't look like they were ready to go home. As Marga Man followed them to the dressing room, he stopped them.

'Yo, listen.' They could hear the crowd shouting for more. 'Your public needs more,' he said.

The boys turned round and went back on stage, delighting the crowd with another hard-hitter called 'Parental Guidance', about the censorship of musical recordings and television programmes. When they did manage to leave the stage and make it to the dressing room, they were physically exhausted, but mentally high. By the time the band had showered and changed, a large crowd was waiting outside the dressing room. When the signal was given, Marga Man let them in. Kori and her friends were amongst the first in, but the crowd included members of Prem's family, Tyrone's family, record company people and school friends, all bestowing heaps of praise upon the band. Sam made a quick appearance to congratulate the boys and thank Tyrone for the backstage pass, then she disappeared.

As the boys were soaking it all up, Marga Man called the gathering to order and announced that there was an after-show party at his shop. The crowd expressed their happiness and they made their way out of the building. But it was difficult to set out as everyone wanted to talk to the boys.

Outside the venue there were even more people waiting for them. As they were signing autographs and talking to fans, Marga Man tried to persuade them to make their way to the car, but the boys were happy to continue signing. Their first gig had been a success and they wanted to lap up every minute of it.

As Kori and her two friends Lizette and Thara were telling the boys how great they were, they were interrupted by a hooded youth who was surrounded by his hooded friends.

'Have you ladyboys got something to say?' asked the hooded youth.

Ray smiled. 'Hey man, we said everything we wanted to say back there on stage.'

'Your raps are crap, you know that ain't it?' he said, flexing his fists.

'Yeah, whatever,' said Ray, thinking it was an old friend joking and trying to recognise what he could see of the face.

The youth continued. 'You lot are serious non-starters, especially you,' he said, looking at Ray. 'You rap like your tongue's in your arse, man. All you east London people rap shit, your beats are shit, your lyrics are shit, and your girls are shit.'

One of the guys standing behind the ringleader flicked a cigarette over, and it landed near Kori. 'Put your foot on that, bitch.'

'Who do you think you're talking to?' Kori shouted back.

'I'm talking to a bitch, and you're that bitch. Maybe you should stop following these dogs and get to know yourself.'

'Don't talk to me like that, you. Who are you anyway? Afraid of showing you face 'cause you're so ugly?'

'What you want is a slap, bitch.'

Ray moved forward until he was directly in front of the ringleader. 'What's yu problem?' said Ray, suddenly realising that he was much smaller than the guy in front of him.

'We ain't got a problem, we're just concerned environmentalist. We smell bullshit and we come to clean up.'

Tyrone and Prem began to manoeuvre themselves behind Ray. Marga Man shouldered his way over.

'Leave it,' said Marga Man.

'Yeah boy, leave it,' said the hooded youth.

'OK, I'll leave it, but just watch how you talk to my sister, guy,' said Ray, then he turned away to join the others.

'Hey, it's his sister,' the ringleader said, looking around at his followers. He turned to Ray. 'I see where the problem lies now. Tell your sister to close her legs, her breath stinks.'

As soon as he heard that, Ray went for him. Filled with rage, he swung his punches fast and wild, with no game plan, and his opposition responded in kind. A couple of the others went for Tyrone and Prem. For a second Marga Man tried to separate Prem from his aggressor, but after being hit by both Prem and his enemy, he gave up. There was screaming and shouting, and when a couple of bystanders from the Positive Negatives camp got hit many of those bystanders joined in. It all happened very quickly – as did the arrival of several policemen and club security staff. On seeing the police the gang ran away, but Marga Man, the boys, and their friends and relatives made no attempt to run. Some were struggling to get off the ground whilst others tried to find belongings which had fallen from their pockets or been ripped from them during the commotion.

Ray was angriest. He shouted and cursed that the ringleader had got the better of him but that he wanted another shot. Marga Man and Kori were trying to calm him down, but his fury attracted the police, whose first instinct was to try to arrest him. The crowd came to his defence.

'Leave him.'

'You should be getting the others, they started it.'

'That ain't right, why don't you go after that other lot?'

They soon convinced the police that there was more to the situation than met the eye. So the police then tried to get the story but all they got was, 'There were some people who came and started trouble and a fight started.'

Realising that they weren't getting anywhere, the police began to take names and addresses. Then Lizette noticed that one of the Positive Negatives fans was still down and unable to get up.

'Look at him,' she said, pointing. 'He needs help.'

A police officer and Lizette went to help him. He

was a white kid, about seventeen, with spiky brown hair and a camera around his neck.

'Are you all right?' said one of the officers.

'Can't you see he's not?' said Lizette, as she reached down to help him up. Seeing that he made no attempt to reach out to her she stretched down further and took his hand, but as she lifted it she screamed. His upstretched arm revealed blood coming from his side and running underneath him.

The kid looked up. His eyes rolled, focusing nowhere. 'I think I've been stabbed,' he said, panting. 'In my side.'

'Call an ambulance,' shouted the officer to his colleagues.

They kept the knife victim where he was, but kept talking to him. After the ambulance had taken him away the police tried asking a few more questions, but no one knew the victim, and no one saw who had done it. The police could see that they were getting nowhere, the boys wanted to go, and more people began turning up wanting to know what had happened. The police arranged to see the band and Marga Man in the music shop the next day and they went off to file their report. Marga Man got his car, and with the help of a couple of volunteer drivers the band and their entourage were taken to the music shop.

As they drove past the front of the venue Ray thought about his early dream of starting a rap band

and how he had struggled in school. He thought about all the time he had spent freestyling in the park and on the streets, and the hard work he, Tyrone and Prem had put in at the studio. And now, in less than a year, they had a number one hit record, they had recorded an album, and on the fascia of the biggest venue in east London were the words 'TONIGHT, LIVE ON STAGE: POSITIVE NEGATIVES (SOLD OUT)'.

Back at the music shop there was no party, just talk and anger against the gang that had turned up at the stage door, and concern for the boy who had gone out that night to listen to beats and lyrics but ended up with a knife in his side.

It was early morning before Ray and Kori got home, and as soon as Ray opened the door their mother was up to see how the concert went.

'Tell me then, what was it like?'

'It was great,' said Ray. 'You should have come, you would have loved it.'

There was an unfamiliar touch of excitement in their mother's voice. 'So, was there a lot of people there or what?'

'It was packed, Mum,' said Ray, 'the place was bubbling, plenty nice girls too, all come to see me.'

'OK,' said their mother, 'so you had a good time then?'

'It was good, Mum,' said Kori. 'There was some trouble after the concert, but the concert itself was really good.'

'What kind of trouble?' their mother asked, concerned.

Ray replied quickly before Kori said too much. 'It was nothing, just some guys looking for trouble after the gig.'

'What, was there fighting?'

'Don't worry, Mum,' said Ray. 'We're all right, just tired.'

It took Ray ages before he was able to settle down that night. He had to lie in bed and go through the whole concert in his mind before he was able to slow down enough to allow himself to sleep. It seemed like he had only been asleep for a moment when his mobile phone rang. He reached out in the dark and answered it.

'Yo, who's this?'

'It's the Messenger.'

'Who?'

'The Messenger.'

'Stop messing about, who is it?'

'Listen, I'm not messing you about. I've come to tell you that you were lucky tonight but your luck will run out.'

'You're the guy who was down the Rex tonight, are you? If you are, then come again, you don't fret me.'

'Just watch out, great things come from the west. Goodnight, pussy face.'

The phone went dead. Ray looked into the darkness for a while and then he tried to sleep.

CHAPTER 11

The Mix Mag

Hip-hop reviews

Album: *Collective Security*
Artist: *Positive Negatives*

It may be British, but this has to be the hip-hop album of the year. The beats draw you in instantly and the lyrics are very, very phat indeed. Musically the whole thing is hard, tight and very danceable, and the production is polished to perfection but not reliant on studio gimmicks. First-time producer Marga Man has managed to create a virtual speaker's corner that completely complements the deft rhymes. This is truly an amazing piece of writing, full of quick, clever rhymes and intelligent cultural observations performed with verbal gymnastics of the highest order. The single 'War Cry' is exceptional, but don't take my word for it – take a look at the charts. Positive Negatives are young, gifted, and Bad, and it seems as if the whole world has agreed that they look like the first British rap band capable of doing it Stateside.

This is one of those rare collections of beats that encourages you to dance and think at the same time. Feel free to raise your expectations high. You will not be disappointed.

Stella Bella

CHAPTER 12

The Show Must Go On

Two completely different plain-clothed police officers turned up for the interview at the music shop the following day – a small quiet one, and a big loud one. The loud one, Detective Sergeant Horne, did all the talking, and from the outset he insisted on taking the wrong approach.

'Right, understand this. We are not beat cops, we are not even your run of the mill CID, we're from the Serious Crime Squad,' he said, sniffing the air. 'So we're not bothered about you having a bit of weed. We don't chase stolen phones or anything like that. We do serious stuff. And a stabbing is serious. So let's cut to the chase. I'll stop talking, and you tell me what happened last night.'

'We told your brother already,' Marga Man replied.

'My brother?' said the officer.

'Your police friend,' said Marga Man, 'last night.'

'Look, he's my colleague, not my brother or my police friend.' The officer cast an evil eye over Marga Man. 'Now, let's move on. Can't you think of anything you could have done to provoke this gang?'

'What are you saying?' said Ray.

'What I mean is, do you owe anybody any money, or does anybody owe you money that may not want to pay you back? Any unfinished business, or anything like that?'

'We don't know nothing,' Ray said angrily. 'We come out of the gig and these guys come talking rubbish and insulting our girls and things like that, and that's how it happened. We don't drink or smoke weed, and we don't steal. We were minding our own business, you know what I'm saying? We is the victims here.'

'We're only here to help,' said the second officer, trying to calm things down.

'If you want to help, why are you talking to us like that?' said Prem.

'You gotta show some respect,' said Tyrone. 'Yeah, we're the ones that get attacked but you're treating us like the criminals. We're just artists, you know what I'm saying, we never slash anyone, never rob anyone.'

'But as I understand it, you struck the first blow,' said the big officer.

Ray got even angrier. 'Hey, man, if you know that you should know why those people were out for trouble, they came tooled up looking for blood.'

'OK, just be cool,' Marga Man said, bringing order

to the room. He turned to the officers. 'How's de guy dat got stabbed?'

The quiet officer spoke. 'It's serious, but he's going to pull through.'

'OK, are you sure you don't have anything else to tell us?' asked D.S. Horne.

They all shook their heads.

'Well, we may have more questions we would like to ask you, so don't be surprised if you see us again. And let us know if you remember anything that you think is relevant to our enquiries.'

'Goodbye,' said Ray.

The officers said nothing else as they left the shop.

Kori had told their parents about the stabbing incident early that morning. Once again their father had said very little, but their mother was deeply concerned. Ray made it clear to her that there was no way that the band were going to let it get to them. This was the time they had worked towards. Tyrone had to convey a similar message to his parents, and they tried to get him to quit the band, but he wasn't going to. But Prem planned to keep it a secret from his parents. He even made his sister and her friends promise not to say anything. But his parents found out when it made page three of their favourite tabloid newspaper, and the front page of *The Newham Echo*.

To make things worse for all of them there was an item on *Newstalk South East*, the local TV news programme. It caused an almighty row in the Sharma household, which led to Mrs Sharma phoning Marga Man.

'Mr Man, you are doing a good job with the boys, I think my son looks very good on TV, but why are they in all the papers? I mean we want them in the papers, but for good things, not for all these bad things.'

Marga Man was trying to serve customers as he replied. 'Yes, Mrs Sharma, yu right, we want good tings, not bad tings. But trust me, de boys are cool, Prem is just nice, Mrs Sharma. It's like dis, right, some mad guys come bigging up themselves, really I was there. Dem was trouble makers, yu know, terrorist, dem come terrorise and an innocent youth get cut. Dat's how it go, Mrs Sharma, sometimes innocent people can just be in de wrong place at de wrong time.'

'But I heard that there was a big riot.'

'No ma'am, no riot, just some self-defence business.'

'Are you sure, Mr Man?'

'Yes, I was there. Prem was just looking after himself. There are some crazy people out there you know, Mrs Sharma.'

'Yes, and that's why I don't like my son being out there.'

'Don't worry Mrs Sharma, I'm taking care of tings.'

'I am worried, so you better take care of things.'

For the first time in years Ray's mother prayed, and all his father could say was that 'Badness will bring forth badness', but Ray was as determined as ever to keep everything moving. He made sure that Prem and Tyrone continued to attend the centre, and he continued to write and work on new music. Marga Man had a lot to think about, and for the next couple of days, all he did was think. When he had thought, he made another trip to meet the band in the studio.

The moment the boys saw him, they could tell by the thoughtful look on his face that he was in meeting mode, and so once again they gathered around him in the control room.

Marga Man started by telling them what he had told Mrs Sharma, that maybe it was just troublemakers, but Ray wasn't having it either.

'I don't buy that,' Ray said, shaking his head. 'Those guys came for us, I know it.'

'We just don't know,' said Bunny. 'But I've been getting strange phone calls here, someone rings and then talking some negative stuff.'

'Me too,' said Ray. 'Last night someone called me and chat a whole heap a rubbish in me ears. That's why I know something's happening, someone's stirring things up guy.'

Marga Man began searching his many pockets. 'Yeah, we be getting dat in de shop too, but we have to stand firm, like a rock, we can't let dem sabotage de work.' He took a handful of business cards from his pocket. They were for a personal security company, and he handed one to each of the boys. 'Today I talk wid these people, we can set up a contract wid dem. It works like dis: any time we have official public appearances they provide security, they back us up. Dis would mean at least two bodyguards, any time we need dem, day or night.'

'Who's gonna pay for this?' asked Ray.

'Good question,' said Marga Man. 'If we all agree, I say it should be paid for from de bank account, but from de expenses dat we receive from de record company, in other words from tour support money, and not royalties money.'

'I think that's cool,' said Prem.

'Me too,' said Tyrone.

'I don't know,' said Ray, looking quite unhappy. 'That's not going to save us if someone comes for us. I reckon we should be prepared to fight and that's it. These bodyguard people, they can't be with us all de time.'

'No of course dem can't,' said Marga Man. 'But it's better dan nothing. When you guys are doing your ting on stage or dealing wid your fans, they will be looking out for yu.'

'It's better than nothing,' said Prem.

'True,' said Ray, nodding thoughtfully.

'OK,' said Marga Man, 'I'll go ahead wid de deal. So remember, dis is for any public appearances, dat means gigs, signings, press conferences, and anyting dat we do dat de public has knowledge of. I will organise it but yu have cards just in case. At all other times we just have to be vigilant.'

Ray put his card away, then said, 'I think we should take a trip to the hospital to see that kid that got stabbed.'

'Yeah,' said Prem. 'The guy was a fan, a true fan.'

'True,' Tyrone said. 'We shouldn't just forget the guy.'

'Dat's a good idea. I'll find out where he is,' said Marga Man. 'There's two ways to do dis. We could just go there one visiting time as normal, unannounced, or we could let de press know. Dat way de people will know dat we care about our fans.'

Ray responded quickly. 'No, I don't think we should let anyone know. We do it for him, not for the press and not even for us.'

No one could argue with that.

'OK,' said Marga Man. 'We done wid dat now. Now let's deal wid some good news. De record company doesn't want to wait for two years before de next album. On de strength of all de pre-sales and sales to date, dem want to tek up de option for de next album straightaway.'

'Yes,' said Ray. 'We've started work on that already.'

'And there's even more good news,' said Marga Man, producing another one of his big smiles. 'I am proud to announce dat Positive Negatives have been nominated for four MOBO Awards.'

The boys flew up off their seats in celebration. They touched fists, slapped palms and touched shoulders. Bunny danced around the room and Marga Man looked on like a proud father.

'Best Newcomer, Best Album, Best Hip-Hop Act and Best Video,' he said, smiling contentedly.

The next day Marga Man took them to Newham Parkside Hospital to see the stabbed teenager. When they arrived at his bedside his sister and father were already there, and made it clear to the band that they did not blame them for what happened. The teenager's name was Thomas, but he was known as Fingers. He described himself as a hardcore Positive Negatives fan. He knew every word on the album and had read everything published about the band. His stab wound was deep but luckily no vital organs were damaged. He was due to go home the next day but said happily, 'I'd stay longer if it meant that you guys would visit me again.'

He explained that he had been hanging around waiting for an autograph and taking photos when the fight started, and a couple of boys went for him and one of them stabbed him. 'That's all that happened,' he said. 'The police keep asking me for more, but that's all I know.'

The boys thought that Fingers had the hip-hop spirit about him, unsentimental and uncompromising; they all got on well together.

'I want to thank you for coming, makes me feel good.'

'No problem,' said Ray.

'I wanna ask you something.'

'Do it,' said Prem.

'Why haven't you guys got a website?'

They all looked at each other cluelessly.

'It looks like we don't know,' said Ray.

'When I get free can I build one for you?'

'Yeah,' Ray replied.

'Cool.'

Marga Man took Fingers's phone number, then they left him with a signed limited edition copy of the CD, and told him to check out the MOBO Awards on television.

A week later and there they were, all dressed in expensive threads, and chilling out in the Al-Fayed Hotel. The ceremony was being hosted by the American soul singer Matt Cliff and the British radio DJ Miss Issy.

As the show was about to start, Ray looked around. All around him he saw faces that he had only previously seen on television. Everything in the room seemed to glitter: the chandeliers, the windows, the walls, the food, even the people. The band's two newly acquired bodyguards sat quietly at the table. Dressed in black suits and wearing sunglasses, they looked like saxophone players from a jazz band.

Ray sat in between Tyrone and Prem. He put his arms around their necks and drew them to him and said, 'Just think, if we'd walked in this place last year, we would have been kicked out.'

'You mean arrested,' Tyrone said.

'Or given a cleaning job,' Prem added.

The show was about to start. The television cameras began to roll and a bodiless voice came from the ceiling.

'Ladies and gentlemen, welcome to the MOBO Awards. Please welcome on stage your hosts for the night, all the way from the USA, the soul man himself, Matt Cliff, and your very own superwoman Miss Issy.'

The soul man entered stage left wearing a bright red suit that was a couple of sizes too big for him, and Miss Issy entered stage right wearing very little. The men in the audience whistled and cheered as she strode on stage in what looked like a green bra and a matching belt.

Together they introduced the guests to give awards

to the winners. The guests comprised of actors who were trying to keep up their public profile, former pop stars, sports people and game show hosts. Categories included the best R'n'B band, best soul band and best reggae act, plus their respective videos. As the awards were being given out, the competing artists would look at each other and smile, sometimes wishing each other the best, whilst secretly hoping that they would drop dead. This was repeated throughout the evening, as was the ritual of accepting the awards. The winners would take to the stage and repeat the same words over and over again, only changing the order.

'I really wasn't expecting this.
I would like to thank my manager,
and my mum,
I want to thank my record company for having faith in me.
I want to big up my crew,
I want to thank God.
But most of all I want to thank you the fans, because without you I wouldn't be here.'

Which oddly always seemed to go down well, considering that the audience consisted mainly of other nominees and invited VIPs. Very few fans were actually present. Ray noticed this. He leaned over his table.

'Hey Marga Man, so where are the fans?'

Marga Man pointed to the camera. 'At home.'

After the lifetime achievement award was given out, Miss Issy went on stage to introduce another guest.

'Now it gives me great pleasure to welcome on stage an actor who just goes from strength to strength. His talent knows no end, he's everybody's friend – it's Kenny Morgan.'

Kenny Morgan walked on stage holding an envelope. He told a joke and people laughed, then he began to list the nominees for the next award.

'The nominees for the Best Newcomer Awards are: The Full Force Crew, Tony Manchester, Legal Eyes, Sharon Easy and Positive Negatives.'

He opened the envelope.

'And the award goes to … Positive Negatives.'

The crowd clapped and the boys headed up to the stage with the two bodyguards following them. The nearer they got to the stage the louder the crowd got, but once on the stage they couldn't help but notice some rather stony faces looking up at them from the Western Alliance table. They were not clapping.

The award itself was a plastic representation of the word MOBO. Ray took the award from Miss Issy and then the boys all took the opportunity to kiss her on both cheeks.

Tyrone put his head to the microphone. 'Marga Man, this is for you, and you too Sam.'

Prem put his head to the microphone. 'Mum, this is for you.'

Ray put his head to the microphone. 'Hey you, this is for me.'

There were cheers and laughter from the crowd, and the boys began to walk back to their table to more applause.

Next the best album category was announced; again the band were nominated alongside Sharon Easy, Love Lite and the Western Alliance. Once again Positive Negatives won. But the most important award as far as the band were concerned was the award for the best hip-hop act. The nominees for this category were Positive Negatives, a band from Birmingham called Roots Culture, a black Irish rapper called Fhil the Flow, Little Sista, and the Western Alliance.

Matt Cliff invited supermodel Lulu Obeng on stage to announce the winner, and the award went to Positive Negatives. The band casually went back to the stage with their bodyguards in tow. This time Prem took the award, but only Ray spoke.

'First of all I wanna say to Fingers over there in Parkside, we're with you, brother, you supported us and we're supporting you. Get well soon man, and stay on the beat. Also I wanna say that all music is good, I wanna say to my sister Kori that Beyoncé is cool, all music is cool, and we all just finding musical ways to express ourselves. My man Marga Man just told me that MOBO stands for music of black origin, but I say that all music has black origins, life has black origins, but at the same time music is colour-free.'

The crowd clapped and shouted words of agreement; many rose to their feet. Ray continued.

'Now we, Positive Negatives, are accepting this award for the best hip-hop act, but I gotta tell you that we are not a hip-hop act, we don't act, we are hip-hop, we live and breathe hip-hop. This is true, we are the real deal.'

Just then there was an interruption. A voice shouted from the audience, 'You ain't hip-hop, you just puppy dogs.'

Everyone turned to see where the voice came from. It was from the table of the Western Alliance. They were laughing and congratulating the speaker. The speaker stood up and Ray could tell straightaway that it was Dragon, the front man of the Western Alliance.

Ray continued, 'Puppy dogs bark and run away. We don't run, we represent ourselves, we say hip-hop is about being upfront. What do you say?'

'We say you're pussy cats,' shouted Dragon.

'Hey what, you jealous?' shouted Ray, looking directly at Dragon.

'You baby rappers, why should we be jealous of you?' Dragon said, cupping his hands and doing a swinging motion as if rocking a baby.

The crowd reacted with a mixture of laughter and whispering as they tried to understand what was happening. Remembering that this was being recorded for television, Miss Issy tried to regain some order. 'OK lads, let's all be friends. It's only an awards ceremony.'

Prem held the award high over his head, Tyrone didn't take his eyes off the Western Alliance table and Ray shouted, 'This is us, this is hip-hop, and right now no one can touch us.'

As the boys walked back to their table another member of the Alliance shouted, 'We can touch you, and don't be worried, children, you will be touched.'

As the other awards were being handed out, the Western Alliance members and the Positive Negatives table kept a close eye on each other. Then the nominations for the best video were announced. They included both the Western Alliance and Positive Negatives. A distinguished newsreader was brought on stage to announce the winner.

'And the winner is,' she said slowly, 'the Western Alliance.'

Four members of the Western Alliance went to the stage, led by Dragon, who took the award without any hand-shaking. With his free hand he took the microphone from its stand and put it to his mouth.

'I ain't gonna say too much, just wanna let people know that we are the Western Alliance. Maybe we ain't picking up loads of awards but then again we don't go around running our mouths like some nursery rhymers in the area. You see we stay true to the music, but if anyone crosses us, we deal with them. Remember we are the Western Alliance.'

The applause was nervous and muted. The two camps kept a watch on each other for the rest of the proceedings; everybody could feel the tension between them. The night ended with a live performance by Sharon Easy who managed to get everyone on their feet and clapping their hands to her up-beat R'n'B songs. As she sang, Marga Man suggested that they slip away. But Dragon and other members of the Western Alliance were waiting outside.

'Go home babies, it's your bedtime,' shouted one of them.

'Keep walking and never mind dem,' said Marga Man.

Their bodyguards stiffened up and prepared themselves for trouble. They had turned away and headed in the direction of the hotel car park when a plastic water bottle hit Tyrone on the head. Ray couldn't take it any more and he turned to face them.

'Come on then, who first?'

About five of the Western Alliance moved forward to volunteer themselves.

'Come on,' shouted Ray.

'No problem baby,' said Dragon.

'You're gonna get some,' shouted another voice from the Alliance.

Marga Man stepped in front of Ray to calm him down, and the bodyguard stepped in between Marga Man and the Alliance.

'OK, next time baby,' shouted Dragon.

'Yeah, next time,' shouted Ray.

CHAPTER 13

Negative Positives

The awards ceremony was transmitted on Channel Four the next night and very little was edited out of the programme. News about the event had made it into some of the morning papers so the programme got top ratings. On the streets of east London the band were becoming even bigger heroes. Fans thought the music was great, but many gave the band even more respect for standing up to the west Londoners who outnumbered them and were older than them.

The controversy pushed up CD sales for both bands, and for one week the Western Alliance's album 'Mass Distraction' overtook Positive Negatives – but it was not to last. The success of the 'War Cry' single and their appearance on *Top of the Pops* and other TV programmes gave Positive Negatives an advantage.

The press began to request more interviews, but the band wanted to concentrate on recording the next album. The beats were flowing easily enough, but they were finding it increasingly difficult to write raps. Ray had told the others that they had to try not to simply repeat the sentiments of the first album. He knew that second albums were always difficult. They had crammed their lives' experience into the first album, and now they had to fill another album having experienced very little new except fame.

One morning after a late session in the studio, Ray received a call on his mobile phone. He was still in bed and sleeping when the phone rang. He picked it up, pressed the answer button and put it to his ear without opening his eyes.

'Who's this?'

'It's me, Prem. Did you hear what happened last night?'

'No, what happened?'

'A guy got shot, man, right in the head, right in front of everyone. A west London guy.'

'That's bad man. Where that happen?'

Prem was speaking very fast. 'Happened in the Alleyway Club in the West End.'

'That's bad man,' said Ray, his eyes still closed.

'Things are getting rough, there's pure friction out here.'

'Yeah, guy. Let's talk later.'

Ray went back to sleep but then ten minutes later the phone rang again. This time it was Tyrone.

'Ray, it's me.'

'Yeah, what?'

'Did you hear what happened?'

'Yeah, I heard what happened. Call me back later, I'm tired.'

'You can't sleep now. Someone's dead.'

Tyrone was sounding very agitated, there was an urgency in his voice. Ray tried to cool him down. 'OK, someone got shot. It's bad but let's just talk about it later.'

'We can't just leave it till later. The press are trying to find us right now.'

'What they want us for? It's got nothing to do with us, we wasn't there.'

'Don't you know? They're saying it's an east London versus west London thing. They're saying it's like some Western Alliance fans and some Positive Negatives fans started arguing, and then an East Ender shot a West Ender.'

Ray sat up in bed. 'Are you serious?' he asked, eyes now wide open.

'Very serious.'

'OK,' said Ray. 'I'll ring Marga Man.' Ray put the phone down and got out of bed, but before he had time to do anything the phone rang again. He picked it up.

'Hello.'

There was silence.

'Hello?'

Then a voice slowly uttered, 'This is war.' And the phone went dead.

Ray rang Marga Man immediately.

'Marga Man, what's happening?'

Marga Man's voice was calm and reassuring. 'If any newspaper people find you, don't speak to dem, don't talk to anybody about anyting. Tell your family not to say anyting. Just come to de music shop now.'

Ray washed and dressed at breakneck speed and ran all the way to the music shop where Prem, Tyrone and Marga Man were already in conversation. Ray joined straight in. 'What's it all about, what's going on?'

'This is what I heard,' said Tyrone, already sounding as if he had told the story a hundred times before. 'DJ Rapcity and Ali Fire were playing at the Alleyway Club and some guy gets on Ali Fire's microphone and starts to run down the east London crew, saying that east London people this and that, and then him start say that Positive Negatives is rubbish and we only win MOBOs because we go on *Top of the Pops*. So then Omar, you know Omar?'

Ray looked at everyone. 'Who's Omar?'

'De brother always come in de music shop, always wear some type of bowler hat ting,' said Marga Man.

'You know him,' said Prem, 'Red Eye Omar.'

'Oh yeah, Red Eye.'

'Yeah, him,' Tyrone continued. 'Well, he gets on

Rapcity's mic and starts to run down the west London crew. I heard that he cursed them bad, and tell them that no west London man can rap. Anyway, I don't know everything that happened, but I heard that the DJs and the management get everyone to cool down and then when people start to leave the club some east London and west London man start a fight and one of the east man shoot a west man.'

'So did anyone get locked up?' asked Ray.

'I heard that they arrested Red Eye at home early this morning,' said Tyrone. 'But then they let him go because he had already gone when it happened and no witnesses described him.'

'OK,' said Marga Man. 'All we have to do is stay cool, don't go chatting to people and keep working. We have to focus on de music and nothing else.'

'Yeah, I wanna focus on the music too,' said Ray. 'But how we gonna focus on the music when all this is going on? And this morning somebody ring me on my mobile and tell me that this is war.'

'Me too,' said Prem.

'And me,' said Tyrone.

'And me too,' said Marga Man. 'Dis could be anyone, dis could just be people trying to scare us. We have to be on our guard, but we can't stop working.'

Ray stood up and began to pace around the shop. 'You're right Marga Man. We got to keep it positive, got to keep it hip-hop.'

Just as Ray was speaking, there was a loud noise at the back of the shop, followed by the sound of people moving towards them. Then the front door was kicked in and what seemed like hundreds of policemen came through the door shouting 'Police' and waving their truncheons around. Marga Man was the first to be grabbed, quickly followed by the others.

'So what's this about?' shouted Ray.

'You are under arrest for conspiracy to murder,' said an officer who was just entering the shop. It was D.S. Horne, the officer who did all the questioning when the stabbing happened outside the Rex.

'Yeah,' said Ray, 'I suppose you want us to help you with your enquiries.'

'That's right,' said the officer holding him.

'So you want us to beat ourselves up?' shouted Prem.

'This is no time for joking,' said D.S. Horne, who seemed to be the one in control of the raid. 'You are all being arrested for conspiring to murder Alton Benn last night in the West End. We don't know who pulled the trigger, but you can be sure that we will find out.'

Each of the Positive Negatives crew had two officers holding their arms. Ray began complaining. 'Hey, careful how you touch me you know. I don't like when people rough me up, I ain't done nothing to you, so just ease up.'

'This is stupid, you lot must be desperate. You know that we didn't have anything to do with last night,' Prem said, staring wildly at the officers.

'I'm not having a conversation here. We're all going back to the station and we'll deal with it there,' said D.S. Horne.

Ray began to struggle, twisting from side to side, trying to get away from the officers. 'I'm not going anywhere,' he shouted. 'This is rubbish, we're the victims.' Ray struggled more as the police began to head out to the vans that were waiting outside.

'Just be cool,' said Marga Man.

'If we're any cooler, they'll kill us,' said Prem.

'Don't say nothing to dem,' said Marga Man. 'Refuse to answer all questions until you get legal people, and leave dat to me.'

In the station their mobile phones, money and other personal effects were taken from them. They all refused to answer any questions but demanded their right to a phone call. Marga Man rang Skelly at Deaf Defying Records and arranged for some legal support.

The boys waited for an hour until a solicitor from the record company arrived. By now everyone was being held in separate rooms, so he went and introduced himself to each of them and instructed the boys not to say anything until at least one parent was present.

The solicitor sat in as Marga Man was being questioned. But it didn't take long for the police to establish that he had a strong alibi, and that Marga Man was not interested in any east versus west war. Just as it looked like Marga Man's interview was about to end, D.S. Horne rested back on his chair and tried to act reasonable.

'Look, we know that neither you nor your lads were at the club last night, we know that none of you pulled the trigger. But anyone can see that there's some kind of gang warfare going on here and somehow it does involve your boys and the Western Alliance. There's no murder charge coming your way, but you must know some of the East Enders that were out in the West End last night. We just need a few names to go on. Look, you're a mature guy. The kid that got shot last night was just a teenager, just a kid. It could have been your son.'

'Marga Man rested back in his chair. 'Listen, Mr Policeman, I don't know anyting about anyting. Last night de only place I went out to was de cash point, and I'm sure you have dat on film somewhere. Then I went home, ordered some food in, I'm sure you also have dat recorded on film, and then I spent the evening in wid me woman. And it wouldn't surprise me if you have dat recorded too.'

'So where were the boys?'

'Well, you will have to ask them dat.'

'I advise that you do not answer that question,' said the solicitor. He turned to the questioning officer. 'My client will only answer questions that are relevant to him. I suggest that you address questions about others' whereabouts to the persons concerned.'

The questioning ended abruptly. The police knew that Marga Man was telling the truth and so it wasn't long before the police gathered them all into a room to announce that they were to be released. No charges were to be made, no cautions were to be given. The solicitor oversaw their release, but after all the papers were signed, a policewoman who had been looking out of the window turned to the solicitor and said, 'You can use the back door to leave if you like.'

'Is there a problem?' said the solicitor.

'Well, yes,' said the officer. 'It looks like there's a few press reporters waiting for you.'

The boys all went over to the windows to see the reporters waiting around. When the solicitor saw them he said, 'Yes, I think that would be wise.'

'No,' said Ray. 'We haven't done anything wrong, we have nothing to hide. I say we go out of the front door and we go about our business. What do you guys say?' he asked the others.

They all nodded in agreement. And so they planned to walk the short distance to the music shop with the solicitor, where they were to continue the meeting that had been disturbed earlier that morning. Once they had received their possessions they left via the front door. As soon as they stepped out, cameras started flashing. The solicitor and Marga Man pushed a path through the reporters and photographers. The boys held their heads high but said nothing as the press shouted.

'Pro Justice, this way.'

'X-Ray-X, this way.'

'What do you think about the death of Alton? Do you think that there is a war between east London gangs and west London gangs?'

'Don't you think that you're being bad role models?'

But they all stayed silent and headed towards the shop. As they walked down West Ham Lane, the press followed them. Camera operators with sound recorders connected to them jostled with photographers and journalists. Soon there were members of the public and fans. When they reached the shop, they could not believe their eyes. Not only were the front and back doors still open from the raid, but the shop had been looted. As Ray raced around the shop to see what had been stolen, Marga Man, Tyrone and Prem just looked around at the wrecked shop, and the solicitor asked the press to 'stand back and have some respect.' Then he began to take notes.

'This is the police's fault,' shouted Ray. 'If it

wasn't for them, this wouldn't have happened. They wouldn't even let us lock up.'

'They gotta pay for this,' said Prem to the solicitor.

'Is there any money missing?' said the solicitor as he examined the door.

'No,' replied Marga Man. 'None at all. Dis morning when they came we were having a meeting, I do no business today. But look at de shop man, look at all dis damage, just look at dis.'

'Well, Mr Jolly,' said the solicitor to Marga Man, 'I can't say for certain, but it looks to me that you may be able to claim damages or some form of compensation from the police for this. If they did not allow you to lock the premises, then I think that you will have a strong case.'

'What do we do now?' asked Marga Man.

'Call the police,' said the solicitor. 'The crime has to be reported.'

Marga Man shook his head.

'I know,' said the solicitor. 'Very ironic, but it has to be done. The crime has to be reported before any action can be taken.'

Marga Man phoned the police and reported the matter, and then he called the security service and requested a couple of heavies. But outside the press were becoming impatient. The solicitor went to the door and requested that they go away.

'As you can see, the members of the group have a

lot to deal with right now,' he said. 'They would really appreciate it if you could leave them alone for a while until they are ready to speak to the press.'

'Can't we talk to them now?' shouted one of the reporters.

'I'm sorry, that's just not possible,' replied the solicitor.

But then Marga Man interrupted. 'No, let dem come in. Let dem see what happened here, yes man, take photos, photographic evidence.'

'Yeah,' said Ray. 'Let them come and see what happens when you get arrested without reason. One morning in the police station equals years of a man's hard work down the drain.'

'OK,' said the solicitor. 'Ten minutes for photos, but no questions, and please take care not to move anything or touch anything.'

The reporters entered, photographing and filming everything in sight. Although they still tried to question the boys, the band replied to none of their questions. They simply lined up with Marga Man like suspected criminals on an identification parade and allowed themselves to be photographed. After ten minutes the solicitor began to get the press out, but they all wanted their last photos or to try to tease words from the band members.

Once the two bodyguards turned up, however, it didn't take long for the shop to empty, and when the police arrived all they did was look around for five minutes, issue Marga Man with a reference number, and promise they would make enquiries. Soon after the police left, the locksmiths turned up to secure the property and then everybody got into taxis and went to the studio.

The boys filled Bunny in on what had been happening and then they talked for hours. Their biggest worries were their relationships with their public and their parents. Tyrone rang home explaining as much as he could, and Prem did the same. Ray didn't.

When Ray was taken home he went straight to the kitchen, helped himself to some cold rice and fish, and then went to his room. He spoke to nobody. He was sitting quietly in his room thinking about all that was happening, when there was a knock on the door.

'Ray, it's me, Kori. Can I come in?'

'Come.'

Kori entered the room, closed the door behind her and slid down it until she was sitting on the floor. 'Ray, what's going on?'

'I don't know,' said Ray.

Ray's head was bowed, his voice was quiet. Kori could see that he really didn't know what was going on.

'It looks like when you get a bit of success all these things come to test you,' Ray continued, head still low. 'One of our fans gets stabbed, we get threatening phone calls, we get arrested for murder, and the music shop gets robbed.'

'Maybe it's time to drop the band,' said Kori.

'It's all we have. If we drop the band what else do we do? We worked hard for this.'

'Yeah, I know, but look at all the trouble it's causing.'

'We've only just started, things have got to get better.'

'And what if this east versus west thing gets bigger? The Western Alliance were on TV today saying you guys are their sworn enemies. What if it just gets worse and worse?'

'We're here for the hip-hop, we're here because we love what we do, but if the Western Alliance come we can't back down, we can't run away.'

'Is this one of those boys to men things?'

'No, Kori, this is a self-defence thing, this is a self-protection thing.'

'All I know is, right now it doesn't look good and it doesn't feel good, so just take it easy, try to make it good,' said Kori, standing up.

'I'm working on it,' said Ray, taking a deep breath.

Kori left the room and Ray sat still. He raised his head, breathing steadily and slowly as if in a state of meditation, looking straight ahead, hardly blinking, staring at a CD that was next to the player. Then he went over to put the CD on. It was his favourite album of all time, 'Collective Security'. He fell asleep listening to it.

CHAPTER 14

Newstalk South East

'The controversial rap group Positive Negatives have been making the headlines again. Yesterday the three band members and their manager were arrested in connection with the murder of Alton Benn. Alton Benn was a young black man who is believed to be the latest victim of a gang war that is taking place between east and west London gangs.

'Many believe that the animosity between the gangs was started by Positive Negatives and another rap band from west London, the Western Alliance. No representatives from either of the groups were willing to speak to us, but on the streets of Hammersmith this morning many of the Western Alliance fans were calling for revenge.

'After being held for three hours the Positive Negatives members were released without charge, but when they returned to their base, a music shop on West Ham Lane, which, coincidentally, is just across the road from the police station, they found that it had been robbed.

'This morning the group's record company, Deaf Defying Records, issued a statement, part of which claimed that "Positive Negatives were wrongly arrested and the robbery of the music shop happened as a consequence of the manner in which the raid was executed. The band are at present considering all the options open to them – this includes taking legal action against the Metropolitan Police".

'We did contact the police, but they refused to comment.'

CHAPTER 15

Graduation Ceremonies

'Look at that,' said Ray's father as he turned away from the TV, putting on his coat. 'Every time I hear about your band it has nothing to do with music. Someone even asked me at work if my son is a controversial rapper, as if controversial is a style of music.'

Ray was tucking into his breakfast cereal and watching the weather forecast. 'That's their business. People can call us what they like, we just deal in music.'

'OK, you should know what you are doing,' his father said as he left the house.

'He's got a point,' said Ray's mother, who was rushing around the living room and kitchen preparing for work.

'I know,' said Ray. 'But we can't control what those media people say.'

'I'm off,' said Kori as she left the house.

Ray's mother slowed down. She picked up the remote control and turned the volume of the television down. 'Ray, this is too serious, and I'm worried.

Fights at your concerts, people getting killed, police, solicitors, threatening phone calls.'

'What threatening phone calls?' asked Ray. 'Are you getting threatening phone calls too?'

'I've had about three, on the house phone. Your father doesn't know. I don't know what he would do if he did.'

'What did they say?'

'Well, they don't say much, just nasty things. The other day one said "Not long left", and yesterday one said I must "say goodbye to my son". How do you think that makes me feel? This is not like school fights, this is not a scrap in the park. I don't know if I can take it. I'm not sleeping well.'

Ray wanted to answer his mother, but his mobile phone rang.

'Is I, Marga Man.'

'What's happening?'

'Hey, what are yu doing today?'

'Me and the boys are going to the Positivity Centre, progress meeting, kind of thing.'

'Dat's cool, I'll call yu back.'

Ray ended the call and picked up the conversation with his mother. 'Mum, I know what it feels like. I don't want fights at our concerts, I don't want people to get killed, but this is not something that we're doing. We're getting threatening phone calls too, so I know what it's like, but what do you want us to do?'

'Just stop all this rap music business. Do something else, and just rap as a hobby,' his mother said abruptly.

Ray responded just as quickly. 'Come on Mum, stop sounding like Dad. You know that's not happening so don't go there.' After a short silence Ray tried to reassure his mother. 'Don't worry Mum, we'll sort it out, I promise you.'

A few minutes later Marga Man rang back. He had arranged to be in on the meeting at the centre. Ray's mother left for work and an hour later Marga Man knocked on the front door. Prem was already in the car.

'Where's Tyrone?' asked Ray.

'He said he's tired, he had a late night out celebrating his birthday with a friend. He's making his own way over,' said Marga Man.

Ray looked towards Prem and then back to Marga Man. 'Celebrating his birthday, since when has he started celebrating birthdays? And why weren't we invited?'

'Dat's not important,' said Marga Man. 'Hurry up, let's go.'

When they arrived at Positivity, Skelly was just locking his car. Tyrone was already inside; as they entered, Sam greeted them and introduced herself to those who she didn't know.

'Hello, my name is Samina Mirza, but that doesn't matter because everybody calls me Sam.'

'Hi, I'm Skelly from Deaf Defying Records.'

'Oh yes, we spoke on the phone,' said Sam, shaking Skelly's hand.

'And I'm Marga Man.'

'Oh yes,' she said, smiling broadly, 'I've heard so much about you. It's about time we met.'

'Yeah, well I pleased to meet you too,' said Marga Man.

They sat in a circle in a private room. Sam initiated the proceedings.

'When I heard that there was going to be an opportunity to get you all here this morning, I thought it would be a great idea. I was going to have a meeting with the boys anyway before we write our report for the school, but I think with all that is happening now we should also think a little about the bigger picture. So if it's OK with you, I'd like to just talk about the progress so far and then I think it would be great if we could just talk about the band. Is that OK?'

Everyone nodded yes, so Sam continued.

'Well as far as we're concerned, here at Positivity you have been a great success. I know the music thing has been good, but even the work that you've been doing in the classroom has been good. We are proud of you. There's only a month to go now before you leave here, and as I understand it you will be leaving school to pursue your careers in music, so we wish you all the best. When you first came here, the word was that you guys would be really difficult and out of control, but you proved that wrong. It goes without saying that the report that we will be giving to the school on the three of you will be very positive; full of positivity, you could say. So congratulations.'

Skelly, Sam and Marga Man clapped as the boys sat proud in their seats and nodded their heads saying, 'I told you we could do it,' without speaking.

'Do any of you want to say anything?' asked Sam.

Ray smiled. 'Just wanna say I'm glad we didn't stick with Mr David Oak of The Strolling Rollers fame. Bunny has the touch, you know what I'm saying?'

'I know what you're saying,' smiled Sam, lowering her head, and moving swiftly on. 'OK, in a way it's none of our business, we wanted to help you get your foot on the musical ladder, but now that you're on it, everything's gone crazy. How do you plan to deal with it, and is there anything that we can do to help you?'

'The boys haven't done a thing wrong. They have made a brilliant first album that thousands of people have gone out and bought,' said Skelly. 'We want them to keep making good music and not get distract-ed by what's going on out there, which is why we are now paying for the legal representation and for the claim against the police for the looting of the shop, and within reason we shall pay for any legal represen-tation the band as a whole may need.'

'But it has to be said, what's going on out there is very serious – I mean, murder?' said Sam.

Marga Man shook his head at Sam and then said, 'Hey look, sister, yu should know better. Dat murder happened fifteen miles away from where these guys were, these guys were in bed, de police know exactly where we all were, so if yu link dat murder to us, you're doing exactly what de press are doing.'

'Yeah,' said Ray, 'we are not murderers, we are hip-hop.'

'And everyone's talking about east London, west London – the last time I went to west London was like three years ago to see my auntie. We ain't got no argument with people from west London,' said Prem.

'You saw the awards on television, didn't you?' Ray asked Sam.

'Yes,' she replied. 'And I know that you were nowhere near the murder.'

Ray continued. 'Well, you heard what those Western Alliance guys were going on with, you saw it. It was them running up their mouths, anyone could see that.'

'OK, I understand all that, but where do you go from here?' asked Sam.

'We're just gonna go and make more breaks, we got a Bom album in the making,' said Ray.

'And we're going to support them as they do what they do,' said Skelly.

'And I'm just gonna hang easy,' said Marga Man. 'De boys gotta stay creative, I gotta stay wid dem.'

'What I would say,' said Skelly, 'is that no one should talk to the press, certainly not without checking with me. There's good press and there's bad press, and anyway, soon we want to set up a press conference so that you can set the record straight.'

'Yeah', said Ray. 'A press conference.'

'Yeah, so we can tell it as it is,' said Prem.

'Directly to the people,' said Tyrone.

'And one more thing,' said Skelly, 'you should do a tour, a nationwide tour.'

Skelly was waiting for big celebrations, but the room fell silent. It was the last thing everyone expected to hear.

Ray whispered, as if he was talking to himself, 'A nationwide tour.'

'That's right,' said Skelly, 'a nationwide tour. I got it from the boss, you know, the powers that be. There's lots of money to be spent on a Positive Negatives tour, and they don't spend lots of money on tours often.'

'But,' Sam said, leaving a pause and then choosing her words carefully, 'don't you think that a tour right now may be a bit risky? On the one hand you are saying don't talk to the press, be cool, lay low, then on the other hand you're saying get right out there.'

'I said they should not get distracted, and keep

making good music. Basically I'm saying they should still keep working. Going out and doing gigs is just one of the things bands do.'

'And you think it's safe?' Sam added.

'Well, nothing's going to be a hundred per cent safe, but the company will make sure that there's a good team around them and they get tight security.' Skelly dropped his voice and looked around as if he was going to reveal a secret. 'I've been told no expense spared.'

From deep in thought, Ray smiled. 'Yeah, a nation-wide tour, we can do that.'

Sam looked towards Tyrone. 'You're quiet Tyrone, what do you think?'

'I think we should do it. Hip-hop is our lives.' He smiled uncharacteristically at her. 'And who really knows what will happen in the future?'

'Who knows?' said Sam, smiling back. She looked towards Prem. 'And your thoughts?'

'I wanna do it,' said Prem.

Ray looked towards Marga Man. 'You're not saying much.'

'I'm not saying much but I'm listening to every-ting,' he replied.

'So what do you say?' asked Prem.

'It's going to be hard work,' Marga Man said, still thinking.

'We know,' said Ray.

'It's not like de one-off you did de other night, you have to be focused, you have to have discipline.'

'We know,' said Prem and Ray together.

'And all dem days and nights on the road together will really test your friendships.'

'We know,' said all three.

'Well,' said Marga Man, taking up his role as a manager. 'The conditions must be right and the timing must be right. Remember there's still plenty of work to do on de new album.'

'We'll talk about the deal later,' said Skelly. 'The important thing is to keep the momentum up, keep things moving. I think a tour is just what the fans want right now.'

'Hey, Skelly,' said Marga Man, nodding his head very slowly and looking very seriously at him, 'we know dat it may be just what de fans want, but it's also just what de record company wants.'

The band went back to the studio and Marga Man went back to begin restocking his shop and filling in his insurance claim forms. A couple of weeks later Marga Man received good news and bad news. The bad news was that the solicitor thought that it would be difficult to successfully sue the police and advised him to drop the proceedings, but the good news was that the insurance company were going to pay him a substantial amount. All the boys were still receiving threats on their phones and they continued getting negative media attention, but they kept working. The beats for the new album were soon done and awaiting lyrics and they had begun to practise for their live tour.

When the time had come for them to sign off from the Social Inclusion Project and officially leave school, there were no exams, no ceremony, just another meeting at the headmaster's office with the mothers. This time the meeting was different. Word of the meeting had reached the press and they gathered outside the school gate. Other pupils at the school were excited and keen to see the local boys turned good and turned bad. As they drove into the school gate in black taxis, photographers put their cameras to the windscreens of the cars, desperate to get a picture of the boys with their parents. Two bodyguards were in a car behind watching carefully. It was more like a visit by the Prime Minister than the rude boys' farewell, and when the boys and their parents went into the office the bodyguards stood silently on guard outside. Whereas once most people were glad to see the back of the boys, now everyone wanted to get a glimpse of them, even the school office workers.

Inside the office Mr Lang took up his informal position at the front of the desk. The boys and the mothers sat in exactly the same positions as they had on their previous visit, but this time the boys looked a lot more confident.

'Well, a lot has happened since you were last here. Before I say anything else I want to congratulate you on the success of "Collective Security". It really is a great piece of work and it deserves the success that it has achieved. My daughter loves it. Suddenly she has gone off grunge and punk, now she wants to get down with the brothers.'

Ray clapped his hands and rubbed them together. 'I told you that we're going to be the baddest fucking hip-hop band since Adam and Eve.'

His mother slapped him on the back of his head.

'It's true,' said Ray. 'That's what I said, and that's what we are.'

'You may be good, but that's no reason to use language like that,' his mother said in his ear.

Mr Lang looked down at the notes on his desk. 'Tomorrow is your last day –'

'It's not,' Ray interrupted.

Mr Lang looked down to double check. 'This school breaks up next week but according to the report I have from Positivity, your time with them ends tomorrow.'

'Yeah, but what I mean is we're still gonna be working.'

'They live in that studio,' said Mrs Sharma. 'Day and night they're in there.'

'That may not be such a bad thing,' said Mr Lang.

'Well, at least I know where he is,' Mrs Sharma conceded.

'Hey,' said Prem, 'if you think the first album was bad, you wanna hear the second one.'

'Do you have it with you?' Mr Lang asked, looking towards the computer.

'No, it's not finished yet,' Prem replied. 'We just know in advance it's gonna be bad.'

'I have no doubt about your ability to produce a good second album.' Mr Lang cleared his throat as if to signal a change of mood. 'At this point I should be giving you a talk about your careers and the real world, but your careers have started already, and the real world – well, I suspect that you know quite a bit about that.'

'They know, all right,' said Mrs Sharma. 'It's nice that they have a bit of success and it's good to see them earning a bit of money, but this rubbish about fighting and gang wars is no good.'

'They can't go anywhere without their bodyguards now,' said Tyrone's mother.

'How did it get to this?' asked Mr Lang.

Ray started. 'We don't really know. We do a gig at the Rex, some guys come looking for trouble, a fight started and a guy got stabbed. Almost died, but he's all right now. Then there's this band from west London called the Western Alliance, they do hip-hop and we

189

say, "That's cool", then we heard that they start to diss us in public.'

'Yeah,' said Prem. 'We don't know them you know, we don't go west London, we don't say anything about them, and they start to diss us.'

Ray continued, 'Then when we go to collect our MOBO awards, they start to chat rubbish at us and everybody starts to say there's a Positive Negatives and Western Alliance rivalry going on.'

'Hip-hop don't need rivals,' said Tyrone calmly, 'it needs allies.'

'That's right,' said Ray. 'If you listen to our album we don't diss other rappers. Anyway, we're just carrying on doing our work, we even stopped going out, then we hear about this shooting in the West End.'

'We weren't even there and we got arrested for it,' said Prem.

Mr Lang looked at the mothers.

'It's true,' said Ray's mother. 'Ray was at home when that happened.'

'So was Prem,' said Prem's mother.

'And Tyrone,' said Tyrone's mother.

Ray began to wave his hands about. 'Now police are watching us and everyone's talking about guns on the streets, and east London, west London gang wars, and we're the ones who are supposed to be leading the east Londoners to war. We got no time for that.'

'I saw the awards ceremony on television,' said Mr

Lang. 'I've read many of the news reports and I listen to what the kids are saying in school, and I have no reason to doubt what you are saying. Sometimes events just happen, and they happen with you in the middle of them, but even when that happens you really have to try to keep your nose clean.'

'Yeah, clean noses, that's what we're about,' said Prem.

Mr Lang smiled. 'Speaking of clean, your reports from Positivity are absolutely glowing, they are fantastic, unbelievable. But I knew that you had it in you. The good thing about Positivity is that the courses can be tailored to you and you really made the most of it.'

'It has been very good,' said Mrs Sharma, with the other two mothers nodding in agreement.

'And do you think it's been good?' Mr Lang asked the boys.

'It's cool,' said Tyrone.

'Yeah, it's nice, sweet, yu know,' said Prem.

'Yeah,' said Ray, 'it was a good move. If Marga Man wasn't so great you could have been our manager.'

'Marga Man's doing a great job,' Mr Lang said. 'But look, I know you don't like school . . .'

'That's right,' Ray said quickly.

'And I know that you may want to put school behind you, but I just want to say, if there's anything that I can do for you, please let me know.'

They could all see that he meant it and they all

made various silent gestures of acknowledgement.

Tyrone's mother stood up. 'Thank you Mr Lang, you have been a great help.'

All this time Ray had been thinking. He had wanted to say something but he didn't know how to say what he wanted to say without sounding sloppy. When he could see that the meeting was coming to an end, he said it anyway and hoped for the best.

'Yo Mr Lang. I just wanna say yeah, you're all right. We didn't like school, I suppose that was obvious, and speaking for myself I still don't like school, I was glad when I was excluded, it was freedom. But just because we get excluded doesn't mean we're stupid. Anyway, I just wanna say thanks, for us all, for like giving us a chance. Respect, guy.'

'That's all right,' said Mr Lang as he walked to the door to let them out. 'I wish you all the best. Hopefully all this stuff in the press will blow over and you can get on with finishing another great album.'

As they left the office Mr Lang was once again thanked by the mothers and the boys and just as he was saying his final goodbye, he searched through his pockets nervously.

'Oh, yes,' he said, as he located what he was looking for. He quickly pulled a limited edition copy of 'Collective Security' from his jacket pocket. 'Could you sign this for me, please. It's not for my daughter – it's for me.'

CHAPTER 16

The Newham Echo

Local rap artists Positive Negatives went back to school yesterday. For almost a year the controversial Stratford-based rappers had been attending a special unit away from the school after they had all been permanently excluded from formal education. None of the band members was available for interview yesterday, and staff members at the school would not comment on the relevance of the visit, but it is widely believed that the three ex-pupils went to officially collect their leaving certificates. Pupils at the school were kept well away from the group, whose angry rap music has taken them to the top of the charts in recent months and given them international success.

A spokesman from the band's record company, Deaf Defying Records, told *The Newham Echo* that 'The band have done extremely well considering their circumstances. They have used their energy positively and they have a bright future ahead of them. Very few people can claim the success they've had when they've just turned sixteen. Newham should be proud of them.' The spokesman refused to comment on the band members' recent arrests, saying, 'That was in the past, and they were released without charge. It's a non-issue.'

Local fans and press from all over the world gathered to get a glimpse of the band, to the amusement of many of the residents nearby. Mrs Winterton, a seventy-one-year-old retired shop assistant, said, 'I don't know what all the fuss is about. That school is full of talented kids. I should know, I used to be one.'

CHAPTER 17

A Woman's Touch

During a Saturday night rehearsal session at the studio Sam made an appearance. Ray was surprised to see her.

'Sam, cool, what are you doing here?' he asked.

'I thought I'd just pop in to see you and Prem. I haven't seen this place for a while now and I think we may use it for some other projects in the future. But don't worry, I'm off duty, and anyway, you're free now.'

'I'm not worried,' said Ray, 'everything's nice. So you come to see me and Prem. What about Tyrone?'

'Oh, and Tyrone too,' she added. 'Good to see you again.'

'Good to see you too,' said Tyrone.

'So is it all right if I stay for a while? I'd like to see you at work,' said Sam.

Bunny waved his hand over the mixing desk. 'At your service,' he smiled. 'At Rock It Science Studio, we bring musicality to the community, at reasonable rates.'

'Why don't you sit down and watch us work out?' said Tyrone.

'I will,' replied Sam. 'Please carry on.'

Sam watched and listened, then late into the night Marga Man suggested that they all go out for a meal, Bunny and Sam included. Bunny and Tyrone went in Sam's car, and Prem and Ray went in Marga Man's. He drove them to a plush Nigerian Restaurant on Green Street where they ate and talked about American hip-hop until one am.

It was a happy, high-spirited gathering that did not go unnoticed by two girls a couple of tables away. The girls, who were a little bit older than the boys, had finished eating, but they found entertainment in watching and listening in on the band's conversation, using the slow drinking of red wine as cover. When the girls saw Marga Man paying the bill they knew that if they didn't speak to them soon they would be gone.

'You go,' said one to the other.

'No, you go,' said the other.

'You bought the CD.'

'You saw them first.'

'OK, let's just both go together.'

'OK, let's go.'

They both went and stood next to the band's table.

'Hello, my name is Mallam and this is my friend Yinka. We don't normally do this and we don't want to be rude, but could we have your autographs please?'

'No problem,' said Ray. 'You can have anything you want, trust me.'

Mallam had very dark skin and around face, and she wore purple lipstick. She handed a notepad to Prem. 'I'm sorry,' she said, 'I haven't got anything else. I write my bits and pieces in there.'

'I haven't got anything either,' said Yinka. 'Only this, you can sign it anywhere.' She handed a small diary to Ray.

Ray held the diary for a moment and looked at her. The pupils of her eyes were perfectly black and the whites of her eyes perfectly white. Her skin was dark, her face slim with high, gentle cheekbones. Her hair was plaited close to her head in patterns that could have been designed by an award-winning artist.

'So your name's Yinka? That's a great name,' said Ray as his eyes began to explore the rest of her.

'I like it too. It's Nigerian, both my parents come from Nigeria.'

When Prem had signed Mallam's notebook, he passed it on to Tyrone. It was normal for them to pass around whatever they were signing in this way. But after Ray had scribbled in Yinka's diary he handed it straight back to her. She took it, looked for his signature but saw no signature, just a phone number. She was silently delighted. She quickly turned the page and handed it to Prem. When the autographs were done, the girls went back to their table. Bunny, Sam, Marga Man and the boys waved goodbye to them and headed out of the restaurant.

Sam volunteered to take Bunny and Tyrone home in her car, and Marga Man took Prem and Ray. As they were on their way to Ray's house, his phone rang. Ray was in the front of the car. He looked at the screen but did not recognise the number, and, expecting the worst, he said, 'Yeah, who's this?'

'Hi, it's Yinka.'

Ray's mood suddenly changed. 'Yeah, how you going?'

'I'm fine.'

'Where you at?'

'We've just left the restaurant. Why did you give me your digits?' she asked.

'Because I wanna check you.' It was difficult, but Ray was trying his best to keep the conversation private. There was a CD playing – he leaned forward and turned up the volume.

'What's going down?' said Marga Man. 'Let me know.'

'Everything's cool,' said Ray.

'Who is it?' asked Prem.

'An admirer,' said Ray, putting his thumb over the phone's mouthpiece.

'Don't trust him, I'm your man,' shouted Prem.

Ray continued the conversation with Yinka. 'So where you going now?'

'Home.'

'How you getting there?'

'We're going to the taxi office now.'

'Which one?'

'The one at the bottom of Green Street.'

'Hey, do me a favour. Meet me by Upton Park tube station.'

'What, now?'

'Yeah, now.'

'Can't do, it's too late and Mallam's really tired.'

'This is about me and you, come on.'

'Me and you what?'

'Me and you, come on, I'll bring you some nice chocolates.'

Yinka laughed down the phone. 'All right then, how long will you be?'

'I'll be there in ten minutes.'

'OK. If you take longer, I'll be gone.'

'Don't worry, I'll be there.'

'OK, bye.'

'Later.'

Marga Man was just turning into Ray's road when Ray realised where he was. 'No, spin round, guy, take me to a minicab place.'

'Are you mad?' said Marga Man. 'Where are you

going now?'

'Didn't you hear?' said Prem. 'He's gonna meet some girl.'

'Who is it?' asked Marga Man. 'I bet you it's one of those girls from de restaurant.'

'No,' said Prem shaking his head, 'there was no digital exchange. But then again you never know with Ray, he's quick.'

Marga Man stopped the car. 'Are you serious?' he asked, slumping over the steering wheel.

'Yeah,' said Ray. 'Come on, I gotta hurry.'

'Do you want me to take you?' asked Marga Man.

'No, just take me to a minicab office,' Ray said, and Marga Man did.

'Ray, just be careful now,' he said, as Ray was leaving the car. 'Ring anytime, and don't forget where you live.'

Ray moved so quickly that within a minute he was out of one car and in another. When he arrived at the underground station Yinka was there. She looked lovely.

'Where's your friend?' said Ray, closing the car door.

'She's gone home, I told you she was tired. Why did you want to meet me so soon?'

'Because I like you. Why did you ring me so soon?'

'Just curious, and how can you like me so quickly?'

'It was love at first bite.'

'Very funny, and what do you want to do now?'

'Just walk,' said Ray. 'By the way, here's a present.'
He put his hands in his pocket and pulled out a handful of thin chocolate wafers.

'Very clever. You nicked them from the restaurant.'

'No I didn't,' he said, straight-faced.

She put her hand in her pocket and pulled out
more of the same. 'I got some of my own.'

'See, you nicked some as well.'

'No, I didn't,' Yinka said, smiling. 'One of the
waiters told me to take as many as I like. He said
chocolate suited me.'

They walked down the road towards Stratford.
Taking it for granted that Yinka knew all about him,
Ray questioned her. She was rather shy at first, not
quite believing that she was now walking with the
person she had not long before asked for an autograph, but the more they walked the more she opened
up. Her parents, both immigrants from Nigeria, were
in the import-export business; she was attending college on a business course. She told Ray that she
bought the 'Collective Security' album after being
told by friends that it was full of progressive lyrics.
But she wasn't convinced.

'It's a good album,' she said. 'But I wouldn't call it
progressive.'

'So what would you call it?' asked Ray, disappointed.

'Well, what you're doing is sounding off about how bad life is for you, and what a raw deal you've had, and how tough you are, and how united your posse is, and that's OK, your first album can be like that, it's about letting off steam. But if you do the same thing on your second album and your third one it won't be long before Positive Negatives fade away into oblivion. You got to find something new to say.'

Ray got thoughtful. 'Yeah, we've been thinking about lyrics for the new album. We got mad beats but the lyrics ain't flowing, you know what I'm saying? And yeah, we don't wanna say the same thing over again, I keep telling the others that.'

'It's not just about making up lyrics, you have to believe in something. The thing is, you lot are rebellious, but you're not revolutionaries.'

'You got some big words there, break it down for me?' Ray asked, slowing down the walking pace.

'What I mean is, you are rebels, right?'

'Yes. Of course.' Ray stopped walking.

'That means you rebel, you don't take on bull, you're angry with the system and you want to tear it down.'

'Yeah, well what do you expect? The system stinks.'

Yinka began to point at Ray as she spoke. 'That's it, you see, breaking things is not that difficult. Anyone can break things, but when you mash everything up what do you put in its place? The whole world can't live on rap music, so what's your alternative? You see, when you have some ideas of your own, *that's* revolutionary. True rebels are responsible, true rebels know why they rebel and what they're rebelling for.'

'Hey, easy. So you expect me to have all the answers?'

'No one has all the answers. I don't have all the answers, but at least I've started to think about the questions, and at least I have some principles in place to build my ideas on.'

'So what are these principles?' Ray asked.

'Equality for a start, and justice. Not the way we have it now, where there's one kind of justice for the rich and another for the poor – real justice. And then there's knowledge of self, which would mean creating an education system that is not just about teaching you how to be a good worker and an obedient citizen, it would also tap into your true potential.'

Ray shook his head. 'Heavy shit. You ain't serious right? Now you sound like the guy who stands outside the tube station selling that anti-everything newspaper.'

Yinka shook her head. 'You still don't get it, do you? This is not simply about what you're *against*, this is about what you're *for*.'

Ray could see that she was very serious. 'OK, so what's that gotta do with our music?'

'Come on, Mr X-Ray-X. Look, if you had a direction you would be writing now, you wouldn't have a problem coming up with lyrics. If you knew exactly what you stood for, and if you had some vision, you wouldn't have to struggle to express your ideas.'

They walked for another half an hour and Ray forgot about Yinka's beauty and became captivated by her mind. In her spare time she studied the history of the world and theology, and she even had her own theory on how everything had started. They walked slowly as if they had nowhere to go, while Ray listened.

'I have to go now,' Yinka said, seeing a taxi office. 'It's that time of the morning.'

'But hey, you chat sense, I like the way you drop science. Lyrics me some more.'

'Yeah, but it's bedtime.'

'So, let's call it night school and be cool, you know what I'm saying?'

Yinka tried unsuccessfully to sound serious. 'No, I have to go.'

'I tell you what, come to my place, just for a short time, half hour, twenty minutes.'

'No.'

'Oh please.'

'I have to go home.'

Ray put his hands together as if praying. 'Now don't let me have to go down on me hands and knees to beg you.'

Yinka smiled and looked skywards. 'Where's your place?'

'Five minutes away.'

'So do you live in a house with all your bad boy rebel friends?'

Ray looked around, trying to hide his embarrassment. 'No, with my parents and my sister, but I'll be getting my own place soon.'

Yinka laughed. 'Hey, there's nothing wrong with living with your parents. I do, I think it's great. But I suppose it doesn't fit your tough image.'

'It ain't that.'

'What is it, then?'

'Nothing,' said Ray, unable to come up with a convincing response.

'Let's be sensible,' Yinka said, trying to be serious again. 'You go home to your parents and I'll go home to mine.'

'Come on, I'll get down on my knees and I'll beg till morning.'

As Ray began to go down, she stopped him. 'OK, stop. Just for a short while. But what will your parents say?'

'Yes. Don't worry about my parents, they're cool. As long as we don't make loads of noise they're safe.'

'Like I said, I'm not staying long.'

Outside the house Yinka began to rethink. 'Are you sure about this?'

'Of course,' said Ray. 'Just follow me and things will be good. Trust me, you're with me so you don't

205

have to worry about a thing. I'm a big man you know.'
Ray opened the front door and Yinka quietly followed
him up to his room. She was amused by the room.
She looked around it, smiling.

'What's so funny?' asked Ray.

'Well, it's weird, there you are on television, and in
the papers, and your face is all over the streets on
posters, but your room looks like any schoolboy's
room.'

'I ain't a schoolboy any more, I got nuff money in
the bank. Soon I gonna get me own place, I may even
fly in one of those top interior designers from France
to design it for me.'

'Yeah,' Yinka replied doubtfully.

'Yeah,' Ray said positively. 'Sit down and give me
more of that mind food,' he said, pointing to the bed.

'OK,' she said, sitting on a chair near the CD
player. 'What do you want to talk about?'

'I dunno, something educational, some of that deep
shit.' He paused. 'I know, tell me what you want to do
in the future?'

'I'm not sure,' she replied. 'I know that I want to go
into business, but I'm not sure what kind of business
yet. I can remember when my parents were really
poor. For ages they were unemployed, then my dad
begged a man for a job, but the man said he wouldn't
give him one, and my dad couldn't believe it because
this man was supposed to be a good family friend.

206

Then one day the man came to our house and said to my dad what he would do is give him a loan so that he could start his own business. He said my father had the ability to be independent. My dad had no idea how to run a business but he took the money, did a short business course and studied hard, I mean really hard. He hardly slept, all he did was work on his business plan. He was just so desperate that he didn't want to miss the opportunity. And he did it, he started an import-export business with my mother, and his first big contract was with the man who gave him the loan in the first place. I don't really want to go into that kind of business, I want to do something which helps other people to get jobs; I want to do my bit to cut the unemployment figures.'

Ray was deeply impressed. 'You're a real shero.'

'Not really.'

'What you mean, not really? You're well conscious.'

'I'm just trying to do my bit. I really think I should go now,' Yinka said, standing up.

Ray stood up quickly. 'Hey, that was quick.'

'I said I was only staying for a while.' She stepped towards the door.

Ray moved quickly towards the CD player. 'You gotta hear this tune,' he said, putting a CD into the drawer. 'Tell me what you think of it.'

As the tune began to play, Yinka looked puzzled. 'The beat's OK, but where's the words?'

'Here are the words,' Ray said, as he began to improvise a rap around the beauty and intelligence of the girl in front of him. He walked towards her and put his hand on the handle of the door. Yinka was now in between the door and Ray. He ended the rap with a line that implored her to stay, and then he leaned forward to kiss her. Yinka turned away and burst into laughter.

'You know I like you,' Ray whispered.

'Yeah, well I don't kiss on first dates. I mean this is not even a date, this is just a detour, I'm basically on my way home.'

'But I like you and I might never see you again.'

Yinka pushed him away gently and folded her arms. 'So because you might never see me again you want to exchange saliva with me?'

'No, it's not like that,' Ray panicked, 'what I mean is, you're nice, right, and I never want to let you go. Yeah that's right, me and you, I can see it now, house, car, children, holidays and everything.'

Yinka laughed even more. 'How do you know that I want children? Look, why don't you just slow down, put your lips back on your face and take one step at the time. You could start by asking me out on a proper date.'

'Good idea,' said Ray, as if he had come up with it himself. 'Will you go out with me on a proper date, I wanna wine and dine you, I wanna tease and please you, I wanna drop phat sophisticated verbals on you and touch your tenderness in the mellowness of the morning?'

'You what?'

'I wanna buy you a burger.'

'OK.'

'Yes,' said Ray, strutting around the room.

'When?'

'Tonight,' Ray replied without thinking about it.

'What, tonight?'

'Yes, tonight, I can't waste any time, I wanna marry you before the end of the year.'

She laughed more. 'Hey, forget the burger.'

Ray went to the other side of the room and just as he was turning off the music his father pushed the door open, knocking Yinka forward.

'Keep your noise down.' His father's words were slurred and the usual smell of alcohol accompanied him. 'You may be a big star, but you still have to have respect for others in this house.'

'Dad, please, give it a rest will you?' Ray shouted back.

'Give it a rest? You think you are a big man but you is not. So you start to earn a little money eh, and you feel big eh, well if you are so big pay me some rent boy.'

'What rent?

'Rent money, boy, pay your way.'

'What's wrong with you?'

His father looked at Yinka and back to Ray. 'What's wrong with you, and when have you started bringing girls home?'

'I'm sorry, I'm going now,' said Yinka, as she made for the door.

'Don't go,' shouted Ray.

'No, it's all right, I'm going.'

'Don't. It's OK, he's drunk,' said Ray, pointing at his father.

'No, I'm late anyway,' said Yinka hurriedly.

Ray shouted even louder at his father. 'You see what you've done now, you make me sick. You're just jealous.'

'All I'm saying to you is to keep your noise down.'

'I'm sorry,' said Yinka. 'It's my fault.'

Yinka left the room and rushed downstairs to the front door. Ray ran after her. 'I'm sorry,' he said, opening the door for her. 'So what about tonight?'

'I'll call you,' she said quickly.

'Will you really?' asked Ray, doubting her.

She smiled. 'I'll call you, I promise. Now go and make peace with your father.'

By the time Ray was back upstairs, his father had returned to his own bedroom. Ray went straight in and turned on the light. His mother and father sat up in bed.

'Why are you trying to do, show me up?' Ray shouted.

'Get out of this room,' his father shouted back.

'You're trying to shame me, innit?'

'It's not 'bout me trying to shame you, it's about you not allowing us to sleep.'

Ray looked at his father with pure hatred. 'Fuck you.'

His mother shook her head. 'Ray, you can't speak to your father like that.'

'Look how he speaks to me.'

'OK, I'll stop speaking, I'll break your stinking neck,' his father said, getting out of bed and heading for Ray.

His mother jumped up and stood between them. 'Stop it, both of you.'

'You have a lot to learn,' his father said, pointing his finger at Ray.

'Well, I'm not going to learn it in this house.'

Ray left their room and went back to his own. His instinct was to leave the house, but this time he sat on his bed and thought until he fell asleep fully clothed. When he woke up he immediately continued his line of thought from when he had fallen asleep. Fifteen minutes later he rang Marga Man.

'Marga Man, I need your help.'

'I'm here to help you,' said Marga Man's mellow voice back.

'I need to find a place to live. I can't stay in this house any longer.'

'Are you sure?'

'Yeah, I'm sure man.'

'What's going down?'

'My dad man, I can't take it any more. Please don't give me a lecture, I know what's what. Can you help me?

'When do you want to do de move?'

'Soon, anytime, tonight.'

'Tonight may be difficult, but I'll see what I can do.'

'Thanks, man.'

Once Ray had made the decision to leave, it was as if he had made peace with his father. He didn't see him that often anyway, but he wasn't trying to avoid him any more. Ray spent the day being cool about it all, and he was polite and civil to his father.

After a long phone conversation with Yinka later in the afternoon, they met in the early evening at a Thai restaurant. Ray tried to apologise for what had happened in the early hours of that morning, but Yinka wasn't having it, as she saw no need for him to apologise and no need for him to be embarrassed. Once again he did more listening than speaking. Even when Yinka started by saying, 'I don't know much about this but . . .', she would go on to enlighten Ray. He took no risks with Yinka that night, but he didn't need to – as he dropped her off in a taxi she promised to call him the next day. And she did – in fact for the next few days she called him every day, and their phone conversations got longer and longer.

It took Marga Man a couple of days to find a flat for Ray. It had two furnished rooms and was on the first floor of a small house near Stratford bus station where Ray had slept on a bench. It quickly became a place where the boys spent much of their time when not in the studio. Yinka also began visiting him there, and Ray gradually learnt how to maintain a home. And it didn't take long for Marga Man, Tyrone and Prem to see that for the first time Ray was taking a relationship very seriously and that Yinka was having a profound effect on him. Before really getting down to writing the lyrics for the new album, Ray insisted on having 'reasoning sessions' in his flat where they would talk about a chosen topic. Ray thought that the band should have an ideology, just like a revolutionary political party. This impressed Marga Man, and soon Tyrone and Prem got the idea.

The lyrics they began to write began to take on a new character. The first rap ready for the recording was called 'Ever Ready Reasoning', a slow jam that reflected the journey the band had taken. Its message was that through reasoning band members would be in tune with each other and have a greater sense of purpose. The second rap was called 'Mental Inquilab',

'Inquilab' being the Urdu word for revolution. Then a third rap was written called 'Made in Poorland', a lyric exploration of how many of the things we take for granted are made in the poorest countries of the world by people who receive very little pay. Yinka made sure she didn't hang around the band too much and she was also careful not to tell Ray what he should be writing. For his part, Ray did not go to Yinka for answers, but he did go to her for questions. At no time did the others feel that Yinka was getting in the way.

During a week of intensive recording, a reasoning session was called in the studio. They were all present: Tyrone, Prem, Ray, Marga Man and Bunny. But unusually, this session was called by Tyrone. For a while all he talked about was how well he thought the new recordings were going. Then he spoke about how much he loved working with the band and for a while it began to sound as if he was talking about the past.

'What's up?' asked Ray, fearing he was about to announce his resignation or a solo career.

Tyrone was thoughtful and calm. 'It's like this, I'm gonna be a big daddy rapper, 'cause I got a small baby rapper on the way.'

There was a pause as everyone wondered if he was serious.

'Don't play,' said Prem.

'He's not serious,' said Ray. 'This must be some new rap he's got going on.'

'I'm serious,' Tyrone said.

'You want to be a father now?' asked Marga Man.

'Yes,' replied Tyrone.

'Why?' asked Marga Man. 'It's an expensive business, an yu can't just give up when tings get rough.'

'Yeah, that's right,' said Prem. 'You have to plan ahead and start taking life seriously.'

'I take life seriously already, and anyway, it's not a case of wanting to be a father, I'm going to be a father,' Tyrone said.

'But Tyrone, yu is just a youth, tek my advice, let de good times roll, be a youth for as long as yu can,' said Marga Man.

'Listen,' Tyrone said firmly, 'I know what I'm doing, I've thought about everything, I'm not running away, there's no abortion thing happening here. I'm the daddy, and that's that.'

'You can't be clearer than that,' said Marga Man.

Bunny tried to contribute to the conversation. 'The thing is, nowadays things are getting confused. Children are having children. The statistics show that teenage pregnancies are on the increase.'

'Bunny man, yu read too many newspapers,' said Marga Man.

'And anyway,' added Tyrone, 'I'm not a statistic.'

There was a short silence whilst everyone took it

215

all in, then Marga Man asked, 'Are yu sure yu gonna be all right?

'I'm all right,' said Tyrone, 'No, I'm more than all right, I'm happy.'

They all realised that Tyrone had given it some thought and so they then began to congratulate him, until something occurred to Ray.

'Hey man, you didn't do it on your own, so who's mummy?'

'Don't you worry who mummy is, mummy's cool,' said Tyrone smiling. 'That's all you need to know, mummy's cool.'

CHAPTER 18

Freedom or Death?

The record company employed the world-famous promoter Tony Oldsmith to promote the tour. Marga Man said he was the best money could buy, an expert. The tour was going to cover most of the major cities in Scotland, Wales and England. Bunny was now working freelance as the band were having to pay him for his studio time, but record sales were going so well that they could afford to. Within a couple of months they had made thousands of pounds each. They now had individual bank accounts and money was going directly to them from sponsorship. Their faces began appearing on billboards advertising cool clothes, wrapping paper and a well-known soft drink.

All was all going well, and weeks before the tour was to start the second album was ready. The advance payment for the album was in the bank, but the plan was to wait until the tour was over before releasing it. The tour was the next big thing and this tour was still riding on the success of the first album. Things couldn't have been better.

A press conference was called in the newly re-decorated and newly re-stocked Flip Discs music shop. Marga Man was keen to show off his new-look shop to the press and get some free publicity at the same time. But on the day it became clear that it was going to be difficult. The press conference did publicise the shop and let people know that Marga Man was back in business, but the shop could barely contain the crowd. Conferences of this kind were usually only of interest to the music press, but this one attracted many of the daily newspapers, a few television cameras and a sizeable number of reporters from foreign publications.

It was a press conference with a difference: the press conference became the news. The band took questions standing behind the counter with Skelly on one side and Marga Man on the other. Yinka stood watching quietly to the side, and Sam, who had made a surprise visit, stood on the opposite side. In front of the counter stood the two bodyguards, and two extra guards stood at the entrance of the shop.

The questions came fast from all directions.

'Has winning those MOBO awards made any difference to you?'

'It may make a difference to the way you see us,' said Ray. 'But it doesn't make any difference to us. I haven't written a MOBO rap yet.'

'Don't you think that hip-hop is an American art form that will never really take off here – aren't you just playing around?'

'We're not playing,' said Prem. 'We're serious. Right now hip-hop lives in Africa, Canada, France, all over the world. Even my old headmaster knows that. Hip-hop is not limited by political borders.'

'Is rap important?'

'No,' said Ray adamantly. 'When you get right down to it rap is just the thing we do. You can rap the news, you can rap on rock tunes, you can rap on R'n'B, you can rap on folk music. Rap is just a way of speaking. Rap isn't important, hip-hop is important. Hip-hop is a philosophy, hip-hop is about the way we live, it's about the way we see life. We are outsiders and we survive by creating new families for ourselves.'

'What do you think of the Western Alliance?'

There was a tangible pause and then Prem spoke. 'We don't have a problem with the Western Alliance, and we hope that they don't have a problem with us. The press are just blowing this thing up because they want a story. They represent the west and we represent the east, and that's that.'

'But they accuse you of being behind the killing of one of their fans. They say they keep getting threatening calls from you and your crew and that last night one of you phoned one of their girls saying that, and I quote, "If you come to the eastside, baby, you can get some real man, and you need real men to do it for you. Western boys can't do you good, come here so we can put a smile on your face, and other parts of your anatomy." Unquote.'

'That's rubbish,' Ray said, waving the idea away. 'You think that we have time for that? We haven't got time to waste on that stuff, we're too busy being creative, we're on a mission.'

'So you've sent no messages at all to the Western Alliance.'

'That's right,' said Ray. 'We do have a message for them, but it the same message we have for everybody. Our motto is, *Let wordy great minds think alike, sweet Hip-Hop be our guiding light*. We want unity in the hip-hop community, we wanna bring people together, for ever. That's our message.'

'This is all good talk, but let's be honest, wouldn't it be fair to say that hip-hop is about violence?'

Tyrone answered this time. He spoke slowly, and the seriousness in his tone was notable. 'Hip-hop is not about violence. The worst violence being done on this planet right now is being done by politicians, but when you interview politicians you don't say that politics is about violence. Soldiers actually carry guns and are trained to be violent but you call them heroes and you make statues of them.'

'But it could be said that they are defending the country.'

'Well,' said Ray, 'you say the soldier is defending the country even though he may be fighting thousands of miles away. But look at us, we are here, walking the streets where we live and when we defend ourselves we're called violent. Watch us as we circulate from day to day. When we meet and greet we say peace, because hip-hop is about peace, we keep saying peace because we want to live in peace. But hip-hop is also about defending the self, it's not about invading other people's land, it is not about being a hero, it is simply about self-preservation, the right to defend one's self, you know what I'm saying?'

'You say it's not about creating heroes and you say it's not about violence, but Tupac Shakur is a hero of yours, and didn't he both live and die by the gun?'

Ray's response verged on anger. 'If you think it's as simple as that you can't have any idea of the conditions my man Tupac lived in. Your ignorance must be caused by some bullshit that you've read in some newspaper. Or did you print it? Tupac had to survive in the ghetto, he had to be creative and constructive in a situation of pure negativity. He was about freedom. Just like Bob Marley was for freedom, so Tupac Shakur was for freedom.'

A Japanese reporter with a film crew behind him put his hand up as he spoke. 'But Tupac carried a gun and was convicted of rape. Bob Marley was never known to carry a gun, and although he had lots of children, no one seems to know how many, he was never accused of rape.'

Ray shook his head. 'You just don't get it. Bob Marley lived under different circumstances to Tupac, but they both reacted according to their situation, and they both made mistakes. The important thing was that they both came from poor places, they both saw poverty, they both had raw deals, and they both realised that other people would suffer the same as them if they didn't fight for freedom. In their own way both of them were saying freedom or death.'

'Come on, Tupac was a thug. He said he stood for what he called thug life.'

'Tupac wouldn't take no bullshit,' Ray replied, banging his fist on the counter. 'Tupac defended himself, but it was freedom or death, and he got death.'

'So is Tupac your hero then?'

'What's wrong with you lot, you just don't get it, do you?' Ray was trying to keep cool but everyone could see that he was being pushed to the edge. 'Tupac said and did some great things, but he also made some mistakes. Look where I live. Here in the East End of London the way we live is very different to the way that Tupac lived, and no doubt the way we die will differ too.'

'Do you think Tupac was a revolutionary?'

Skelly quickly interrupted. 'Now let's remember why we are here. This is about Positive Negatives and not about Tupac Shakur. I would like to suggest that your questions be relevant to the talent in front of you.'

The band fended off more questions about violence and the predicted death of hip-hop before Skelly moved to the centre. 'I'm afraid that's all we have time for, but before we go I'd like to make an announcement and make an offer. First the announcement. The first gig of the tour will be at the Pavilion in Brighton. This will be a benefit gig with all the proceeds going to The Nation Foundation, the organisation that works with young people who have been excluded from mainstream education. And the offer. In order to show that Positive Negatives are about working together we would like to offer the Western Alliance the support spot on this tour.'

The boys were taken by surprise; they looked at each other, trying not to make it obvious that they knew nothing about this.

A reporter raised his hand. 'Are you really saying that you would be willing to share the bill with the Western Alliance?'

'That's right,' said Skelly. 'Well, not exactly – they would be sharing the bill with us, we would still be the headliners.'

'One last question,' another reporter shouted. 'Pro Justice, I understand that you're going to be a father. How does it feel, and do you have any plans for the baby?'

Tyrone cracked a baby smile. 'Well, it feels good. It's my first time and I have no idea how it happened – all we did was hold hands,' he said, tongue in cheek. 'But it feels good. And as for future plans, I don't know, first things first, we'll get the newborn a record deal and take it from there.'

After the press conference the boys and Marga Man confronted Skelly.

'What's this about the Western Alliance and us?' said Prem.

'Don't worry,' Skelly replied. 'It's just something they came up with in the office. The Western Alliance ain't going to say yes, but it's the thought that counts, and it's great publicity. People can't say you hate them if you invite them on tour with you.'

Marga Man pointed a threatening finger at Skelly. 'Listen, man, don't pull one like dat again. I see where you're coming from but de next time yu have any of dem bright ideas mek sure yu run dem pass me first.'

Just over an hour after the end of the press conference Marga Man was answering phone calls in the shop about the tour. But there was another from the unknown. 'The Messenger here. Can't you see that the Western Alliance will never tour with you nothings. You have declared war. The fight will be to the very end.'

* * *

The press conference had the desired effect. No British hip-hop band had ever had a tour covered by the press in such a big way. Almost every venue was sold out. Tyrone's parents and Ray's mother began to welcome their boys' fame; Ray's father said very little, and Ray felt he was quietly jealous. But even Prem's mother was beginning to be happy with the positive coverage of her son's activities.

The night before the start of the tour, Marga Man arranged for the band to have a meal at the Nigerian restaurant on Green Street where Yinka and Ray had first met. One half of the restaurant was given over to the band to accommodate their friends. Marga Man brought his wife Pauline with him. The boys had heard a lot about her, but this was the first time they met her. Like Marga Man she spoke with a heavy Jamaican accent, and like Marga Man she was large, but unlike Marga Man she seemed rather serious, although quiet and polite. Along with Bunny they were the first to arrive. They were quickly followed by Ray and Tyrone, and ten minutes later Prem arrived with Anita Das holding on to his arm. As he entered the restaurant Ray and Tyrone cheered and clapped. Anita was a pupil at their school, a pretty, dark-skinned Hindu girl. Prem had been chasing her for years. Tyrone and Ray were just glad to see them together at last. Next to arrive was Yinka with her friend Mallam, and the last person to turn up was Sam from Positivity. Prem and Ray were overjoyed to see her, she wasn't expected, but Tyrone was very cool about it all. Ray introduced her to Yinka, Mallam, Anita and Pauline and they began to order their meals. As they waited for the food the conversation turned to the press conference.

'You lot were good,' said Sam, 'you stood your ground.'

'I don't trust them,' said Ray. 'The only thing those reporters know about hip-hop and Tupac is what they read by other reporters who lied in the first place anyway.'

'And none of them bought any tunes,' said Marga Man. 'In me shop so long and spend no money.'

'But I liked the way you ended it,' Ray said to Tyrone. 'That stuff about your baby, and that stuff about the record deal, was nice, guy.'

Ray turned to Sam. 'Listen to this, Sam, you'll never believe it. Tyrone is going to be a dad right, the guy done a thing and is actually starting a family, and he won't tell us who the mother is. Look how long we've been friends, look how close we are, and he still won't tell us who the lucky lady is.'

Sam sipped her juice, put down the glass and said, 'That's because he wanted me to tell you myself.'

Everyone except Tyrone and Sam seemed to freeze. In unison they looked at Sam and then Tyrone. Tyrone and Sam were looking at each other and transmitting happiness between themselves.

'No,' said Ray.

'Yes,' said Sam.

'You joking,' said Prem.

'I'm not,' said Sam.

'You playing,' said Ray.

'I'm not,' said Sam, patting her belly. 'I'm two months gone.'

Marga Man raised his eyebrows high and took a deep breath in and a deep breath out. 'Wow.'

'That must be unethical, illegal or something like that,' said Ray.

'It's ethical and legal,' said Tyrone. 'I'm over sixteen. I checked it out.'

'Is it like some kind of extra-curricular activity thing?' asked Bunny.

Sam took a fork and lightly tapped the table. 'Just for the record, I should say that when you were attending the Positivity Centre Tyrone and I were just friends. We talked a lot on the phone and we met up sometimes, but it wasn't serious.'

'Yeah, I bet,' said Ray, drawing the words out to make them sound naughty.

'It's true,' Sam continued. 'Then, well, then it did get serious.'

'It sounds like it,' said Prem.

Sam tapped the table again. 'No, but the thing is, right, when it comes to the baby, I mean the concep-

tion of it . . . you know what I mean . . . you lot . . .'
She stopped, highly embarrassed, and looked to
Tyrone for help.

'What?' said Ray, pointing a finger each at Tyrone
and Sam. 'You mean the creative process?'

There was an outburst of laughter. Tyrone held his
head down and looked up shyly under his eyebrows.

'Hear me,' Sam went on. 'When it comes to that
stuff, right, it was legal. You weren't attending the
centre and he was the right age.'

'The right age, are you sure?' asked Ray.

'Of course we are,' said Sam. 'We waited before we
got together.'

'You got together all right, but it must have been
difficult waiting,' Ray said, laughing aloud.

'We're responsible people,' Sam continued, 'we
know what we're doing you know, we talk to each
other about stuff. All right, we didn't actually plan to
have a baby, but as soon as we knew there was one on
the way we talked about everything – being together,
being a family, money, music, love, and the in-laws.
You name it, we went heart to heart on it.'

'Rude boy Tyrone, I was wondering who mummy
was,' said Ray, 'so why the big secret?'

'Seriously man,' replied Tyrone, 'I didn't want it to
distract from the work.'

'That wouldn't have distracted me,' said Prem,
'that would have inspired me.'

'Tyrone man, you're bad,' said Ray.

'Yu is a dark horse,' said Marga Man.

'Both of you are dark horses, if you ask me,' said Ray in disbelief. 'Real dark.'

'Well done, girl,' said Pauline.

Yinka, not knowing what all the fuss was about, said the right thing. 'Well, they don't look like dark horses to me, and even if they are dark horses, whatever that means, I think congratulations are called for, if not celebrations.'

'Yes, that's right,' Prem said, raising his glass. 'Congratulations, and good luck to all three of you.'

Before all the glasses had time to settle back on the tables, Ray stood up. 'And I have an announcement to make.' Everyone froze, looking at Yinka, who shrugged her shoulders and looked towards Ray, confused.

'I would like to say,' Ray said, glass raised high, 'that hip-hop is great because it brings people together.'

Yinka's heart started beating again and they all celebrated until past midnight.

They kicked off the tour with the charity concert at the Pavilion in Brighton. The idea was that the concert would act as a warm-up gig, giving them a chance to identify weak points in the set which could be improved upon. Few changes were needed; they performed as if they had been on the road all their life. Bunny had done a great job of making sure that the sound mix was right, and the boys made sure that they performed each rap with the right amount of energy and emotion, based on the guidance they had been given by Marga Man when recording the tracks.

That night the boys stayed in a hotel for the first time in their lives. The first thing Ray did when he got to his room was ring Yinka.

'Hi Yinka.'

'Hello, how did it go?'

'It was wack. You should have been there, the crowd loved it.'

'Well, I knew they would. But how was it for you?'

'Great. Everything was just right, the sound, the atmosphere, and the stage was massive, even bigger than the Rex, but we had no problem filling it. I think they said that after all the costs have been taken out we've raised about six thousand pounds for the cause, that's including T-shirt sales and stuff like that. We doing the business, girl.'

'So no after-show party?'

'No, we got an early sound check in Southampton tomorrow, so we're taking it easy. We gonna leave the partying until we get up to London. I don't want to party with no one but you.'

They did more gigs in Bristol, Oxford and Ipswich before getting to London. Two gigs were lined up in

London. The first would be a return to the Rex and the second would be at the Brixton Academy. From there they would make their way north. To keep the momentum and reinforce their unity, the band stayed in the East End the night before the gig. There was a great sense of anticipation.

When the band turned up at the Rex the next afternoon, fans had already started to gather. Autographs had to be signed at the stage door before and after the sound check, and just as they were getting into the tour bus a teenage girl stopped them.

'Please, please, can I have your autographs?' she pleaded.

'No problem,' said Ray. 'A nice girl like you should have our autographs.'

She passed Ray an autograph book. 'In there please, and can you put my name? It's Annabel. My dad used to be your head teacher.'

'What?' gasped Prem. 'Is Mr Lang your dad?'

'Yeah, I'm sorry, he's OK when you get to know him.'

'He's OK,' said Tyrone. 'You look a bit like him.'

'He said you're into punk, not rap,' said Ray.

'Things change,' she replied, and when all there had signed her book she skipped away. Then as they turned to board the bus again they heard a friendly voice.

231

'Hey X-Ray-X, Pro Justice, Prem de la Prem, look, they've fixed me.'

As they looked in the direction of the voice there was the flash of a camera. It was Fingers. They called him over. 'How you going?' asked Ray.

'I'm feeling good. I would ask you for your autographs but I have them already. Have you guys been on the internet lately?'

'Don't really have much time for that,' said Ray.

'Well,' said Fingers, smiling mischievously, 'you should check out Positive Negatives dot com the next time you're on.'

'Have you done it?' asked Prem, excited.

'I'm not completely happy with it, but it's a start,' said Fingers. 'To get it good I need some more stuff from you. I've got photos but I need some tour information, permission to reproduce some lyrics and them kind of things.'

'That's coming to you,' said Ray, 'along with a cheque.'

'Don't worry about paying me.'

'No, we must, and we will,' said Marga Man. 'Why are yu here so early? Yu trying to get right up front?'

'Now, that's where I'm not feeling so good, you see money can't buy you everything,' said Fingers, tilting his head towards the ground. 'The gig's sold out, I can't get a ticket anywhere. They sold out so quickly and I ain't got credit cards and shit like that so, by the time I got the cash together –'

'Don't worry,' Ray said, interrupting. He turned to Marga Man. 'Make sure my man Fingers is on the guest list.'

'No problem,' said Marga Man, searching his multi-pocketed coat for his notepad. 'OK, Fingers, you're on de guest list, you plus one, so bring a friend and I'm putting you down for de after-show party if you want to come.'

The London gig was to be the big night out. Yinka and Mallam turned up at the hotel in the late afternoon, followed by Sam. Then not long before they left for the Rex, Kori and her two friends Lizette and Thara arrived, quickly followed by Anita with Prem's sister and three of their friends. They were all looking their best, but none of them could match the rocks, or bling bling, otherwise known as jewellery, that the boys were wearing. The colour scheme for the night was gold. They were wearing baggy gold-coloured denim suits and their wrists, fingers and necks were covered with gold. These were just casual before-gig clothes. To wear on stage they also took shiny gold suits with shiny gold buttons.

When Positive Negatives arrived at the Rex they did so like three kings surrounded by beautiful women of all shades. It looked like a rap video, with cameras flashing, fans cheering, and bodyguards guarding. They entered the building with attitude, and performed like masters. The previous gigs had been great but this was the best. They touched fists, recited their motto, and from the moment they walked out on stage the crowd went wild. They really were playing at home.

The crowd rapped along with most tunes and there were times when the band would point the microphones into the crowd to let them take the lead. Fingers was at the front of the crowd taking as many photos as he could and chanting the lyrics to the raps. He was right up against the stage making his presence felt. When a rap called 'It's All About Living' was dedicated to him he shouted his happiness out loud. The band had given their all, and after three encores they had nothing else to perform, but the crowd demanded more, as did Yinka, Sam, Anita and the others who were standing at the side of the stage. Ray started thinking aloud.

'So you want some more?'

'Yeah,' came back thousands of voices.

'Well, I got this idea, and maybe my man Bunny at mission control can help me out here. If he can set it up, we can do for you, exclusively, for the first time in public, a joint from our next project. The joint I have in mind is a thing called 'Refugee Me', and let me tell you now this next album is full of positivity. Bunny, my man, can we do this?'

Bunny had just finished setting up the backing track tape and so gave the thumbs up.

'OK, let's do this,' said Ray, looking round at Prem and Tyrone, and they rocked.

Even as they left the stage the crowd shouted for more.

'See you in Brixton,' shouted Ray.

Marga Man had hired a small hall near the music shop for the after-show party, but getting there wasn't easy. The stage door area was completely blocked with fans who were waiting for autographs, so Marga Man told the boys to sign a few while he went to get the tour bus. They tried to sign as much as they could but it was impossible to sign everything – books, scraps of paper, tickets and CDs came to them from every angle. Their bodyguards watched carefully over the crowd, knowing that they were on the very spot where the fight broke out the last time the band played the Rex. But that was the last thing on the boys' minds; they just signed as many things as they could until they were rescued by Marga Man. The band jumped into the back of the bus along with Yinka, Sam and Anita, and they drove off followed by three other cars carrying the rest of their entourage.

The vehicles stopped at a set of traffic lights at Stratford Broadway, a massive roundabout with a shopping centre in the middle of it. The tour bus was still at the front of the convoy. Inside the bus it was unusually quiet – no music was being played, nobody was talking. It was as if they were all thinking about the enormity of the night. The lights turned green and Marga Man began to move off when suddenly he was forced to hit the brakes. A motorbike had pulled up in front of them. Marga Man slapped his horn and shouted in anger.

'Get out of de way, are yu stupid, or what?'

Marga Man looked to the side when he saw another motorbike rider who took out a gun and pointed it at the back window.

'Get down!' Marga Man shouted.

Two shots were fired through the windows at head level but everybody got down flat and the bullets passed over their heads, shattering the glass. One of the bodyguards managed to open the door on the opposite side and get out, but, being unarmed, there was nothing he could do except avoid getting hit. Inside the bus everyone held each other tightly and the people in the cars behind began to sound their horns. Marga Man saw the man on the motorbike in front of him struggling to get something from the pocket of his leather riding-suit, but Marga Man wasn't going to give him a chance. As the second rider aimed to fire, Marga Man accelerated, knocking the rider off his bike, and the shot went wide. Marga Man drove right over the motorbike, just missing the rider, who limped as fast as he could over to the other rider's bike and jumped on the back. The bikers made their getaway, leaving one bike wrecked in the road. The cars all stopped and Kori came running out from one of them.

'Ray, are you all right?' she shouted, pulling open the bus door. Shattered glass fell on to her.

'Yeah, we're all OK here. Are any of you lot hurt?'

'No,' Kori said, with tears in her eyes.

They all started to get out of the bus, making sure everyone was unhurt, and other people from the cars also began to get out.

'Are you sure you're all right?' Kori asked Ray.

'I'm OK,' he replied. 'What about you, are you OK?'

'Yes.'

'Have you been hurt?

'No,' said Kori, 'I'm all right.'

Ray glanced over at Yinka who looked completely shaken. For the first time since he'd known her she looked absolutely vulnerable as she looked back at him. He went over and put his arms around her and held her tight, whispering in her ear, 'Don't worry, it will be all right. I love you, girl.'

Just then there was a scream from Anita, and she shouted, 'Watch out, it's them, they've come back.'

The gunmen had gone around the roundabout and were coming down the other carriageway.

'Get down!' the bodyguards shouted. The biker riding pillion began to shoot again. There were more screams and then Yinka slumped against Ray.

'Oh shit, Yinka's fainted,' Ray shouted, unsure what to do next. As he tried to adjust his arms to give her better support, her head flopped back and her eyes rolled over. He looked down and saw blood soaking her dress and dripping on to the ground.

'Help, somebody help! Yinka's been hit!' he shouted as loud as he could. There was confusion as everybody got on their phones to call for an ambulance, but Ray ignored them. 'Yinka,' Ray said as he held her. 'Yinka.'

But there was no reply. Yinka's eyes were open but she wasn't looking anywhere, and her body was completely limp in Ray's arms.

'We can't wait. Put her in the bus,' Ray shouted to Marga Man, who was giving their location to the ambulance service on his phone.

Marga Man stopped the conversation and went to help Ray. With the help of the two bodyguards they began to lift her.

'It's too late. Put her down,' said one of the bodyguards.

'Put her in the bus!' shouted Ray desperately.

'Put her down,' said the bodyguard. 'She's not with us.'

'No,' said Ray. 'There's still a chance! Hurry up,

come on, let's go.'

'She's not with us,' said the bodyguard.

Ray looked into Yinka's eyes. She was lifeless. Her eyes were fixed on him as if he were the last person she ever saw in her life. Everyone took a step back. Ray placed his body over hers and hugged her tightly, and everything else in the world faded into insignificance as he held her and wept.

CHAPTER 19

Question Time

A large group gathered in the waiting area of the hospital where Yinka's body had been taken. Ray was allowed behind the scenes where he attempted to get rid of all the blood that covered him. Here he also tried to explain to the doctors and the police officers what had happened but he was so distressed that he was unable to concentrate his mind to give any useful replies. A police interview with the band was arranged for the next day. Mallam, sobbing, and with tears streaming down her face, barely managed to give the hospital staff details about how to contact Yinka's next of kin, and when Yinka's parents did arrive they spoke to nobody. Anita, Prem, Tyrone and the others who were in the waiting room offered condolences but Yinka's parents did not respond. They were expressionless, although it seemed their lack of expression was not malicious, but caused by the shock of losing their daughter.

Although Ray too was in a state of shock, he managed to tell Yinka's parents how sorry he was. He offered to help them in whatever way he could but her father just replied very solemnly, 'Thank you, we will be able to take care of everything.'

There was great concern for Ray. He had lots of offers of accommodation or company, but he wanted to be alone, so as a compromise he allowed Kori to ride home with him. One of the bodyguards drove them and when they got to his place Kori walked him right to the door, and she squeezed his hand in a way that she had never done before and said goodnight. She went back to join her friends, and he went inside and began searching through his collection for a Tupac CD. He selected a track called 'I Wonder if Heaven Got a Ghetto'. He put his headphones on, set the player to repeat, and listened to it over and over again.

The next morning after very little sleep Ray got a taxi to the music shop where the whole crew were to be interviewed by the police. Ray's original plan was to be as helpful to the police as possible, but, on seeing that the officers who arrived to do the interview were the same officers who had interviewed them after the stabbing of Fingers, Ray's mood changed. To make things worse Detective Sergeant Horne greeted him in all too friendly a manner.

'Hello, Ray, my mate. How's it going?'

'It's not going, and I'd rather you not call me mate.

Let's face it, I'm no mate of yours,' he replied.

'Can we get on wid de interview? said Marga Man. 'This is a difficult time.'

'Yes, I understand,' said the sergeant. He looked at the two bodyguards standing at the door of the shop. 'Who are they?'

'Dem come from a private security firm dat we use from time to time,' Marga Man replied.

'Were they there when the shooting happened?'

'Yes, they were there, and I believe dat they have submitted a written statement.' As Marga Man spoke, he looked towards them, and the bodyguards both nodded back in agreement.

D.S. Horne turned to Ray. 'Now, mate, I believe the young lady was your girlfriend.'

'Will you stop calling me mate?' Ray shouted. 'I'm not your bloody mate, don't you get it?'

'Calm down,' said the sergeant. 'There has been a serious incident here and we need to get all the information we can.'

'Well, stop acting like me and you are friends,' Ray said, spitting the words towards the offending officer.

'Will you just ask the questions?' said Prem.

'OK. So, was she your girlfriend?'

'Yes,' Ray answered quietly.

'Tell me what happened.'

'We just finished doing a concert at the Rex and we

were driving to an after-show party on Bryant Street. We stopped at the traffic lights at the Broadway, and these two guys on motorbikes drove up and started shooting at us. We all ducked down, I'm not sure how many shots were fired, about four I think. One of them came off his bike and then they rode off.'

'Now I understand that that's not the time the young lady got shot,' D.S. Horne said as he took notes.

'Her name is Yinka, and no, that's not when she got shot.'

The sergeant turned to Marga Man. 'Were you driving?'

'Yes, I was driving. What happened den was we all got out of de bus checking dat everyone was OK, and den they came down de other side of de road and dem start shoot up de place again, dat's when dem shoot Yinka.'

Without looking up from his notepad the sergeant said, 'When they came back the second time they were on one bike, I believe?'

'Yes. Dat's right,' said Marga Man. 'Do you have de motorbike?'

'Yes.'

'So who does de motorbike belong to?'

The officer who had been silent so far responded. 'I'm afraid the bike was stolen a couple of nights ago in west London.'

'So have you checked out the owner?' Tyrone asked.

'Yes we have, and we know it wasn't the owner. The owner has a watertight alibi.'

Marga Man pressed on. 'How do you know? Sometimes watertight things spring leaks.'

'We know,' said the officer, sounding embarrassed and looking at the floor, 'because the motorbike was stolen from outside a police station.'

'Outside a police station? So who does it belong to?' asked Prem.

'You're not going to believe this,' D.S. Horne continued, 'but the owner is a police officer. He was in the station at the time.'

There was muffled laughter of disbelief from the boys. Marga Man continued to question the police. 'So, wait a minute. Yu mean to tell me dat somebody come an thief de big motorbike from outside de big police station and it belong to de big police officer?'

'That's right,' said the two officers in unison.

The boys laughed again in disbelief.

'Bullshit,' said Marga Man loudly, bringing the room to silence. 'Absolute bullshit. I know dat yu big police station would have big cameras all over de place.'

'Yes, you're right,' said D.S. Horne. 'You're right, but no one was watching the monitors at the time.'

The boys began to verbally express their disbelief.

'This can't be true.'

'It's some kind of test guy, one of those questioning tactics.'

'So there you go, the police can't police the police.'

The officers sank into a state of even deeper embarrassment. But Marga Man was still not letting up. 'OK, so de big officer, who was supposed to be watching de big monitor fell asleep, big problem, but not so big. Let's view de tape.'

'Yeah,' said Prem, 'good idea, let's view the video tape.'

The officers looked at each other nervously, then D.S. Horne spoke again. 'Could any of you describe either of the two people on the motorbikes?'

'Of course not,' said Tyrone. 'They both had full-face helmets on.'

'That's our problem too,' the sergeant said. 'We have them on film, and we can see them taking the bike, but they were quick, and they had those same helmets on.'

There were more sighs of disbelief from the boys and a strange disbelieving smile from Marga Man. 'Me tink is time for yu to go,' said Marga Man.

'You lot are rubbish,' shouted Ray. 'You know that, don't ya? You're rubbish, and I can see that you don't care. We will never get justice if you have your way, never. As far as you're concerned we're just black people killing each other. This is just another black on black statistic for you, ain't it, and all you're doing now is just going through the motions. This is just a job for you, but this is our lives. My girlfriend has been killed, we could have all been killed, and to you we're just paperwork.'

Sergeant Horne was putting his notepad away and the second officer responded. 'We are not calling this a black on black killing, we're not giving it any title whatsoever. As far as we're concerned this is murder, and we will treat it as such.'

'Yeah, but it's a dead black woman,' said Ray. 'And you got better things to do, haven't you?'

'I understand you're upset,' the officer said, trying to sound sympathetic.

'It's time for you to go,' said Marga Man.

'I think you're right,' said the officer. 'But you must understand we may need to speak to you again. And if you have any leads, or you remember something that may be of interest to us, please let us know.'

'Yeah, talk to those guys on the door. Maybe they can offer you some advice on security for your police station,' said Prem.

The officers left, without saying goodbye.

CHAPTER 20

Rhythm TV

'It has just been announced that British hip-hop band Positive Negatives have called off their first major UK tour. The band had just started the tour when seventeen-year-old Yinka Molara, the girl-friend of X-Ray-X, one of the band members, was shot and killed. The fatal shooting happened in their hometown of Stratford, east London, after a concert. The band were driving from the venue to a party when two men on motorbikes rode alongside the band's tour bus and started to shoot at the bus. The controversial rap band have been linked to a spate of gang fights that have been taking place between east and west London hip-hop fans. Earlier on this year a follower of rival west London band the Western Alliance was shot and killed in a West End nightclub.

'The Metropolitan Police refused to speculate on rumours that the murder of Ms Molara was a revenge killing and said that they were following up several lines of enquiries. The managers and representatives of both bands would not be inter-viewed on camera but sources on the music scene say that many stabbings and minor affrays have been attributed to the band's followers. The televi-sion presenter and music journalist Stella Bella said today that "There is no doubt that a great deal of animosity exists between the bands, and that this animosity has spilled over to their followers. However, whether the bands have actually done anything to provoke the hatred that we now see is debatable."

'Any tickets for concerts returned within the next two weeks will be refunded, and organisers of the tour say that at the moment there are no plans to reschedule the tour.'

CHAPTER 21

Ashes to African Ashes

For the first time since its formation Positive Negatives halted all its activities and Marga Man closed Flip Discs 'until further notice'. The boys spent most of their time in their respective homes but stayed in contact with each other by phone. Ray spent much of the time listening to Mallam reminiscing about how she and Yinka first met and how they grew up together. Ray was continuing to learn about Yinka after her death, and the more he learnt about her the more he was convinced that she would have been the woman for him. Now his biggest frustration was being so removed from anything to do with Yinka in his time of mourning. Her family had kept her body and had no contact with him. His only way of knowing anything about what they were thinking was via Mallam, and Mallam was being told very little.

The phone woke Ray at six o'clock one morning. Looking at his caller display he could see that it was Mallam. He answered immediately – she had never rung this early before.

'Mallam, what's up, is there something wrong?'

'You're not going to like this.'

'I'm not going to like what?'

'I spoke to Yinka's parents last night.'

'And?'

'I'm going to the airport now.'

'What do you mean, you're going to the airport?'

'You're not going to like this, Ray.'

Ray sat up in bed. 'Come on, Mallam, I'm not going to like what? Tell me what's happening.'

'OK, please calm down.'

'OK, I'm calm, now tell me.'

'They're taking Yinka to Nigeria.'

'What?'

'They're taking her to Nigeria.'

'What for?'

'They say they want to bury her there.'

Ray just could not believe what he was hearing. 'Why do they want to bury her there?'

'They say she should be buried in the land of her ancestors.'

Ray went quiet as he thought. 'But she's British. Her family are here, what about her friends here?'

'That's what I said to her dad,' Mallam said. 'But he just said that this country killed her. I'm going to the airport.'

'I'm going too,' Ray said, getting out of bed.

'Which airport and what time are they leaving?'

'You can't come.'

'Why not?'

'Because the family want privacy and I'm not supposed to tell anybody anything.'

'Please Mallam, please, tell me what time they're leaving?'

'I can't.'

Ray began to plead like he had never done before and Mallam had tears in her eyes as she listened. 'Mallam, please, you've got to tell me. I'm going to have nothing left of her, no grave, no nothing. I'm not asking for much, I just want to see her before she goes. It was my fault that she died, if she had never met me she would be alive now. It's all my fault and I just want to say sorry. Please Mallam, tell me what's happening.'

There was a long silence. When Mallam replied she did so as if it was being slowly forced out of her. 'They leave at eleven o'clock, from Heathrow Airport. There's some kind of cargo place at Terminal Four where they send and receive bodies. That's where Yinka is now. There will be a chance for friends and family to see her and then they have to leave. I think her mum and dad just check in as normal then. Everything has been arranged for her funeral in Nigeria the day after they arrive.'

'OK,' said Ray, moving around the room trying to

251

get himself together. 'I'll be there.'

'No, you can't,' said Mallam.

'Why not?'

'Slow down and listen, Ray.' Mallam was almost shouting now. 'Not just anybody can go down to the cargo place to see her. I told you, only friends and family, and those have to be approved by her parents.' There was another long silence.

'You've got to understand,' Mallam continued, more quietly. 'They can't just let anyone go there, and her parents are really upset because the press have been trying to speak to them.'

There was another long silence and then Ray spoke. 'What can I do?'

Ray could hear Mallam thinking as she spoke. 'I don't know, it's hard. I've got an idea. It may not work, it could go wrong, it could make things worse, but it's the only thing I can think of right now. I'll call her parents, I'll have a word with them and see if they'll let you join us.'

'OK. Please do that. Tell them that it's really important to me and that I will completely respect their wishes,' said Ray quietly.

'I'll call you back.'

Ray was relieved when Mallam rang back to say that Yinka's parents had agreed to allow him to go to the airport. For his part he had to agree that he would turn up with Mallam and not bring members of the band with him. Ray had no problem with that. He put on the blackest clothes that he could find and went in a taxi to meet with Mallam on her way to the airport.

They met at an underground station and from there the taxi took them to Terminal Four, where they were directed to a large unit where Yinka's mother and father were waiting. Yinka's parents stood silently surrounded by other many members of their family. Although no one acknowledged them, Ray and Mallam went and stood silently with the family members, not quite sure what would happen next.

As they stood waiting, to Ray's dismay his phone began to ring. Everybody looked towards him. Yinka's father shook his head, and Mallam looked away in shame on Ray's behalf. Ray struggled to find his phone and turn it off. As he did so, he looked at the caller display screen to see the number of the caller but all it said was 'Withheld'. He put the phone back in his pocket and whispered, 'I'm sorry.'

Five minutes later, two men dressed in black overalls appeared, pushing the coffin on a high trolley. They carefully opened the lid of the coffin before stepping back. Yinka's mother and father walked silently up to the coffin, followed by the other members of the family. Ray and Mallam waited until last. Ray watched the others carefully and he couldn't help noticing that although some members of the family wept and were obviously disturbed, Yinka's parents seemed to show no emotion at all. They were silent and dignified – as dignified as parents could be, having lost a daughter.

When Ray walked up to the coffin he felt as if he and the world around him began to operate in slow motion. He was aware of every step that he made and every breath that he took. And when he looked down into the coffin, everything stopped. Yinka looked as beautiful as ever. Her hair was plaited in the same way it had been when he first met her, her skin shone, and the bright, patterned traditional dress she wore immediately caused Ray to admire her beauty once again. It was a long moment, in which he realised that he was looking down upon a dead body but without the unease that he had expected. Yinka looked as if she was simply in a peaceful sleep, and for a moment Ray was convinced that if he asked her opinion on an important issue or kissed her forehead she would wake up.

Ray tried to whisper, 'Sorry.' His mouth moved, he heard the word in his head, but it did not seem to pass his lips. Convinced that she still heard him, he snapped back into reality and realised that he had been standing looking at her for some time. He walked away, the men in black closed the coffin and Yinka's father signed the relevant documentation.

The family began to disperse and Ray could see

Yinka's parents heading towards the check-in area. He left Mallam and walked quickly towards them.

'I'm sorry, I'm really sorry. I know that sorry is not enough, but I just don't know what else to say. I really did love Yinka.'

'We still love her,' said Yinka's mother softly. 'We are sorry too, and we still love her.'

'I understand,' said Ray, bowing his head before them.

'Listen, young man,' said Yinka's father. 'We wished she had never met you, maybe if she didn't meet you she would be alive today, but we also know that what happened was not your fault. I am being honest with you, this is how we feel.'

'I understand sir,' said Ray, head still bowed.

After leaving the airport, Ray dropped Mallam off in a taxi and then continued the journey to his flat. He closed his eyes and began to recall the image of Yinka in the coffin, when his phone rang again. He looked at the caller display and saw that the number was withheld. Convinced that the caller was the same person that had called earlier, he answered harshly.

'Who's this?'

'Your bitch is dead, now what you going to do?'

'Who's this?'

'Listen dog, your bitch deserved to die. Long may she be dead, she was a slag anyway.'

'Identify yourself, scared rat, identify yourself and let me come for you.'

'This is a message from the Messenger. Your days are numbered,' the voice said calmly. And the line went dead.

When Ray got home the first thing he did was ring Marga Man, but Marga Man knew exactly why he was ringing – he had just been called by Prem and Tyrone who had both received similar phone calls to Ray. Marga Man played it down, but he had also had a call by someone threatening to burn his shop down.

But Ray was finding it hard to contain himself. As Marga Man was telling Ray to lay low, Ray interrupted him.

'Marga Man, we gotta cut the bullshit and deal with the enemy, this has gone too far. You know where this is all coming from, don't you?'

'Do you?' asked Marga Man.

'Come on, we all know it's those Western Alliance boys. They killed Yinka and if we don't respond they'll kill one of us next.'

'We don't know dat.'

'That's weird, because everyone else does. Every time they're on television they're talking about how much they hate us and what they wanna do to us.'

'Dat don't mean anything, the phone calls could be someone completely different.'

'It's them, they hate us.'

'Just be cool,' Marga Man said, trying to calm Ray down. 'We'll talk about it some other time. Tings are too heated now.'

'This is no time for being cool,' Ray said sharply.

'What is time? We can make of time what we will.'

There was a pause. Ray knew what he wanted to say but he wanted to say it without causing offence to Marga Man.

'You know I respect you Marga Man, and I don't want to disrespect you, but I don't think that this is time for your philosophy and your wise words.'

When Ray called Prem and Tyrone later he found that their attitude was similar to that of Marga Man, but Ray had other things in mind. He waited until midnight, put on a hooded top and got a taxi to drop him at Piccadilly Circus. Then he sat on the steps under Eros watching people rollerblading and juggling. He sat and waited. The rollerbladers and jugglers were replaced by drunks, and as time went on the drunks were replaced by cleaners. The area began to empty and then Ray heard the voice that he had been waiting for. It came from over his shoulder.

'Are you from up north?'

'Do you really care?' said Ray. As he turned he saw Midnight, the man who had approached him when he was last in Piccadilly Circus after leaving home. Midnight didn't recognise him and Ray wanted it to stay that way.

'You wanna make money?' asked Midnight, wide-eyed.

'No, do you?'

Midnight looked Ray up and down thoroughly. 'What, are you with Scotland Yard or something, Double O Seven on Her Majesty's Secret Service?'

'Are you for real or are you just a player?' Ray said, trying to indicate his seriousness with his voice.

'I'm for real,' said Midnight.

'If you're for real, hear me. Let's go for a walk, we both need some exercise,' Ray said, and they headed down Shaftesbury Avenue.

'So this is where you operate?' asked Ray.

'Yeah,' replied Midnight. 'This is where I live, day and night, night and day, from midnight to midnight, everything happens around me.'

'And how well do you know your community?'

'I know everything down here, I even know the rats by name. So what you after, some weed?'

'No, come again.'

'OK, you want something harder – cocaine, women, driving licences, passports?'

'It's more serious than that. Look, I ain't got no time to waste, I'm gonna get to the point. I need a master piece, and some missiles.'

Midnight was unphased by the request. 'Look, youth man, if someone's upset you go and learn a few kung-fu moves and beat them up. No need to get murderous.'

'Don't call me youth man and don't give me any advice. I told you what I want, now can you get it?'

Midnight's voice dropped. 'Are you serious?'

'You can't get more serious than me. Now what can you do? If you have no use, let me move on, if you know the world, let's deal.'

'If you're serious just give me a hour and I can get you a wicked air gun or a pellet gun, no problem.'

Ray threw his arms in the air. 'Forget it,' he said, turning around to walk away in the opposite direction. 'You're just playing man, I'd get better stuff in a toy shop. Thanks for nothing. Later.'

Midnight turned and stepped behind him. 'OK, youth man.'

'I told you, don't call me fucking youth man. Now can you do this shit or what?'

'Calm down brother. I can do it, no problem. So what do you want, sawn off or a hand piece?'

'I wanna hand piece.'

'Any particular make?'

'Look, all I wanna know is that it's got no history and it fires missiles.'

'OK, meet me here tomorrow, nine o'clock.'

'Where, right here?'

'Yeah, right here, you see where we are? The Gielgud Theatre.'

'OK. Who's Gielgud, anyway?' Ray asked, looking up at the theatre.

'I don't know. Anyway, who are you?'

'You don't know and you don't need to know. How much you after?'

'A grand.'

'What?'

'A grand. One hundred thousand pence,' Midnight said slowly.

'Forget it,' said Ray, and he began to walk away again. And once again Midnight quickly stepped after him.

'What's up, man? That's the going rate.'

'Who do you think I am? Listen, talk to me proper, how much?'

'Five hundred.'

'Look,' said Ray, 'I'm gonna go home, 'cause you're wasting my time, and I'm sure you've got better things you could be doing.'

'Five hundred is the going rate,' said Midnight.

'You see,' said Ray, shaking his head, 'you just said a thousand was the rate, and now five hundred is the rate. I'll tell you what, I'll see you here, outside that Gielgud place at nine tomorrow, and you show me what you've got.'

'I don't know you, are you real?'

'I'm real,' replied Ray, placing his fist on his chest by his heart.

'Are you coming with the money?' asked Midnight.

'Don't worry, I'll have money,' said Ray. 'Good morning.' And he walked off to get a taxi home.

The next day Ray was woken by more phone calls from Prem and Tyrone informing him of even more telephone threats they had received the previous night. A meeting was called at Flip Discs where Marga Man said that he was going to reopen the shop and try to get back to normality. He suggested that the band begin to think about rescheduling the tour and go to the record company with a suggested release date for the new album. Prem and Tyrone were willing to go ahead with Marga Man's suggestions, but Ray wasn't having it.

'I don't wanna do anything,' said Ray.

'Listen, man,' said Marga Man. 'It's hard, it's difficult times, but life must go on.'

'Life is not going on,' said Ray. 'Death is going on.'

No one had a reply. All Tyrone could do was suggest that they go away and think about it, and all Marga Man could do was agree.

That evening Ray went back to Shaftesbury Avenue and waited outside the Gielgud Theatre. Nine o'clock came and went and as twenty past nine came he began to get nervous. Every time a police car went past it was as if they were looking at him. He wondered if it had been wise to deal with someone like Midnight, who was nowhere near low profile, and could be working for the police. As doubt began to set in a car pulled up.

'Get in,' said a voice from the back. It was Midnight, and he gestured frantically. 'Get in, man.'

'Who's this?' asked Ray, pointing to the driver, a twenty-something white guy, wearing a dark woolly hat that came right down to his eyes.

'Don't worry about him, he's safe. Come on, let's move, we're holding up traffic.'

Ray felt unsafe in the car and he let it be known. 'Where we going? And I thought I was meeting you, on your own.'

'You're safe,' said Midnight. 'This is Rick, my driver. He's cool, so be cool. And we can't do business there anyway, this whole area is covered by cameras. You only work there if you wanna be on TV.'

As they drove off, Midnight reached under the seat in front of him and pulled out a plastic bag, from which he took a towel which he placed on the seat between him and Ray. Then he slowly unwrapped the towel to reveal a black gun and four small boxes.

'There it is,' Midnight said, savouring the moment as if he had his favourite meal in front of him. 'That's it, a twenty-two. It won't let you down.'

Ray's heart raced at the sight of it. He reached out and stroked it as if it were a small pet. When he withdrew his hand Midnight picked up the gun and whispered, 'It's beautiful.'

Ray shook his head slowly. 'It's not beautiful, it's necessary. Is it safe?'

'What do you mean?' asked Midnight in a raised voice.

'Has it got a history?'

'It's safe, man. It's not wanted, it hasn't touched anyone, and it's fresh on the streets.'

'Are you sure?' asked Ray, reaching out and taking it from Midnight. It was surprisingly light and it fitted Ray's hand perfectly.

'I'm sure,' said Midnight. 'This piece of iron comes straight from the cop shop, yeah man, this is from the source, the Metropolitan Police recycling service, and you can't get better than that.'

Ray turned the gun in his hands and looked at its details carefully. He had no idea what he should be looking for, but he thought he should look as if he did. He picked up one of the boxes and looked inside to find the bullets. He took one of the bullets out and examined it, caressing it with his fingertips, then he put them all back on the towel.

'I'll give you three hundred pounds for the lot.'

'Are you mad?' shrieked Midnight. 'Do you know what the going rate is?'

'Never mind the stupid going rate,' said Ray. 'The going rate is whatever you want it to be. Take three and be happy.'

'I can't, five's the best I can do.'

'OK, stop the car,' said Ray. 'Let me out.'

The driver, who had just been driving round and round the block, saying nothing, pulled over.

'No, keep moving,' said Midnight. 'OK, gimme four.'

'No,' said Ray. 'Three, and if that's no good let me out.'

'Three fifty,' Midnight said quickly, expecting a deal.

'I'm going,' said Ray.

Midnight conceded. 'OK, give me three. You're getting a bargain, you know. You won't get a deal like this anywhere else, but hey, I like your face.'

'Never mind my face, forget my face,' Ray said, handing him six fifty pound notes. 'I just hope this shit works.'

'Don't worry,' said Midnight, 'I told you, it came straight from the station, they got strict quality control there. Look, let me show you how to load.'

Midnight gave Ray a quick lesson in how to load the gun, then Ray wrapped it up in the towel with the bullets and placed it back in the bag. He had no idea where he was but he ordered the driver to stop, and he got out and walked for a few nervous minutes before he found a taxi and went home.

Before Ray went to bed he unrolled the towel to have another look at his purchase. The killing machine looked innocent lying on his bed. Ray admired it. He picked it up, pointed it at an empty glass and looked down the barrel like he had seen it done in films. He was fascinated by the shape and form of the piece. For a minute he stroked it like he had in the back of the car, but then he realised the morbidity of his ways. Suddenly it struck him that the small piece of metal in front of him was built for one purpose only. He wanted it out of sight. After a moment of thought he decided to put it under the floorboards. He moved his bed, peeled back the carpet, then, using a screwdriver and a hammer, he levered up a single floorboard. He placed the gun in its wrapping in the space as if he were burying a small animal, then he whispered 'Goodbye' to it, and put everything back.

Ray knew that he had taken a giant step. He wasn't sure if the others would approve but he had no plans to tell them. He had no idea what his next move would be but he did know that his girl was dead and that he was being threatened; now he was ready to defend himself, by any means necessary.

CHAPTER 22

The Banned Band

For a week Ray did nothing but listen to music and eat, mostly take-away. He did no writing and his only contact with the outside world was by phone. At a time when he knew that his father wasn't around he made one trip to see his mother and Kori, who both tried to persuade him to come back for a few days, but he wasn't having it. The house still brought back memories of his relationship with his father. He stayed for less than an hour, and to try and compensate his mother for such a short visit, he left a cheque for a sum twice her weekly wage.

Marga Man could see that the inactivity of the boys could quickly bring the band down. He knew that Prem and Tyrone were easy and would go with the flow but he wasn't so sure about Ray. Ray just didn't seem to be recovering. Marga Man called a late meeting in his shop and this time he was making demands.

'If Positive Negatives is over, tell me now so dat I can prepare de paperwork. If not, tell me now so dat we can get on wid de business. I tell yu guys already, me is a survivor, I pass through great tribulation, and right now yu have to make your minds up. Are yu going to survive, or are yu going to do de boy band ting and give up as soon as de going gets tough? Me is de manager, so me is going to manage, unless you're going to sack me.'

He stopped for a response but there was none, so he continued.

'People still want Positive Negatives. Every day I'm selling your tunes, and every day people are asking about yu. Yu need to get back on de scene, but we can do it gradually if yu like. I've already spoken to Skelly and de record company are cool wid releasing a single from de new album, and that would be followed by de release of de album itself. And I've spoken to Tony Oldsmith and we feel dat when de album is out and penetrating de hearts and minds of de people, we should hit de road wid a tour. And listen to dis, de record company say dat after de tour yu should tek a break and den go to de States.'

Tyrone and Prem quickly warmed to the idea. Prem punched the air. 'Yeah, the States.' Tyrone nodded positively.

'That's cool,' said Ray.

'Ray, what's happening, man?' said Marga Man. 'You're usually the motivator, get wid de project, man.'

Ray responded angrily. 'I told you, didn't I, what did I just say? I said I'm cool.'

Marga Man looked hard at Ray.

'I'm sorry, man,' Ray said, shaking his head. 'You're right, we need to get the vibe back.'

They all agreed that Marga Man should get things moving and set up a timetable for rehearsals. As they were leaving, Marga Man pulled Ray aside.

'I know yu can do this yu know, but do yu want to, do you feel dat you're up to it?'

Ray could see genuine concern on Marga Man's face. 'I'm all right,' Ray replied. 'It's tough, man, but I'm trying to be like you, a survivor.'

Marga Man reached out and put his hand on Ray's shoulder. 'However you do it, just be yourself, and don't be afraid to ask for help.'

'Thanks. I'll remember that,' said Ray.

The band quickly got back into rehearsals and it didn't take long for them to find their old form. Ray added a new rap to the set, called 'It Ain't Da Same'. It was a tribute to Yinka that also referred to himself and the fact that he had changed. But soon they were making headlines again.

The Newham Echo
Local Hip-Hop Heroes Banned from Major Venues

The Western Voice
Venues Say Let's Stop Hip-Hop

Peckham Post
Positive Negatives Get the Negative

The Weekly Londoner
London Venues Say No to Gangsta Rap

As soon as Marga Man and Tony Oldsmith began to organise the tour it became apparent that many venues around the country had collectively decided to boycott the band. Tony's office and Marga Man began working hard behind the scenes trying to find alternative venues, but there were still some cities where the band had nowhere to perform. Marga Man tried to reassure the band by letting them know that the lack of venues available had nothing to do with a lack of fans, as the sales of CDs had increased and the venues that had booked the band were completely sold out. But it didn't help when there were more media reports about more fights between east and west London gangs, and every time there was a report they never failed to mention Positive Negatives.

Sam was openly spending more time with Tyrone and she would often listen in on rehearsals. Everyone was beginning to get excited about her giving birth and they were all watching carefully as Sam grew in size. Prem began to speak about Anita much more seriously and Kori had become a much closer sister to Ray. Mallam still kept in touch with Ray. Their friendship had developed into one in its own right. Having to concentrate on rehearsals and interact with the other band members helped Ray to take his mind off Yinka.

By the time the tour was ready to hit the road Ray was raring to go, but there were still some major cities where no venue would accept them. Their plan was to do a tour that was so peaceful and so successful that these venues would regret their decisions. This time the tour started in Manchester at the Apollo. There was a small fight after the concert but this had nothing to do with the troubles down in London. As before, the first gig was a benefit fund raise for The Nation Foundation. Then they went on to perform in Liverpool, Newcastle, Birmingham and Leicester before going to London. No central London venues would book them but they did manage to get two venues further out: their friendly local venue the Rex, and another venue which would not have been their first choice. It was important that the band do more than one London gig but the only other large venue outside the East End was the Hammersmith Palais – a great place but it was right in the Western Alliance's territory. As they always did, the band had a meeting to debate the pros and cons and it didn't take long for them to agree that the west London gig should go ahead, but with even tighter security than they had been employing at the other gigs.

As everyone expected, playing their first London gig at the Rex brought out the very best of the band. It was as if the audience had been going through everything the band had been going through. Now they were shouting not just words of encouragement, but also personal messages to Ray about Yinka. As Ray introduced 'It Ain't da Same', an instant hush came over the crowd and the silence lingered as the band performed the rap, with hardly any dancing as the crowd listened. But that changed when the band performed the next tune, a noisy, uplifting track called 'Da Revenge of da Good'. It was an unreleased jam from the new album, and although it was about poor people rising up having a revolution, most of the audience seemed to think it was about Positive Negatives rising up against the Western Alliance.

The band played for two and a half hours before saying goodbye to the faithful, but even then the faithful demanded more. After they had done an encore of four raps they had performed all the raps on both albums plus the dedication to Yinka. When the band came off stage they were pouring with sweat. Marga Man, Mallam, Sam, Kori and all the others who had been watching in the wings knew that this was the best performance the band had ever given, and the fans knew they had been a part of something very special.

A ring of security guards surrounded them as they made their way back to the dressing room, and once in the dressing room the guards made sure that no one outside the band's inner circle had access to them. Their family and friends treated their backstage passes like precious passports.

The boys had always liked meeting fans and signing autographs, but for the London gigs all the advice said that there should be no signings after the shows. So there was a long wait for the fans to disperse, and then the few that did wait around barely got a glimpse of them. The tour bus pulled up right next to the stage door, the guards made a human corridor that allowed the band to walk straight on to the bus, and as advised the boys looked straight ahead and said nothing. Even on the bus they couldn't be seen because all the curtains had been drawn.

This time Marga Man had hired the banqueting hall of an expensive Docklands hotel for the after-show party, and once again the security was tight. The DJ Rapcity provided the music, and his contract stressed that no Positive Negatives tunes should be played, and that at least sixty per cent of his tunes should be by British bands. Marga Man had invited many of the usual suspects but he had also invited many dedicated fans who he had recognised as such when they turned up at the music shop partly to buy CDs but also to make enquiries about the band. By doing this Marga Man gave at least some fans an opportunity to make contact with the band.

Amongst the fans was Fingers, who had turned up with a friend. On seeing Ray, Fingers approached him with his arms wide open.

'X-Ray-X,' he called out to him. They hugged and touched fists. 'Every night's a night to remember with you guys, but tonight was even more than that. I got some wicked photos too. Every hip-hop band in the world should have seen you perform tonight, that's how it should be done. And that new joint is dark, man, those lyrics kill me. People love the website, but everyone including me wants to know when you guys going Stateside? You gotta go and spread the word, let them know what's happening.'

'The States may be happening,' said Ray.

'For real?' Fingers asked excitedly.

'For real,' said Ray.

'Yeah, Positive Negatives in the Big Apple, I can see it now. Can I come?' asked Fingers, straight-faced.

Ray laughed. 'I'll see what I can do.'

The guy who was with Fingers joined the conversation. 'Any plans to go anywhere else?' he asked.

'Well, I've heard a little talk about certain parts of

Asia. Our beats are selling there, and Australia, but they're just all in the pipeline, nothing's for sure right now.'

'You should go to Africa, I'm from there, Africa needs you. And I want to thank you for that rap you done called "Refugee Me". That tune is intelligent, yes, that tune means a lot to me. I brought you a present.' He handed Ray a small book the size of a matchbox. Ray looked at it, amused by its size and intrigued by its title, *Wise Words of Africa*.

'Thanks,' said Ray. 'I haven't even read it yet but I know that it's a good book.'

'Don't forget. I wanna be on your Stateside tour, hey, and your African one.'

'I'll speak to a friend in a high place,' laughed Ray.

Ray was also being pressured by others in the nicest possible way. Just after Fingers and his friend left, the three band members were confronted by Kori and her two friends Lizette and Thara.

'First of all,' said Thara, 'we want to say that you did a great performance tonight, and second of all we want you to listen.'

Kori raised her hand as a signal to DJ Rapcity, who then stopped playing and the three girls began to sing. Kori took the lead and the others harmonised. It was a soulful, quirky song about the need for women to control their men, and it didn't take long for the trio to attract the attention of everyone in the room.

As the song progressed into the third verse everyone began to clap along in time and Prem began to hum a bass line. The song ended on a high note with all three girls holding a close three-part harmony in perfect time. The crowd was enthralled. They clapped enthusiastically and called for more, but the girls shied away. When the applause died down the band members began to praise the girls' vocal skills.

'You hear that,' said Ray, 'my little sister, voice like an angel. A superstar, believe me.'

'Majestic,' said Tyrone.

Kori put her arms around Prem and Ray. 'Never mind all the praise, I say no praise without a raise, so can we tour with you? We've almost rehearsed a full show, and if you have us as support you won't have to go looking anywhere else, will you? So when you're ready, we're right here, and we're called Zen.'

Ray laughed out loud. 'Zen, what kinda name's that?'

'It's deep,' said Kori. 'So deep you wouldn't understand. Just think of us starting the show for you, it'd be cool, we'd bring some niceness to the show.'

'I was just thinking that,' said Prem.

Ray wasn't too sure. 'You're good, no, you're great, but you got a soul and R'n'B thing going there. Our fans are hardcore hip-hop fans, they may not be into it, you know what I'm saying?'

Kori used her arm around Ray's neck to give him a

shake. 'Don't I remember you at the MOBO Awards saying that all music is cool, and that we're all finding ways to express ourselves? So what's changed now?'

'Nothing,' said Ray. 'I'm just saying that when fans come to our gigs they expect to hear hip-hop and not other stuff. And I'm not saying other stuff is bad, it's just the fans.'

'Well you'll just have to educate them,' said Kori.

'You can't argue with that,' said Prem.

'I can,' said Ray.

'Don't,' said Prem. 'I don't know about you but I don't want to be strangled.'

After Ray, Prem and Tyrone had agreed to think about it, Kori let go and peace reigned once again.

It had been a good night. Even the after-show party was a success, so the fans were happy, the crew were happy, and the band were happy. Marga Man smiled contentedly. Positive Negatives were back.

CHAPTER 23

Good Morning TV

'The hip-hop rapper known as Reel Steel has been arrested for the possession of a firearm. The arrest took place last night at a concert being given by hip-hop band Positive Negatives. Reel Steel, whose real name is Lawrence Dale, is a prominent member of the group the Western Alliance, who are believed to be sworn enemies of Positive Negatives. Dale was stopped and searched by security staff as he tried to enter the concert. Whilst conducting the search the security staff discovered a small hand gun. Officers who were on duty outside the venue were called and an arrest was made. The band's management had no comment to make. Dale will appear in court later this morning.'

CHAPTER 24

All Chaos on the Western Front

Ray rushed out of the taxi and threw a twenty-pound note on the seat. 'Keep the change.'

'This is twenty mate – the fare's only four pounds,' said the taxi driver.

But Ray ignored him and raced into the music shop. The newspaper in his hand was opened at the appropriate page. He handed it to Marga Man.

'Have you seen that? They came to our concert armed, and we have to play on their territory tonight. What are we going to do?'

'What can we do?' Marga Man said, unmoved. 'We just do what we do, we can't not do de concert because of their antics.'

Ray pointed to the newspaper in his hand. 'Come on, Marga Man, what would one of their crew be doing at one of our concerts with a gun?'

'We don't know.'

'I think we should call the concert off,' said Ray sternly.

'No way,' Marga Man said, scanning quickly over

the newspaper article. 'You have fans, they await you. You can't let these thugs stop you. I have already organised even tighter security, so rest easy. You are an artist, Positive Negatives is a creative force, do your art, be creative. Let me worry about security matters.'

'I don't know,' said Ray.

'I do,' said Marga Man.

Just then, Prem and Tyrone entered the shop, both clutching different newspapers that were carrying the story. 'Did you hear what happened at our gig last night?' asked Prem in a raised voice.

'We know,' Ray replied.

'Serves them right,' Prem said. 'Who told them to come to our gig with armoury?'

'It's tonight that bothers me,' Ray said. 'I don't think we should do the gig.'

But both Prem and Tyrone disagreed with Ray.

'We have to do it,' said Marga Man.

'True,' said Tyrone.

'OK. Whatever,' said Ray. 'What time are we leaving?'

Marga Man handed the newspaper back to Ray. 'Don't worry about these people. I'll pick you up in the bus at three, we must sound check around five.'

'I see it differently from you guys,' Ray said. 'These guys are out for us. There is war, can't you see it? These are the guys who killed Yinka. OK, I'll go to

279

the concert but I'm not going to be an easy target for them. If they fuck with me I'll fuck with them back. This is serious, we're going on their territory. I'll see you later.' Ray walked out, leaving the others with raised eyebrows.

'Don't worry,' said Marga Man. 'Yu can't blame him, him just lose him woman and him still dealing wid dat.'

Later that afternoon they travelled to west London on the tour bus, and just as they arrived Ray's phone rang. He looked for the caller's number, but there was none. He answered.

'Welcome to hell, baby rappers.'

It was the same voice as always. Ray's face twisted with rage as he switched off his phone. 'There it is again.'

'Don't let it get to you,' said Tyrone. 'We had calls this morning too.'

'Did you? So why didn't you tell me?' said Ray, his temper rising.

'Because it's no big thing,' said Tyrone.

Ray turned on Tyrone. 'No big thing? Your girl hasn't been taken out, that's why you can say it's no big thing. You have your girl and everything's cool with you, yeah your baby's coming and you're earning, but look at me, man, you lot don't give a fuck about me.'

Tyrone was badly hurt by Ray's words but he didn't say anything back. He just gave a cold stare right into Ray's eyes. It was left to Marga Man to cool things down.

'Come on, we got work to do, let's do it. Or do you want to start a fight amongst yourselves? Dat would be very positive. Come on, look at de amount of back-up we have.' Marga Man did a one hundred and eighty degree turn and as he did so the various security guards nodded their heads, acknowledging their presence.

'I'm sorry,' said Ray softly.

'It's cool,' replied Tyrone.

Hammersmith Palais was another large venue. Bunny and the sound crew had brought an extra powerful PA system that caused the venue to seriously vibrate. Fans from east London, many of whom were at the previous night's concert, had travelled over to see them, and soon after the sound check word reached the band that queues had begun to form outside. The boys ordered food in and after eating they stayed around the dressing rooms reading newspaper reports and keeping each other's spirits high.

Time passed quickly and soon it was time for action. As the band stood at the side waiting to go on stage there was an edginess about the boys. Prem was nodding his head as if he were listening to music of

281

his own, Tyrone was standing still as if in deep con-
templation, and Ray was playing around shadow-
boxing and whispering lines from his raps. The
bodyguards looked on like mourners at a funeral,
expressionless and silent. When Marga Man turned
up the mood changed.

'Right, yu ready for dis?' he asked, upbeat.

The boys all answered 'Yes.' But not as enthusiastically as Marga Man would have liked. He wanted
more.

'I said are yu ready for dis?'

This time they replied with more volume.

'OK, well let's go mek some noise in west London.'
He clenched his fist and stretched it forward, the boys
gathered around and, with all fists connected at their
centre, Marga Man started to speak and the rest
joined in.

*'Let wordy great minds think alike, sweet Hip-Hop be
our guiding light.'*

'Your public awaits you,' Marga Man, said before
walking on stage.

As Marga Man arrived on stage the sound system
music stopped and everyone turned towards him. He
had said nothing but still he received applause. He
waited for a moment before speaking, to make sure
that the audience was in place and ready to hear what
he had to say. Then he spoke, proclaiming as if

announcing the coming of new prophets.

'Hip-hop comes from de angry streets, it goes into de recording studio, and den it goes back on de streets. It is created by real people for real people, without de people dis music means nothing. Dis is de music dat record companies can't control because it is de music of de soul, dis music is hated by politicians because dis music is powerful but it seeks no vote. De media people hate dis music because it is not created for television programmes and it is not created by men in suits. Lately yu may have heard de media people talking whole heap a bullshit about hip-hop.'

There was a great roar from the audience accompanied by boos.

'Yes,' Marga Man continued. 'Whole heap a bullshit. But don't let dem fool yu, de music yu are about to hear is about unity, unity of all people against boredom and conformity. De music yu are about to hear is de music of resistance, de music yu are about to hear may have come out of de East End but it is for de people of de north, south, east and west.'

There was another great roar.

'De music yu are 'bout to hear is de music of Positive Negatives.'

The roar rose in decibels and intensity.

'Let's do this,' said Ray.

As they walked on, the venue's line of security men at the front of the stage tightened and the band's own security took up positions on the sides of the stage. If there was anyone in the crowd being hostile they were completely drowned out by the cheers of joy coming from the majority, and the nervousness of the band quickly melted away as they began to musically hypnotise the crowds. The crowd stayed under the influence of the music, completely in tune with every word that was rapped by the boys, regardless of speed, accent or inflection. It was another long, hot and energetic gig, and nothing went wrong, everything went very right. Once again the band had to do four encores before the crowd would begin to consider going home.

After the show the security blocked off all routes backstage while the boys cooled down, washed and changed. The feeling was good. The crowd had been as welcoming as an east London crowd or any of the crowds that they had encountered at other gigs. Tyrone was raving inside, but calm outside, Ray was raving outside and inside, raving about how good it had gone and making up lines of rap about the gig, Prem was dancing around contentedly, and Marga Man was quietly content too.

Soon Marga Man gave the security guards permission to let the guests in. Skelly from the record company made an appearance before leaving for another gig, and Fingers turned up, followed by many other guests including Kori, Lizette, Thara and Sam. A mini party began backstage, and as always Fingers was in high spirits, trying to photograph everyone in sight, and he had plenty to say.

'Positive Negatives rule the world,' he shouted out loud as the people mingled.

'We know that,' shouted Kori in response.

Ray approached Fingers. 'To sleep with your eyes open is to dream out loud.'

'Yeah, right,' said Fingers.

Ray smiled and said, 'No matter how long a log stays in the water it will never become a crocodile.'

'What are you going on about?' Fingers asked.

'It's wisdom man, I got them from that book your mate gave me last night.'

'OK,' said Fingers, as he thought back to the night before. 'Yeah, he's always reading books and saying mystical things. You know that track of yours, "Refugee Me"? He knows it by heart, the guy studied it as if it was college coursework, I tell ya.'

'Well, when you see him, tell him I said it's a cool little book, I've been dipping into it all night,' Ray said, pulling out a copy of the new CD from one of the large side pockets of his trousers. 'Give him this for me.'

'He's got a copy already,' Fingers said.

Ray pulled out a pen. 'Well, give him this one anyway; I'll sign it for him. What's his name?'

'Alem,' said Fingers.

Ray signed the CD and handed it to Fingers. 'I'm not sure if this has as much wisdom as the book but it's the thought that counts.' Ray was smiling, but Fingers looked scared. Then Ray realised that Fingers was not looking at him but over his shoulder. Ray turned round, and standing in the doorway was Dragon, surrounded by six other members of the Western Alliance.

'Look what's happening here,' Dragon shouted. He was looking straight ahead but speaking to his followers. 'The children are having a party.'

'What's your problem?' Ray said, carefully watching them.

'The problem is you. If you got something to say, why don't you say it up front?'

'We got nothing to say to you,' said Ray.

'Are you running scared now?' Dragon said, focusing on Ray.

Ray was the closest to the intruders, too close for comfort. Marga Man went and stood in front of Ray. 'How yu get in here?' he asked, glancing around at the security guards, who were taking no action.

Dragon pointed to a backstage pass hanging around his neck. 'Hey old man, we got backstage passes, and that's no way to speak to your guest.'

'Yu are not wanted here, yu better leave now,' said Marga Man.

286

'That's not what we heard. Look old man, we just come. This party has possibilities. It was a shit gig so let's have a good time now.'

Marga Man looked towards the two security men who were also standing by the door. 'These people are not welcome here, they should have never been allowed in here. Make sure they leave.'

Outnumbered, the guards began to speak to their colleagues using their radio links hidden under their jacket collars, but as they began to call for reinforcements, Dragon took a swipe and punched Marga Man in the face. It was so unexpected, and such a clean shot, that Marga Man went down. Dragon then went straight for Ray, and the rest of the Alliance boys streamed into the room and went for Tyrone, Prem and other males. Fists flew everywhere and screams rang out. Sam crouched down in a corner to protect herself, and Kori, Lizette and Thara tried to protect themselves as well as Sam, but Lizette and Thara were pushed to the ground.

Dragon and his gang were getting the better of the rest until the bouncers arrived. The bouncers were all too big and powerful for them. They just seemed to be picking the Western Alliance boys up and throwing them out of the room. But Dragon was still putting up a fight, until one of the band's bouncers brought his knee up and connected it with Dragon's ribcage and the fight went out of him. As Dragon went down, two venue security guards picked him up and threw him out of the door. Ray was still on the floor, and Dragon got up, took a step into the room and kicked Ray in the back as he lay there. Dragon then ran out of the building, with the others being chased and pushed on by the security guards.

Marga Man's nose was bleeding, and he was in a rage. 'How did they get in here? Who let them in?'

'They had access all area passes, boss,' replied one of the guards.

Everybody began to pick themselves up and check with each other that they were all OK. When Ray got to his feet the first thing he did was to let Marga Man know how he felt.

'You just wouldn't listen to me, would you? I said we should never do this gig, but you wouldn't listen. All the tight security didn't help, all these security people do is pose, all they do is look hard. I don't listen to you any more, now I'm defending myself. No more Mr fucking nice rapper guy, now I'm getting pro-active, you know what I'm saying?'

Marga Man had nothing to say in reply. He looked away, then walked off gesturing to the security guards to follow him. Once he had gathered the main security guys together he questioned them as to why the Western Alliance members were able to get in, but he learnt nothing new. They had got passes, and no one knew where the passes had come from.

Most of the people in the room had been hit or pushed over but no one was in need of hospitalisation. Prem had a badly sprained wrist, and Tyrone was a little bruised. Ray was in the worst shape, but his anger cancelled out his pain.

Word had reached outside of the attack, so as the band and their entourage made their way from the stage door to the tour bus fans and media people were waiting. The band made no comment and the bus made its way back to east London.

There were heated arguments on the journey; one of the arguments concerned the next gig, which was to be in Cardiff two days later. There was a look of determination on the boys' faces. They wanted to go ahead with the next gig but their girlfriends and relatives thought they should call it off. And then there was the question of the police; the band thought that it wasn't worth going to the police because they would do very little about it, whilst others thought that it should be reported.

After being dropped home that night Ray had a long soak in the bath. He played no music, he was in need of silence. Once out of the bath he sat quietly and thought even harder. As far as he was concerned, it had all come together. The Western Alliance were making the malicious phone calls and they were definitely to blame for the murder of Yinka. The arrest of Reel Steel and the attack backstage confirmed everything he had believed. Now he wanted justice to be done, but this kind of justice could not be administered by people in uniforms. He wanted to administer his own justice.

CHAPTER 25

The Messenger

When Ray woke up the next day his mood had not changed. He lay in bed and continued thinking until the phone rang. The number was withheld, the voice was the same.

'So how's your recovery, boy?'

'I'm gonna get you,' Ray said calmly.

'I was hoping you would say that, chickenhead. Why don't we just meet up and let me kick the shit out of you. You need to die, you know that, don't you?'

Ray was as cool as ever. 'OK, three of you and three of us.'

'No,' said the voice. 'One on one.'

There was a long pause. The Messenger broke the silence. 'What's the matter, little piggy, are you running scared?'

'You don't scare me,' Ray said. 'Just me and you. Name the place, I'll show you what's what.'

'That's what I like to hear. We should forget this east–west thing and go north, neutral ground, you know what I'm saying? So how about King's Cross?'

291

'Anywhere,' Ray replied.

'When you leave King's Cross station and head down York Way, after about quarter of a mile you'll see some large gates on the left. Go through the gates. You'll see it's a disused factory yard, an old freight depot. Be there at midnight.'

Ray thought for a while. 'That's OK with me, but how do I know you won't have company?'

'Don't worry about that, this is a solo mission. Just make sure you have some way of getting home. I suggest an ambulance.'

'Which one are you?'

'All you need to know is who you are.'

'I know myself,' Ray said, still cool and calm.

'OK. Midnight. In the yard, just the two of us.'

'I'll be there,' said Ray and he ended the call.

Ray got out of bed and got dressed. He had biscuits and orange squash for breakfast. Then he pushed his bed aside and peeled back the carpet. Using his screwdriver and hammer he levered up the floorboard and carefully lifted out the plastic bag. He put the plastic bag on the bed and took the towel out, then he unwrapped the towel and took the gun in his hand. After he had familiarised himself with the weapon again he replaced the floorboard and put everything back into the plastic bag, then he put the plastic bag into a sports bag.

* * *

About midday Ray rang for a taxi. He was dressed in a blue tracksuit and his black, lightweight parka jacket. He took the taxi to Leytonstone station and then he took the underground train to Epping at the end of the line. He had been there before – it was where his mother used to take him and Kori when they were small and she wanted to get away from his father. Once out of the tube station he headed for Epping Forest with his bag slung over his back, looking like an athlete jogging to a training session.

Deep in the forest he found some cover and nervously began to do what he needed to do. He looked around to make sure there were no people, then, putting the bag on the ground, he unwrapped the gun without taking it out of the sports bag. Then he walked around the bag to check for people. When he was sure that all was clear he bent down over the sports bag again and fumbled for one of the small boxes containing the bullets, and loaded up the gun just as Midnight had shown him. He put the gun down and circled the bag again. He still saw no one but he began to tremble. Suddenly he felt very hungry, suddenly he wanted to go to the toilet, suddenly he began to feel very light-headed and his bottom lip began to shake. He walked an even larger circle; he could hear every squirrel rustling in the trees for a mile and every bird watching over him.

Then the time came. He marched to the bag,

picked up the gun, released the safety catch and fired it about ten yards away into the ground. He wasn't happy. The moment he had pulled the trigger he had closed his eyes tight and bitten his lip. He had no composure, and he knew that that wouldn't work in the real world. He stayed still for a while and thought about his effort. Although he didn't know what to expect he knew he could do better. There had been a slight recoil and the bang wasn't too loud. He was going to do it again. He waited for a moment and listened for any signs of people and then he shot the gun again and again. This time he relaxed his face and kept his eyes open and saw where the bullets were penetrating the ground.

Happier but still anxious, he then quickly wrapped up the gun, placed it back in the sports bag and began running back. About a quarter of a mile on he came across an elderly man and a woman walking towards him.

'Training for the marathon, are we?' asked the man.

'That's right,' said Ray, running on the spot. 'I don't know why I do it.'

'Charity,' said the woman.

'How did you guess?' Ray replied, grateful for the suggestion.

The woman looked out into the distance. 'Are they hunting again?'

'It sounds like it,' said Ray. 'I just hope no one mistakes me for whatever it is that they hunt.'

'No way,' said the man. 'We know who that is, it's all done on private property. It sounds like they're behind you, but they're miles away. Good day to you.'

'Take care,' said Ray as he turned, jogged off and did the reverse journey home.

When Ray got home he could see on his phone that Prem and Tyrone had been trying to get to him. But he did not call them back, he just sat around waiting for midnight. At about eight the phone rang. It was Prem. Ray hesitated but then he answered.

'Ray, what's up, brother?'

'Everything's safe,' Ray replied.

'Hey, we're going to get together at the shop for a mini meeting. Marga Man said he wants to share some ideas, you know how he is. We've been calling you guy, where have you been?'

'Nowhere.'

'We'll come and pick you up.'

'No,' Ray said sharply, 'I can't come.'

'What do ya mean you can't come?'

'I just can't come, just have the meeting without me.'

Prem dropped his voice. 'Are you all right man, have you got some hurts from last night?'

'No, I said I'm OK, just go without me.'

'We can't, we need you. You're one third of the band.'

Ray shouted, 'Well I'm not coming, I got work to do.'

There were five long seconds of silence before Prem spoke. 'What do you mean, work, where are you going?'

'I'm not going anywhere,' said Ray, realising his slip-up.

'So what's this work, then?'

'Nothing,' Ray said, struggling for an excuse. 'I got some rhymes I wanna write.'

'You don't need to stay in for a night to write rhymes, I know you better than that.'

'You know nothing, Prem,' Ray snarled down the phone. 'Just leave me alone.' Ray pressed his disconnect button, leaving Prem listening to the tone.

The phone rang a few times more that evening but Ray didn't answer any calls. He was mentally preparing. The house was silent and he was focused. At eleven o'clock he replaced the spent bullets and put the gun in the inside pocket of his jacket. He took a taxi to King's Cross station and began to walk down York Way. As he started the journey he was approached by a drunk who could hardly stand. The drunk waved his can of beer around, spilling its contents everywhere.

'Yu wanna fight me boy,' he said, simulating a headbutt and almost falling over in the process. 'I'll kill ya, I've killed people like you before, come on, I'll have ya. Come here, let me sing you a song.'

Ray quickened his pace, leaving the drunk staggering behind him. Fifty yards down the road he spotted three women standing in separate doorways. They were dressed in the shortest of skirts. The first girl's hair was so blonde that it was brighter than the headlights of the cars that were slowly circulating. Her legs were so pale and bloodless it was as if she had painted them white.

'Are you looking for business, mate?' she asked as he walked by. Ray just walked on.

The second was a black girl, she looked barely fifteen. Her hair was so straight and stiff and without movement that it could have been made out of wire. Ray looked down as he walked and saw that her legs had long scars on them as if she had been slashed with a sharp instrument.

'Do you want it, Mister?' she asked in a voice that made her sound like a ten-year-old.

Ray kept walking. He walked past the next girl, a well-built brunette who looked like a real prostitute. She had big hair, big legs and fishnet stockings. She stepped out on to the pavement behind him, put her hand on her hips and in a voice that was unmistakeably masculine shouted, 'Hey, baby, if you're not sure what you're after I can do everything. You know, tricycle bicycle, hotel motel, import export . . .'

Ray took a quick glance back but kept walking.

Soon Ray had reached a quieter part of the road where there were warehouses and what looked like industrial estates. He slowed down to make sure he had made no mistake, then he saw the gates of the yard to his left. He turned back and walked for a few yards before stopping and moving the gun from the inside pocket of the coat to the right-hand side pocket. He released the safety catch and walked back with his hands in his pockets and his right hand firmly on the gun.

As he pushed open the heavy wooden gates and stepped into the yard the noise of the street faded away. It was dark, the only artificial light was that which leaked in from the streetlamps. It took a minute for Ray's eyes to adjust, and when they did he could see very little – two large warehouses with smashed windows, bits of broken-down machinery and an array of scrapped heavy vehicles. Ray's eyes darted all around for signs of another human being. He could feel his breathing getting shorter and shorter as he became more tense. Convinced there was no one around he took a deep breath in and a long breath out and he dropped his shoulders which had been coming up towards his ears with tension. Then a well-built figure stepped out from behind one of the scrapped vans. It was Dragon.

Ray nodded his head. 'So it's you.'

Dragon raised his eyebrows and nodded his head. 'So it's you,' he said, punching his right fist into his left palm. 'Are you sure you don't want to go home?'

'Don't ask me any questions,' Ray said, without taking his eyes off him. 'Just do what you gotta do, come with it.'

Ray's plan was to get as close as he could to Dragon and put at least two missiles into his belly. Dragon began to walk towards him fearlessly. But it was nothing like he had seen in the films. Ray tried to do a fast draw but before his shooting hand even left his pocket a blow struck him on the face and his feet were kicked away from him. It was the previous night all over again. Dragon kicked and punched Ray as he pleased, and all Ray could do was roll into a ball. But then a powerful kick to the back of his head sent a rush of adrenaline running through Ray – it was as if a temper button had been pressed. He jumped up and punched and kicked wildly, and for a while Dragon went on the defensive. Then they both fell on the ground holding each other and exchanging very few blows. Dragon's superior strength began to show, as he wriggled until he was able to get his arm around Ray's neck, and then he began to squeeze. Ray's attempt to fight back was futile. He was getting weak, he was beginning to lose consciousness, but with the little bit of strength he had he tried desperately to find his pocket. All he could think was that the gun would turn things round. It wasn't happening, Ray was losing it, he began to give in, he was just getting weaker and weaker. Dragon began to talk to his victim.

'This is it, baby rapper, this is what you get when you cross me. You're gonna die here, and you won't be found until some prostitute comes to service a taxi driver. What a way to go, baby rapper, and I bet you wanted to die on stage.'

Just then there was a loud thud and Dragon's grip loosened. It was followed by what seemed like hundreds of kicks and punches. Ray looked up. It was Prem and Tyrone, who were paying no attention to Ray, concentrating all their efforts on Dragon. Ray jumped up, shook himself back to life and joined in. Dragon rolled in agony. Now all he could do was curl up into a ball. When Ray was directly over him, he pulled out the gun and pointed it at Dragon's head. The action suddenly stopped, as if someone had turned everything off.

'What da fuck do ya think ya doing, Ray?' said Prem, frozen like a dummy.

Ray was gasping for breath but he managed to spit the words out. 'It's called revenge, it's about an eye for an eye.'

Tyrone shook his head. 'Ray man, this ain't the way

to go. Let's rough him up and go make some music.'

'No way, the music is over,' said Ray. His bloodshot eyes looked into Dragon's.

Prem half laughed and stepped towards Ray. 'Come on, Ray, let's rearrange him and get out of here.'

Prem reached out. 'Give us the gun.'

'No,' said Ray, keeping his eyes on Dragon.

'Give it,' said Prem, moving towards Ray.

'No,' Ray shouted, and then to their complete surprise he turned the gun on Prem, then from Prem to Tyrone. 'Stand there.' Ray nodded his head to a place just behind Dragon but no one moved. This time Ray deliberately pointed the gun at Prem's head. 'I said stand there, and you,' he said to Tyrone.

Ray looked as if he was determined to let nothing get in his way. He looked mad; he looked as if he had been possessed. 'How did you know I was here?' he asked.

'I knew something was wrong when I called you,' said Prem. 'So we followed you. Ray, this is getting out of hand, let's go.'

'Shut up. This fucker killed Yinka, now I'm gonna kill him, watch me.'

'I didn't kill her,' Dragon groaned.

'If you didn't kill her one of your lot did, and you're their main man.'

'None of my crew killed her,' Dragon said, before

swallowing the blood in his mouth.

Ray kicked him in the stomach. 'You killed her, then you came here to kill me, didn't you?'

'What are you saying, it was you that called me here.'

'Don't you mess about,' said Ray. 'I'm in no mood to be messed about and you're in no position to start messing about.'

'Come on Ray, leave it,' Prem pleaded.

Ray looked up at Prem and Tyrone. 'You two are my people, man, but you can't stop me.' He looked back down at Dragon. 'And you brought me here to die amongst the condoms and the heroin needles and now look at you.'

'I didn't call you here,' said Dragon. 'I got a message to meet you here.'

'Yeah,' said Ray. 'From who?'

'From your man, the so-called Messenger.'

Ray kicked him again. 'Bullshit, the Messenger's your man.'

'I don't know who he is,' groaned Dragon.

'Hold on a minute,' said Prem. He looked down at Dragon. 'Who told you to come here?'

'The Messenger,' replied Dragon.

Prem continued, 'Who's the Messenger?'

'I don't know.'

Prem kicked him in the head. 'I said, who's the Messenger?'

302

'I told you,' Dragon replied, exhausted. 'I don't know. He works for you, how should we know who he is? We don't know.'

Prem looked up. 'Can't you see it, Ray, something's wrong; you think that he called you here and he thinks that you called him here. They think we keep ringing them and threatening them and we think that they keep threatening us. Something's up.'

Ray could see Dragon thinking it through. He seemed to be genuinely puzzled but Ray wanted to be sure. He kicked him again. 'You're just trying to save your skin, ain't you?'

'I don't know the damn Messenger, I have never called you, it's the truth, man.'

'Think about it, Ray,' said Prem. 'It doesn't make sense. If he came to kill you why ain't he carrying an iron, what was he going to kill you with?'

'We don't know,' Ray replied. 'Search him.'

Tyrone and Prem bent down and began to search Dragon. He was carrying nothing except a phone, keys, cigarettes and money. 'He's clean,' said Tyrone.

Ray bent down and put the gun right on Dragon's forehead. 'I could send you to hell right now but guess what, I'm gonna give you the benefit of the doubt. I'm gonna let you go home tonight and I'm gonna do some research. If what you say is true we should talk again, if not we should fight again, but next time there will be no mercy for the merciless.'

Ray put the gun in his pocket and the three of them ran as fast as they could towards King's Cross. At the station they got a taxi and headed east, hardly speaking as they went. When they reached Stratford, Prem asked the taxi to take them to the Channelsea Business Park.

'What are we going there for?' Ray asked.

'We got something to do there,' Prem replied.

The taxi dropped them off near the business park by a small river called the Channelsea River. Once the taxi had left them, Prem tried to reason with Ray. 'Throw the gun away, Ray.'

'No,' said Ray. 'I paid good money for it and it ain't over yet.'

'Throw it away.'

'No.'

Tyrone leaned on to the bridge and looked at the moon reflected in the dirty water. 'My baby's gonna be born soon. I had this idea that it would be a rapper from birth, but what kind of an example would we be if we teach that the way to survive in hip-hop music is by having a gun? I say the gun should go.'

Ray stood behind Tyrone and spoke to the back of his head. 'Yes, that sounds nice, family man. I know you're gonna be a daddy soon and all that, but this is about life and death, man.'

'No,' said Tyrone. 'What you have in your pocket is death, what Sam has in her womb is life.'

'Never mind the wise bullshit words. If we check this theory out and find that this Messenger guy is not a Western Alliance man I'll throw it away, but if not I'm gonna keep it until I feel safe.'

Tyrone looked at Prem. Prem nodded positively, Tyrone nodded back. 'OK,' said Tyrone, walking away. 'Now let's go home.'

The next day all the concerts for that next week were postponed. The fans were upset but this time they were promised new dates. The press began to sniff around but they found nothing. Both Ray and Dragon were sporting bruises that distorted their faces and weren't too keen to be seen in public. There was an afternoon meeting at Ray's house where Marga Man sat and listened to the boys explaining everything that had happened the night before, everything except the story of the gun. After he had heard all they had to say he began making phone calls. First he rang Damage Limitation Records in west London. Posing as a promoter he got the number of the Western Alliance's manager. Then he rang the manager, identified himself and they arranged a secret meeting that night in the shop.

As the appointed time drew near, Marga Man drove the boys to the music shop under cover of darkness where they waited for the visitors to arrive. They arrived right on time. There was a knock on the door, and Positive Negatives looked out to see the Western Alliance looking in, or at least a few of them. Marga Man went and let them in; the man leading them in was the first to speak.

'How's it going? I'm Pablo, the manager.'

'Cool, and I'm Marga Man.'

Dragon and Ray locked eyes together and the two opposing sides began to size each other up. The Western Alliance were as multi-racial as a band could be. On this night six of them, including their Spanish manager, had made the journey, all shuffling around not sure which attitude to adopt.

'You guys shake hands,' said Marga Man. 'Let's get these peace talks under way.'

The rappers started to shake hands diplomatically.

'That's good,' said Pablo. 'No need for names. If you don't know each other already you will soon.'

They all stood or sat around the counter and let Marga Man lead the discussions.

'Now, yu guys are busy guys and we guys are busy guys so none of us have lots of time to waste. We appreciate dat yu come all dis way to be here and dat also suggests to me dat yu are serious 'bout dis. So let's get to de nitty gritty. Out there people are fighting in de name of our bands. Two people have been killed and over nine people have been stabbed. De police are saying dat there are other deaths dat they feel may be linked to dis warfare and it's impossible to count how many people have really been injured. Now dis is de way it happened from our point of view. We start dropping some lyrics and people love it, we come from nowhere den big hit and tings sweet. But den we go to an award show to pick up some ornaments and yu guys start mouthing at us.'

'You know why,' said one of the Alliance.

'Why?' asked Prem.

'Because we were getting messages from your man mouthing at us, insulting our people.'

'We haven't got a man sending messages,' said Ray.

'Well,' said Dragon, 'the day before the Awards we got lots of calls saying that we were crap rappers and that the only true rappers come from the east.'

'Did he say he was representing us?' asked Tyrone.

'Yeah. Well no, not really. It's difficult to say,' said another member of the Alliance. 'When I heard him he never actually said who he represents, he just went on about what was going to happen to us.'

'But that's it,' said Prem, standing up and gesticulating wildly. 'When he phoned us he didn't say he was from the Western Alliance, he didn't say who he was representing. He just made it sound like he was from the Alliance, he hinted at it. He just kept going on about he's the Messenger.'

'No, he never called anybody by name,' Ray said, thinking aloud. 'We gotta find out who made those calls. Who is the Messenger?'

307

'All right,' said Marga Man. 'I don't want to offend anyone so what I'm now going to say to de Alliance also applies to de Positives. Can you think of anyone in your crew who could be doing dis?'

Pablo shook his head at the thought of having to think about it. 'Do you know how many of us there are? The Western Alliance is seven bands who united into one.'

'I know dat,' said Marga Man. 'But we still have to check every angle, every person. We all have to do de same. Our band's not as big as yours but I'm still thinking of de roadies and de sound people, yu know.'

'What you mean, even Bunny?' asked Prem in a disbelieving voice.

'Even Bunny,' replied Marga Man. 'I trust him one hundred per cent, but dat doesn't mean we shouldn't think of him.'

'So what you saying?' said Ray. 'You saying I gotta suspect Tyrone, and Tyrone gotta suspect Prem, and Prem gotta suspect me?'

'And me,' said Marga Man. 'Come on, it's not about suspecting each other, it's about tinking of every possibility. Please don't give me a hard time.'

'The brother's right,' said Dragon. 'We all gotta do it.'

'Let me quote a rap to you now,' said Marga Man. 'It goes like dis. "We can't go on together with suspicious minds".'

'Who's that, Marga Man?' asked Prem, 'and where's the rhyme?'

'It's Elvis Presley,' replied Marga Man, 'and it doesn't rhyme, not when I do it anyway.'

There were snorts all round as everyone tried to stop themselves from laughing at Marga Man.

'OK,' he continued, 'Elvis couldn't rap. Seriously now, all of us have a mission, to find dis Messenger. We must leave here, we shake hands, and if any of us have anyting to say to any of us we should say it to their face, no matter what it is – take de Messenger outta de loop. Is dat a deal?'

'You got it, man.'

'It's on.'

'For real.'

And various other words of agreement were exchanged, then they shook hands again, this time with feeling.

After the Western Alliance representatives had left, Ray, Prem, Tyrone and Marga Man stayed in the shop for over an hour, talking and trying to think of possible suspects but none of them could think of anybody. They couldn't even recognise the voice of the Messenger. It didn't sound like anyone they knew and it just didn't sound like anyone from the Alliance boys that they had heard.

Back home in his flat Ray found it very difficult to sleep that night. He went through the library in his mind of everyone he knew and he was still getting nowhere. But the next morning he had an idea. He phoned Prem, Tyrone and Marga Man. He was unable to get Tyrone so he left a message on his phone and arranged to meet the others at the shop. They waited for a while hoping that Tyrone would turn up, but when there was no sign of him Ray started getting impatient. Ray wanted to speak to them all together.

Then, just as they were about to start, Tyrone walked in. He looked depressed, and his eyes were watery. He went and sat on a bar stool by the counter and stared into the distance.

'What's up?' Ray asked carefully.

'We lost our baby,' Tyrone said. 'Sam had a miscarriage.'

'Oh no. When did it happen?' asked Ray.

'Last night, when we were at the shop. She was taken to hospital. When I got back home I got a phone call telling me to get to the hospital quickly. I rushed as quickly as I could but it was too late.'

'What? Oh man, sorry Tyrone. Sorry to hear that man,' said Ray.

They all dropped their heads.

'How's Sam coping, is she all right?' asked Prem.

'She's still there with her family. I had an argument with them. Her brother said that it's being around the band that's caused it, so we had a go at each other.

Maybe he has a point. Sam's done a lot of crying but she's dealing with it.'

'That's real bad news,' said Marga Man. 'Look, why don't you go home?'

'No,' said Tyrone. 'What's there for me? I'll see Sam later.'

'I think you should go,' said Ray, resting his hand on Tyrone's shoulder.

'I'm OK,' said Tyrone, hardening his tone. 'I'm here.'

'That's all right,' said Marga Man.

'But I'm off this weekend,' Tyrone continued, shaking his head.

'What do yu mean, yu leaving de country or someting?' Marga Man was confused.

'No, I'm moving in with her. She needs me,' he said. 'What's this meeting about anyway?'

Ray wasn't sure if Tyrone was up to it, so he began by reminding Tyrone he didn't have to stay. 'Tyrone brother, I'm telling you now, I have a little plan. I got a theory that I need to move on, but I mean it, you can leave any time, I won't feel bad, I'll understand. You got other things to think about.'

'I'm with you,' said Tyrone, lifting his head up as if ready for action.

Ray started by asking for confirmation that they had confidence in him. 'You trust me, don't you?'

'Yeah.'

'Yeah.'

'Yes.'

'And you know that we said we should consider all possibilities when we're trying to find out who it is, right?'

They all answered positively again.

'OK,' said Ray, 'do you have your phones with you?' They all did. 'Great, follow me.'

Ray led them out of the shop. Marga Man quickly locked the door behind him. Ray then led them across the road and into the police station. They were all lost for words but went where they were led.

'Can we see Detective Sergeant Horne please?' Ray asked the duty sergeant.

'I'm afraid he's busy right now. Can I help you? What's it about?'

'Well it's about music and television, and hip-hop, and two murders.'

'Are you serious?' asked the duty sergeant.

'We don't joke about murder,' Ray replied.

'I'll get him.' The officer picked up the phone and called D.S. Horne down. Ray asked if they could go somewhere private and they were shown round the back into a room. The others were quiet, leaving Ray to do all the talking when D.S. Horne arrived.

'Have you had any luck at all?'

'No,' said D.S. Horne. 'But let's face it, Ray, you and your community haven't been very helpful, have you?'

'You haven't exactly had it at the top of your priorities either, have you? Anyway, forget that. Look, you know that throughout all this fighting and stuff we've been getting threatening phone calls, right?'

'Yes.'

'Well, so have the west London boys. We thought that they were threatening us and they thought that we were threatening them.'

'So? What does that mean?' D.S. Horne asked, pulling out his notepad in an attempt to look busy.

'Can't you see, someone's stirring it up.'

'And I suppose you think it's me.'

'No, don't be silly,' Ray said. He then turned to the others and held his hand out. 'Give me your phones.'

'What?' said Marga Man.

'Come now, trust me,' said Ray, 'confidence in me, remember now.' They all handed Ray their phones. 'OK, you do some detective work, talk to the phone companies or whatever you do and let us know who's been calling us, and where from. I know you can do that clever stuff.'

'But you lot get hundreds of phone calls, don't you?' the detective sergeant said, not sure how useful it would be.

'Yes,' said Ray, 'but you only need to check the numbers that were withheld. There's only a few of them, and the number we are looking for would appear on all our phones.'

313

It made sense to the detective. The others silently acknowledged that it was a good idea by touching fists, much to the officer's amusement.

'I'll do it,' said D.S. Horne. 'I need twenty-four hours.'

'Great,' said Ray. As they were leaving Ray turned back. 'Hey, I hope you guys mind your own business.'

'What do you mean?' D.S. Horne asked.

'Well, only pay attention to the job in hand, don't start doing market research and ringing up all my friends.'

D.S. Horne laughed. 'Don't worry, we're professionals.'

That night, Marga Man ordered in food from their favourite Nigerian restaurant and they ate in at Ray's place. They knew they were on to something, but Tyrone's mind was on Sam and Ray's mind was still looking for clues. After the meal Marga Man went home, dropping Tyrone off en route to see Sam. Prem stayed, and he ended up staying overnight. They slept fully clothed, two on the bed. When they woke up the next morning they were horrified by how close they had slept to each other, and Ray was even more horrified by the state of his flat. They made a deal, they were to clean up the flat before they did anything else. They tried.

*　　*　　*

About midday, just as Prem was about to leave for home, Marga Man turned up at the house. He was rushing manically.

'Come on, let's go. De police rang me at de shop, said dem have a result.'

Ray rang Tyrone and told him that they were on their way to the police station. Prem and Ray then raced down to the car and with the help of some highly illegal driving they were at the station in less than ten minutes. The desk sergeant was expecting them. He showed them into D.S. Horne's office. As they sat down, Tyrone turned up puffing and panting and looking like he had had no sleep whatsoever.

'Good to see you,' said D.S. Horne. 'We did the check with the phone company and we've found one mobile number that has rung all of you and the caller has always withheld the number. Sometimes he calls from an address in north London, and sometimes from central London.'

'Right,' said Ray, nodding his head, eyes wide and rubbing his hands together. 'Who is it, then?'

D.S. Horne picked up a sheet of paper from his desk and read from it. 'The phone belongs to a Mr D. Sinclair.'

'D. Sinclair?' said Ray. 'Who's that?'

'I don't know. I do know that the phone hasn't been reported stolen, and according to the records of the phone company the owner lives in Bishop's Avenue,

Hampstead. Now there's something.'

'What's so someting about dat?' Marga Man asked.

'Bishop's Avenue is something else. It's leafy, no, it's more than leafy, it's, well, how can I put it? It's like millionaire's row.'

'So what does the D stand for?' Ray asked.

'I'm just having that checked out now,' replied D.S. Horne confidently. 'The phone company doesn't know what it stands for but I got a man working on it now.'

Ray asked for the phones back. Once they were handed over he told Marga Man to phone the Alliance's manager Pablo. When he was on the line Ray took the phone. 'Hey Pablo, is Dragon with you?'

'Yes, he's right here.'

'Can I speak to him?'

'No problem.'

As Ray was waiting for him to come on the phone his mind was working overtime. 'Yo, it's me, X-Ray-X. Tell me something, how did you get the backstage passes into our gig the other night?'

'We got them from you. That caller, whoever it was, after loads of insults, said that if we wanted some revenge we should come backstage and that we would be his guest.'

'Thanks, man, that's all I need for now,' Ray said. 'Later.'

Just as Ray disconnected an officer walked in and handed D.S. Horne a note. He read the name on the paper out loud.

'Duncan Roland Sinclair.'

'That's it,' Ray said. 'Let's go.'

'Where are you going?' asked D.S. Horne. 'What are you up to?'

'Nothing,' said Ray. 'You just do what you have to do.'

'But we haven't got any hard evidence.'

'We'll look for some,' said Ray, smiling.

Ray marched everyone back to the shop. There he got on the computer, logged on to the internet, put the name Duncan Roland Sinclair into a search engine, and everything became clear. There were over three hundred items under his name. Ray clicked on the first one – it was a website full of profiles of businessmen.

Duncan R. Sinclair MA FCA BA (Hons)

Born	18/8/1964
Educated	Morris Moore Grammar School
	Edgbaston Business School, Birmingham
	Queenstown University, Toronto, Canada

Chairman/CEO	Go Girl Cosmetics
	Dizzy Cola
	Sinclair Electronics
Owner	Lickit (Marital Aids)
	Deaf Defying Records
	Damage Limitation Records
Awards	1998 Community Businessman Award
	2001 Adult Entertainment Businessman of the Year

'I knew it. It's the same Duncan we met at the record company office.'

Ray sat back in the chair, and they all leaned over him reading and re-reading what was on the screen. Ray pointed to the screen.

'Not only does he own both Deaf Defying Records and Damage Limitation Records, look, he even owns the sex shop under the record company office.'

The others could not believe their eyes, but Ray could.

'I didn't trust him when I met him. He knew all the moves the Alliance and us were making, and it was him who got the backstage passes for them. Call the Alliance.'

Marga Man called them and two hours later twelve members of the Western Alliance, including Dragon,

318

were in the music shop. Ray explained everything to them and the shop soon became a house full of fury. When the talk was over Ray approached Dragon.

'I'm sorry, man.'

'No need to be sorry, brother. Now we know the truth.'

'But we don't know why,' said Ray. He reached out and they hugged, and the others in the room clapped and cheered.

'We do know why,' said Marga Man. 'Tink about it. Controversy sells. Every time yu make bad news yu records sold more. As soon as both bands got a reputation being bad de kids wanted to be bad, and record sales followed. We started hating each other and fighting each other and killing each other while de man upstairs just got richer and richer. OK, we got paid, but nothing like him. It's like a divide and rule, actually it's divide and profit. We've been manipulated. We have become pawns in a game of death while de man makes his money.'

Ray opened his phone and dialled Skelly's number. 'Hey, Skelly, how you doing?' he asked, sounding quite happy.

'I'm fine, and you?'

'I'm fine too, man. Hey, we're coming into town in an hour or so. It would be great to see you.'

'That's cool, I'll be here.'

'Great, and hey, is Duncan around? We haven't

seen him since the first time we met you. It would be great to see him and talk about the future.'

'Funnily enough, he's due here in ten minutes, we got a meeting.'

'Nice, see you soon.'

Ray looked around the room. He addressed everyone.

'We have to pay Duncan a visit.'

Then he turned to Marga Man. 'But first I need a quick ride home. I have to change my clothes, man, I've been in these for three days. I slept in them last night.'

Marga Man took Ray home and when they returned, everyone was waiting, eager to go. Four cars rode in convoy but then as they were crossing a bridge over the River Lea, Prem demanded that Marga Man stop the car. They stopped and the others stopped behind them.

'Ray, I need to speak to you.'

'OK, speak.'

'No, outside.'

'Why.'

'I just want to speak to you outside.'

Ray stepped out of the car and Prem walked him away from the car to lean over the bridge. 'I know why you went home,' said Prem softly. 'We got stuff to do but not that stuff. Throw the gun away.'

'What are you going on about?' Ray said, faking ignorance.

'Throw the gun away, Ray.'

'It's about death,' came Tyrone's voice from behind. 'There's too much death going down brother, let's think about life.'

There was a pause as police cars raced past to an emergency with lights flashing and sirens blaring.

'Think positive,' said Prem.

'Think life,' said Tyrone.

Ray took the gun out of his inside pocket, looked at it for a moment, and threw it into the river. They touched fists and walked back. None of the others saw what had happened.

On the way Ray rang Fingers. 'Fingers man, where are you?'

'I'm in Brick Lane, having a curry,' said Fingers with his mouth full.

'Have you got your camera with you?'

'Yeah,' replied Fingers.

'We need you man. Get round to the Deaf Defying Records office as soon as you can, like now. Do you know where it is?'

'Of course I do. What's happening?'

'Just hurry up, meet us outside. And be prepared, this is a joint Positive Negatives, Western Alliance mission.'

The journey took forty-five minutes, then it took them half an hour to park the cars. Fingers was already waiting for them. Once they had all assembled at the door of DDR, Marga Man pressed the intercom.

'Hello,' said the receptionist. 'Deaf Defying Records.'

'Positive Negatives,' said Marga Man, and the door opened.

The receptionist smiled like an airline hostess. 'Skelly's in a meeting at the moment. Could you take a seat and wait, please.'

'No,' said Ray as he stepped past her, 'and we didn't come to see Skelly anyway. Fingers, start taking photos.'

When they walked into the office with the receptionist following them in, Duncan and Skelly were in conversation with four young hopefuls. They were both shocked to see the bands together.

'Hey, what are you guys doing here? Surprise, surprise, nice to see you,' said Skelly.

'And you,' said Ray.

'Is there something wrong?' asked Duncan.

'Yeah, you're wrong,' said Marga Man.

Fingers began to take pictures.

Duncan could tell by the look on their faces that his time had come.

Ray smiled and said, 'The Messenger.'

Dragon smiled and said, 'The Messenger.'

Duncan tried to make a run for it, but Marga Man

just stuck his foot out and he tripped over. The four visitors ran out of the room. When Skelly tried to run, some Western Alliance guys grabbed him and pinned him against the wall. He couldn't move.

Tyrone went and stood in the doorway, forcing the receptionist to stay and witness the proceedings.

'We haven't done anything,' said Skelly, fearing for his life. 'What's up?'

'Well, first we're all going to beat him senseless,' said Ray, standing over Duncan.

'But what's he done?' asked Skelly, desperately seeking an answer.

Fingers was now snapping incessantly. Ray replied to Skelly, but directed his energy at Duncan.

'Did you know that your boss, your powers-that-be, is also the powers that be at Damage Limitation Records? He's the one who's been making all the calls, he's the warmonger.'

Dragon joined Ray and Marga Man standing over Duncan. The Western Alliance boys could see that Skelly was genuinely surprised, so they gave him room to move, and he walked over to where Duncan lay, bent down over him.

'Is that true, are you the boss at Damage Limitation?'

'I have many business interests,' Duncan said in a panic. 'Damage Limitation was just a small investment.'

'Yeah,' said Ray, 'investing in war.'

Skelly spat in Duncan's face and Ray raised his foot to kick him, as did Dragon.

'No,' shouted Duncan. 'No, please don't hurt me. I've got high blood pressure, I've got a bad heart. I didn't mean to cause any trouble, honest. Please take my wallet. I'm rich. Please, please, I beg you, please don't hurt me. I'll give you anything. I got money. I've got women, you know bitches, yes bitches, I got plenty of bitches. Please don't hurt me . . . ' He cried and begged pitifully like a man about to die. Skelly looked shocked to see his lord and master begging like this.

Finally Duncan stopped pleading and just lay shivering and crying on his expensive carpet. Not a punch had been thrown but he cried hard, sniffling and gasping for breath. Fingers bent down over Duncan to take one more photo, then Marga Man, Ray and Dragon stepped away as steaming urine oozed out of Duncan's trousers. For a moment they all watched him lying in his pissed-up suit crying pathetically like an abandoned toddler.

'Let's go,' said Ray, 'before we begin to feel sorry for him.'

CHAPTER 26

Channel Six News

'A London businessman appeared in court today and was remanded in custody for over fifteen charges, most relating to the gang fights which have blighted the streets of east and west London for the past year. The fighting had centred on two hip-hop bands, Positive Negatives and the Western Alliance. The accused, Mr Duncan Sinclair, unbeknownst to the band members, was the owner of both their record companies. It is alleged that he used his position and knowledge to provoke both bands using a series of hoax telephone calls.

'Detective Sergeant Horne of the Serious Crime Squad said that, "These callous and malicious calls were the work of an evil, depraved and sinister mind. As young people fought on the streets he enjoyed sitting at home watching the media coverage in the knowledge that he was the cause of it all."

'It is alleged that Sinclair not only found pleasure masterminding these gang fights, but that he also had a financial motive, as the controversy created by the bands made them into two of the biggest selling rap bands in Britain.

'Sinclair, who has a string of business interests, was a well-respected figure in the business community. He has connections in the world of politics and has given donations to charitable causes. Tonight he is behind bars facing charges which include deception, perverting the course of justice, causing a public nuisance, and tax evasion. But this morning, questions were being asked about possible murder charges relating to the deaths of Alton Benn and Yinka Molara, who were both killed as a result of the conflict created by Sinclair. Police dealing with the case say that although they don't doubt that Sinclair was responsible for the gang fights, they believe that the murderers of Benn and Molara were acting independently and that they can only press charges if they are able to find direct links to the businessman.

'Positive Negatives and the Western Alliance have announced that they will be performing together at peace concerts in both east and west London next weekend. Tony Oldsmith, the promoter of the concerts, said, "These concerts are the first of a series of events that will be staged in an attempt to bring the supporters of both bands together."

'The two bands have also said that they will be forming their own independent record label to promote grassroots music and to give other young people the opportunity to make music. Ray Wilkie, also known as X-Ray-X from Positive Negatives, told the *Daily Journal*, "We want to show people that this ain't about being a gangster, this is about being an artist. This ain't about acting up and being fake, this is about being true and keeping it real."'

The Guns

Those twisted irons that men have made
Bring murder to our streets,
And when the makers have been paid
They blame our hip-hop beats,
Their factories make bits of death
With much great legal cover,
And our poor parents hold their breath
As big youth kill each other.

Some die where they once danced with dreams
And great futures ahead,
Some live as they kill us it seems
And laugh when we are dead,
When men on top see weaknesses
Those men will push us further,
And they care not how bleak it is
They make money from murder.

We're not faultless or innocent
We have responsibilities,
We helped to make those guns present
To destroy our communities,
We must wake up and not be used
The death dance has to stop,
And when our beats are not abused
We'll dance to true hip-hop.

BY BENJAMIN ZEPHANIAH